DEATH ANGEL'S SHADOW

KANE
The powerful and forbidding knight of
winter darkness—whose sharp sword
is at the service of anyone who can
command its respect . . .

KANE
Whose eyes burn bright with cold fire—
and whose heart is a steely shield of
ice . . .

KANE
Whose cosmic quest takes him from the
unhallowed Lair of Yslsl, to the castle of
the werewolf—and beyond to the most
cunning and cruel enemy he'd ever
challenged . . .

Also by the same author,
and available in Coronet Books:

Bloodstone
Darkness Weaves
Night Winds

Death Angel's Shadow

Karl Edward Wagner

CORONET BOOKS
Hodder and Stoughton.

To Frances and Manly Wade Wellman,
For their hospitality and encouragement,
When the winter was long . . .

Copyright © 1973 by Warner Books, Inc.

First published in the United States 1973 by
Warner Books, Inc.

Coronet edition 1980

Printed and bound in Great Britain for
Hodder and Stoughton Paperbacks, a
division of Hodder and Stoughton Ltd.,
Mill Road, Dunton Green, Sevenoaks,
Kent (Editorial Office : 47 Bedford
Square, London, WC1 3DP) by
Richard Clay (The Chaucer Press) Ltd,
Bungay, Suffolk

ISBN 0 340 25079 8

Contents

DEATH ANGEL'S SHADOW

I wander through a desolate land,
On a cold and barren day;
I wander beneath a shadow,
Under light so chill, so grey;
My thoughts beneath a shadow,
That will not pass away.
     Death Angel's Shadow.

Faces that avert are pale,
Voices thin with fear;
Silent streets and alleys wind,
Windless skies so drear;
Wither beneath the shadow,
Writhing whispers that I hear.
     Death Angel's Shadow.

What is this grisly visage
That sears their souls with dread?
What demon constant follows me
And tints the sun so red?
What is this fiend whose shadow
Taints lands wherever I tread?
     Death Angel's Shadow.

To turn and look upon its face,
Brought fear I'd never known—
The shadow has ever haunted me,
As I walk the earth so alone—
And when I turned, no face I saw,
For the shadow was my own.
    Death Angel's Shadow.

Reflections for the Winter of My Soul

ince it was obvious that the man was dying, the crowd of watchers had split apart, leaving only the curious or those fascinated by the presence of death. Certainly no man could live with so ghastly a wound; the wonder was that the mangled servant had survived as long as he had.

Outside, the blizzard gathered howling force with each minute—a fury of white crystalline coldness whose blasts penetrated the thick stone walls, raced through dark hallways and billowed the heavy tapestries. Its coldness forced entrance deep within the castle, into this crowded room where an attentive circle of eyes stared down at the thing that gasped futilely in its pool of spreading crimson.

He was one of the baron's servants, a very minor member of the household, whose usual task had been to care for the stables. The blizzard had come with the nightfall, storming suddenly out of the west as the sun was dying. When its first stinging gusts had hit, the court had been filled with scurrying servants, struggling to secure the animals and material within the outbuildings. One man had stayed behind the rest to complete some errand—none remembered what. His scream of terror had almost gone unheard by the last of those stumbling back to the castle gate. But several men had staggered through the near darkness and blinding winds to the darker figure lying in whirling white. They had borne his mangled body into the castle with panic-sped steps, for no man had seen that which had attacked the human with such savage suddenness and vanished again into the blizzard.

The victim lay close to the fire, partially lifted from the stone floor by an improvised pillow of rags. His eyes gaped blankly in stark horror, and scarlet bubbles broke occasionally from his slack lips. Relentless fangs had shredded the flesh about his throat and chest, foiled in their attempt to sever the carotids only by the heavy fur cloak and the intervention of a protecting arm. This much could be determined from scrutiny of the dying man, whose silence had been unbroken since that one shriek of mortal terror. Several had pointed out that the servant probably could not speak even should he come out of shock, for the awful wreckage of his throat would make speech most unlikely.

There seemed to be no end to the flow of blood that streamed through the rough bandages to glisten on the stones. The one who usually tended only to injury to livestock had been called to help—the baron's physician and astrologer could not be found, assuming he would have bothered. The horse surgeon knew it was hopeless of course, but for appearances he made a few half-hearted attempts to forestall imminent death.

The servant uttered one great, wet cough that merged with a final spasm. The horse surgeon considered the limp wrist, critically pried up one eyelid, and shrugged. "Well, he's dead," he proclaimed needlessly. There was disappointment among the watchers, who had hoped to learn from the victim of his assailant's nature. Over them lay a clammy atmosphere of gnawing fear, and several argued louder than necessary, asserting that a wolf, or several wolves, possibly a snow cat had been the killer. Some had darker suspicions as well, for this frozen land of Marsarovj had its legends.

A sudden hideous movement halted their slow withdrawal! The corpse had lurched upward from the slippery stones! Supporting itself with its arms, it sat half-upright and glared at them with wide and sightless eyes. Red slobbering lips fought to form words.

"Death! I see him! Out of the storm he comes for us all!" blubbered that thing which should not speak. "Death comes! A man! A man not man! Death for all!"

The corpse toppled hollowly back upon the stones, now silent.

"He must not have been quite dead," offered the surgeon finally, but not even he believed that.

I. The Rider in the Storm

Kane at last was forced to admit to himself that he was totally lost, that for the past hour he had been without any sense of direction whatsoever. He kicked his plodding horse onward, cursing the fate that had set him abroad in this frozen wasteland during what seemed to be the worst blizzard in his long memory. The shaggy steed was close to floundering with exhaustion, for even its rugged north-bred endurance had been overtaxed by the days of flight which had left them lost in this fantastic ice storm.

Two impressions filled Kane's weary mind. One was a sensation of unbearable, soul crushing cold—cold accumulated during the days of travel through the wintered land and now multiplied by this needled wind of ice. The chill sought for him through the thick folds of heavy fur that surrounded him, and Kane knew that when he stopped moving, he would quickly freeze to death.

The second impression was one of awful necessity to outdistance his pursuers. They had dogged his trail relentlessly for the long, cold days, penetrating every trick this master of deception had employed to hide the signs of his progress. But then with the last powers of the priests of Sataki, his pursuers had little chance of missing a trail that no human eye could discover.

Since noon Kane had often been able to catch sight of them, so close had they gained on him. Knowing that they would almost inevitably overtake him by nightfall, he had welcomed the sudden blizzard when it had come. Although he doubted if even this could cover his tracks from the ken of those grim hunters, he hoped to gain invaluable time—possibly to recover his lead over them. But the storm had become a screaming nightmare of white in which Kane had lost his way completely, and now frozen death joined with those others who sought to bring down the ice-encrusted man who slumped forward in his saddle.

Many days behind him and to the southeast lay the independent principality of Rader, once the northmost province of the old Serranthonian Empire, but now broken away in the collapse of the Empire which had followed the extinction of the line of Halbros-Serrantho. Rader had become a frontier backwater after the dynastic wars had destroyed the strength and wealth of the central states and had created a band of desolation cutting Rader off from the civilization to the south. Law had been lost in the imperial disintegration and never restored. In obedience to ancient principle, brute power shaped chaos into a more orderly framework, and Rader had been ruled for the past century (when it was ruled at all) by a variety of warlords. It had been a motley succession, for the land was of little value or importance. Thus its rulers had usually been petty and relatively unambitious men—old nobility, adventurers, robber barons, and the like.

Until some few days before, Rader had been ruled by the hated exile Orted Ak-Ceddi, onetime bandit leader turned Prophet of Sataki. Under his fanatical command, the dark cult of Sataki had exploded from obscurity into a crimson wave of terror that had overwhelmed the forest land of Shapeli far to the south and had very nearly broken forth to hurl its legions upon the southern kingdoms. But his power had at last been smashed, and

Orted had fled the ruins of his Dark Crusade with only a few of his most loyal followers. Safe in the obscurity of this northern backwater, Orted had seized control of Rader with the last remnant of his former strength and had settled down to ponder the tangled riddles of fortune and power.

To Rader had come Kane in the night. As the mercenary general of the Prophet's cavalry, Kane had both been creator of the fighting arm of the Dark Crusade as well as the cause of its ultimate failure. Treachery on Kane's part had first sundered the Sword of Sataki, but Orted's final insane doublecross had brought on disaster for them both. Orted had escaped the ensuing slaughter of his followers, but Kane was trapped by the victorious army of Jarvo. To avoid capture by his enemies he had entered that unhallowed interdimensional corridor cursed by ancients as the Lair of Yslsl. The torments he encountered within Yslsl's cosmic web of soulless horror were such that it might have been better to have accepted the mere physical torture and death from those he had thus escaped.

But Kane at length accomplished that which no other man could have done. He emerged at the one other place on this world where the Lair of Yslsl impinged. It took him over a year to recover from the ordeal he suffered therein, but when he did recover he set out to kill the man who had driven him within the crawling passages of that elder world nightmare. The trail to Rader had taken him from one end of the known world to the other—a trail that twisted, forked, vanished, and reappeared again. But he followed it with a singleness of purpose unfamiliar even to Kane.

And almost four years after the massacre of the Satakis at Ingoldi, Orted Ak-Ceddi found himself alone in his chambers confronting Kane. The brief, vicious struggle ended most satisfactorily for Kane, who was able to present Orted with a curious gem-like crystal derived from the venom of the now extinct tomb worm of Carsultyal. Embedded in his flesh, the paralyzing venom seeped through Orted's writhing form and silently commenced an ineluctable disintegration of every nerve in his body, working from the tiniest to the largest cords. Kane was forced to cut short his enjoyment of the fantastic contortions of Orted's death throes, when the Prophet's guards finally broke into the chamber.

He had vaulted through the hidden passage by which he had gained entrance to Orted's private chambers— the Prophet had not been able to learn all the secrets of his sanctuary—and fled the city before any organized search could be formed. Since that night Kane had been pushing steadily into the northern wastes. But his pursuers were the last of Orted's fanatics, and Kane knew that only death would halt their relentless pursuit of the slayer of their Prophet. Their fanaticism coupled with the few sorcerous devices left to their dying cult had brought them within sight of their quarry after hard days of searching. And then the blizzard had given Kane respite.

His horse stumbled over some buried obstruction and half-fell to its knees. Kane fought to hold his saddle, noticing the crackle of ice encrusted on his cloak. Gritting teeth he lurched from his mount and helped the exhausted beast erect. The agony of forcing his nearly frozen limbs into action racked his powerful frame, and he swayed on his benumbed feet, clutching the neck of his gasping horse for support.

"Easy, boy," he murmured through his ice-hung beard. "Let you rest just a minute." But only a minute, he told himself, and stamped his frozen boots, wearily brushing off the crust of ice that enclosed his body. A bed of snow beckoned him to its softness, but he hurled aside its temptation. He would not accept defeat this easily. He had cheated death time beyond comprehension, and if he lost here in the storm, his adversary must take him not gracefully, but struggling blindly onward past the extremes of his power. That this frozen elemental fury should be his doom infuriated Kane, and he glared defiantly into the scouring wind. Frustration. His enemy now was utterly intangible—a cosmic entity that heedlessly had engulfed him—whose massive presence now

16

tore at him, smothered his life fire. In no way could he even force his destroyer to take notice of his existence.

Yet it was no ordinary storm, of this Kane was certain. It was too sudden, too violent to be natural; Kane had never encountered anything its equal even on several excursions much farther to the north. It was a witch storm perhaps, for its abrupt ferocity hinted at sorcery. But why any sorcerous power should summon such a blizzard in this wasteland, he could not begin to guess. Surely the Satakis had not evoked it, for it had cheated them of their prey.

The horse whinnied fearfully, and Kane decided he had rested as long as he dared. As he remounted, his steed started in fright. Kane sought to soothe the beast, thinking at first he had somehow startled it in mounting. But the horse was genuinely alarmed, he quickly noted—its nostrils flared and eyes widened in fright. Soon Kane too sensed a presence, an awareness of alien scrutiny. He gave the horse his head, and the animal bolted forward recklessly through the storm. For a tense interval Kane felt the sensation of pursuit, of some entity reaching for him with awful hunger; then the feeling slacked off.

As soon as he felt clear he slowed his mount's headlong flight to a safer pace. "What in the name of Temro was that!" he muttered. At first he had thought his pursuers had blundered upon him, but the horse's reaction and his own sensations dispelled that impression. He had seen nothing, heard nothing—for the howling storm had effectively blotted out and muffled both vision and sound. Yet Kane and his horse had both definitely sensed the presence of something, and Kane knew better than to doubt such extrasensory evidence. The strange workings of his inner mind were not unfamiliar to him, unnatural talents utilized and strengthened throughout his amazing career. And Kane was certain that some form of horrible death had been very close to him in the storm.

Now he strained his senses against the blizzard, while the horse plodded dismally through the rising drifts, his sudden surge of energy dissipated. For a long time there was nothing, until Kane seemed to hear a wild howling that was not of the wind. He inhaled carefully, drawing the frozen air deep into his lungs. Faintly he began to catch the scent of wolf on the stormwind. The horse too caught the scent, and he snorted fitfully.

Suddenly Kane halted. The howling had become more pronounced and seemed to come from many throats. To his keen nostrils came the unmistakable sour scent of damp wolf fur. Somewhere ahead of him—distance was impossible to gauge in the storm—lurked a large pack of wolves. Kane was puzzled once more. From their cries the pack was full in hunt—but it seemed impossible that a wolfpack would be foraging in such a raging blizzard. Perhaps the limits of starvation had driven them abroad, he mused. In that case it was damned lucky that he was downwind.

But this advantage might vanish with a shift of wind, and Kane turned his mount away from the invincible pack, putting the wind to his back. Might as well backtrack, he thought grimly. With no more sense of direction than he now had, any course was as well as another—or as pointless. As he forged onward through the drifts the howling was drowned out in the greater voice of the storm. Just as it was swallowed up altogether, Kane thought he could also hear mingled in the cries of horses and men. But the sounds were too faint for any hope of clarity, and Kane was too exhausted to pursue the fantasies of his tormented senses.

The horse plodded on and on, stumbling more frequently now, but refusing to fall. Kane doubted if the beast would be able to rise once it slid down again—doubted if he would be able to remount if it could regain its feet. Time and distance had no meaning. He was utterly adrift from the world of time and space; there was only himself and the horse caught up in the rushing blizzard. Whether he moved or only the wind moved, Kane could not tell. Nor could he distinguish whether the bits of white moved through the darkness, or flecks of blackness through a sea of white. Now his entire body was growing altogether numb. Soon he would be unable to feel the horse on which he rode, and then there would only be Kane, bobbing helplessly, hopelessly in this maelstrom of ice.

This was infinity.

Abruptly something clawed at Kane's face. He reeled and lashed out at it drunkenly. His frozen hand encountered a tree branch. Several more whipped at him, as the horse painfully slipped its way between several trees.

Kane forced himself out of stupor, gathering together the final dregs of his remarkable strength. If the horse had blundered into a forest there was hope yet. It seemed unlikely, for there had been no body of trees in sight before the storm had hit—but how could he know how far the horse had carried him. The wind's roar became muted, and its force was broken by the trees, causing the snow to fall slowly, sifting through the branches. The blackness of night became settled, and in this darkness Kane's eyes could penetrate—although another man would still be relatively blind.

It was indeed a forest—or at least the grove of trees extended as far as Kane could discover. From the shelter it provided from the stormblast, it seemed likely that this was at any rate a considerable wooded area. Kane urged his faltering mount deeper into the woods. If he could reach a place far enough within to break most of the storm's force, he might build a sort of shelter and possibly get a fire going.

He caught the smell of wood smoke on the wind and pulled up. Had his hunters also found the trees, he wondered—or perhaps he had come upon someone else in this wilderness. He followed the smoke hopefully. Should it be the fire of strangers, he would share it one way or another. If he found the Satakis . . . Well, he had been hunted long enough. Kane loosened his sword from its ice bound scabbard. At least the cold iron would then find warmth. They would not expect an attack, and maybe with surprise, and if his strength had not been fatally drained by the storm. . . .

Visions of carnage passed through his mind, as Kane followed the scent of smoke through the sentinel trees. The ground seemed to rise now, he thought. Revitalized with the tangible before him, hope for shelter and lust to kill, Kane encouraged his horse. The rugged steed was due to collapse at any step, but it too sensed salvation and forced itself beyond endurance.

The trees thinned and then broke into a clearing. As he came through the last of their number, Kane caught sight of several small outbuildings clustered about a walled stone manor house or small castle. The structures loomed darkly against the snow-filled night skies, their silhouette perforated with specks of light from curtained windows. Desperately Kane forced his mount to this unknown castle here in the frozen wastes. Let it be inhabited by demons and he cared not—so long as he found warmth. He shouted hoarsely as he reached the gate. In sudden despair he realized that no gatekeeper would be at his post on such a night, and that no one within the castle manor could hear him above the storm—should they be awake. In his condition he could never climb over the wall. In white fury Kane pounded on the gate with his great sword. To his amazement the gate swung ajar—it had been left unlocked!

Not bothering to puzzle over this good fortune, Kane pushed aside the gate enough to pass through. The horse's hooves clattered hollowly across the courtyard, as Kane shouted wildly, striving to awaken someone within. Just as he reached the manor's main doorway, the animal stumbled and fell, pitching the rider upon the stones. Kane twisted clumsily, too benumbed for his usual lightning reflexes to serve him. He fell heavily before the door, rolling against it.

With his last strength he battered the iron studded oak with his swordhilt. He looked back weakly to the gate through which he had entered. Just before blackness overcame him, he seemed to see something white creeping through that open doorway.

II. Things Found in the Storm

Something white stood blurred in Kane's recovering consciousness. With an effort he forced awareness into his mind, his eyes to focus.

Her eyes widened in startled fright as Kane's baleful gaze suddenly gripped her, but she recovered quickly and said to cover her embarrassment, "Here—try to drink this."

Kane accepted the cup she held to his lips in silent appreciation, even in his condition savoring the excellent brandy. Warmth flowed from the cognac as fully as from the crackling fire they had laid him by. So the people of the manor had heard his call after all, he mused, and quickly he took note of his surroundings.

He was in a small, stone room, furnished by a few benches, some chairs and a heavy table drawn near the large fire that blazed against one wall. An antechamber, he surmised, from its plainness probably where the porter and stewards kept attendance on the main door. Kane's ice-crusted cloak had been removed, and a heavy fur rug was thrown about him. Two servants supported him in a half supine position before the fire; several others and a very sleepy maid milled about the room and doorway.

Holding the cup to his lips was a tousled girl of elfish beauty. From her magnificent robe of white snowcat and the emerald set ring on her delicate hand, Kane knew her to be a lady of high estate. A mane of pale blond tresses framed a perfect face from which a pair of wide, grey eyes shone. Together with a pointed chin and straight, finely chiseled nose, she presented the picture of a somewhat whimsical pixie—a mouth made for quick smiles now set in concern. Her age might be from late teens to early twenties.

"Well, Breenanin, what have you found!" A bear of a man swept into the room, a huge fur robe hastily gathered about him. "Who is it that comes calling on a night fit only for ice phantoms and destroys the sleep of honest folk!" he blustered good-naturedly.

"Hush, Father!" whipped Breenanin. "He's injured and nearly frozen!"

"Eh?" muttered the lord of the castle curiously, and he made a vaguely sympathetic noise to mollify his daughter.

Kane shrugged off the servants' hands and drew himself to his feet, reeling momentarily in pain and dizziness before he straightened. He met his host's curious gaze and announced formally, "Forgive this ill timed and unannounced intrusion. I've been wandering through this waste for several days when the storm caught me, and I had about given out before I happened on this castle. My horse fell in your court, and I was unconscious until a moment ago. Had your servants not found me, I would have frozen solid by morning."

"In the court, you say?" said the other in puzzlement. "How the hell did you make it past the gate?"

"It was unlocked when I tried it," returned Kane. "Most fortunate that someone neglected it."

"Maybe so, but that kind of carelessness can get you murdered in bed. Gregig! Can't you remember your duties just because we get a little snow!"

The porter looked most unhappy. "Milord, I distinctly remember locking the gate when the storm hit. I can't understand it."

"Mmm!" intoned his master. "Well, is it locked now?"

"Yes, milord!" the porter said hurriedly; then uneasily, "It was locked when I checked it—after finding the stranger."

"At least even a near snowman has more sense than some fat porters."

"The wind must have shut it—for I didn't," Kane broke in.

He received a suspicious stare from his host. "That isn't possible," he stated. Then he shrugged, "Perhaps the fall shook up your memory a bit. Not uncommon, I suppose."

Kane remained silent.

"Well, anyway you're inside. Welcome to my somewhat chilly manor! I am Baron Troylin of Carrasahl, and the underfed cupbearer there is my daughter, Breenanin. You are welcome to my hospitality until this blizzard lets up and you feel like moving on. We're always glad for some company from the outside world here—breaks the monotony." He laughed, "The way that blizzard's carrying on, it looks like we're all going to be snowbound for some while."

Kane bowed. "You are most gracious. I am deeply thankful for your hospitality," he said formally, speaking the Carrasahli with little difficulty. He watched his company cautiously. "My name is Kane." There was no reaction, so he went on. "My profession is fighting, but at present I am without a position. I was heading toward Enseljos to see if Winston could use my services in his border war with Chectalos, but I strayed off course trying to save some miles from the usual trails. When the storm caught me, I was very well on my way to being lost."

Troylin showed no signs of disbelieving Kane, although Kane doubted if he was as simple as his rough and easy manner seemed to indicate. The baron was scrutinizing his guest carefully, trying to form an idea of what the storm had brought him.

Kane was a huge man—not much over six feet, but massively built. From an immense barrel of a chest set atop pillarlike legs, Kane's mighty arms hung like great corded tree limbs. His hands were of great size and strength—a strangler's hands, thought Troylin. The man must indeed be powerful, and probably could handle that sword well too. He seemed to be left-handed, as far as the baron could tell. His hair was red and of moderate length; the beard short as well. His features were somewhat coarse and even a bit foreboding, with a fresh scar on one cheek that seemed to be fading.

It was his eyes that bothered Troylin. He had noticed them from the first. It was to be expected, for Kane's eyes were the eyes of Death! They were blue eyes, but eyes that glowed with their own light. In those cold blue gems blazed the fires of blood madness, of the lust to kill

23

and destroy. They poured forth infinite hatred of life and promised violent ruin to those who sought to meet them. Troylin caught an image of that powerful body striding over a battlefield, killer's eyes blazing and red sword dealing carnage to all before it.

The baron hastily avoided those eyes and repressed a shudder. Vaul! What manner of man was this creature! Still, he was a mercenary, a hired killer. Such men were seldom tender poets. And from his bearing, Kane obviously was no common ruffian. His manners and speech indicated a man of culture, possibly of breeding. Sons of the best gentry, bastard or lawful, often took to a military career for fortune or for love of adventure. Kane certainly was impressive enough to have been a high ranking officer, and the rings and fine weapons indicated wealth at some time. His age was strangely difficult to guess. He didn't look physically over thirty, but somehow his bearing made him appear much older.

Troylin decided he would keep entertained untangling the mysteries of his strange guest for the next several days. Probably have some real tales to tell too. A change from that minstrel anyway. Just a few precautions until he was more certain about the man.

"Father! Are you just going to stand there like a stuffed bear!"

Troylin snapped alert. "Ah—yes! Started to doze, I'm afraid. Well, Kane, as I say, welcome. The servants will show you to a room—plenty here, we're sort of under-populated at the moment. Just wintering away from the civilized world for the rest." It occurred to him that Kane had no business still being able to stand after his ordeal, and he realized again the fantastic strength the man must have. "Right! So I hope you'll be recovering from it all by tomorrow." He turned and strode away.

Hugging the fur about himself, Kane followed the servants. It was all he could do to walk and his sight blurred repeatedly, but he didn't wish to show weakness. At least his hosts didn't guess the extent of his plight. With luck he could hole up here from the Satakis—and maybe the bllizzard had finished them.

24

"Damn lucky we found you," offered one servant, as he opened the door to Kane's chamber. "No one was on duty, you know. Fallen asleep with that storm blowing."

"Oh," muttered Kane, too exhausted to feel much interest. "How'd you let me in then?"

"It was the lady, you know. She'd been having trouble sleeping, heard it, and run down, woke the porter, Ing and me."

"Surprised she could hear me even, with the wind." Kane gratefully collapsed onto the bed.

"Oh, it wasn't you she heard," replied the servant, stepping through the door. "It was your horse screaming, you know. Poor thing was pure mad from fear! Something sure had that horse frightened near to death—but there wasn't a thing in the courtyard we could see."

III. Prisoners of the Storm

Kane immediately fell into a trance-like sleep, as his tormented body sought to heal the ravages of days of flight. Occasionally its serenity was shattered by some fitful dream of past adventure or by needles of pain from frostbitten flesh, but not even this could rouse him. At one time he seemed to hear again that eldritch howling of wolves, and in the midst of their cacophony two burning red eyes swam into his fevered vision—inhuman eyes that seared him with savage and abominable hunger.

At length consciousness returned to Kane, and with it came the realization that something hovered near his side. Snapping into instant awareness, Kane hurled himself to one side. His corded arm whipped upward and he grasped a shock of white hair, as his other hand came up with the dirk he had strapped to his side.

"Wait! Mercy!" croaked his terrified victim, and Kane halted the disemboweling thrust just short of its mark. He grasped the beard of a stern and elderly face that projected on a thin neck from dark, impressive robes. The robes flopped in extreme agitation, and a pair of scrawny hands clawed in panic at Kane's grip. Kane released the old man, but retained his knife watchfully.

"By the Seven Eyes of Lord Thro'ellet!" choked the elder, massaging his bearded visage. "Damn near rip off my face and slit my gullet, you did! Vicious killer, that's what! A mad dog! What has my good baron taken in?"

"Who the hell are you?" Kane growled.

"I'd warned him about strangers! The stars tell plainly that these are deadly days for us all—but he won't listen! Brings in a demon from the storm and expects me to concern myself with him. I warn you, you low born spawn of a viper! I don't intend to let this near murder go forgotten!"

"Why were you in here?" snarled Kane dangerously.

The elder looked alarmed once more. He judged the distance to the door, decided it was too far, and collected himself. "I am Lystric, Baron Troylin's personal physician and astrologer. You've been snoring away here better than an entire day now, and the baron told me to look in on you." He glared darkly at Kane. "As if a frolic in the storm would bother an ice phantom! I try to examine your injuries, and you half kill me for my concern! Fine gesture! Nice mannered guest! Troylin should have slaughtered you in your sleep!"

"That's been tried before," returned Kane, swinging to his feet. "Count yourself lucky that I recognized you as a harmless old lecher before I spilled your insides out. But as you have seen, I'm quite all right now."

Lystric reddened in anger. "Damn you! I warn you that my wisdom holds secrets that could blast you to ashes, should I see fit to unleash them! Maybe I will! This is no time for Troylin to bring murdering strangers into his hold! There is death in the stars! I have seen it!"

Kane regained his temper with painful effort. "Would you care to examine me now?" he asked innocently.

"Damn your insolent hide!" shrieked Lystric and stamped toward the door, a stately exit which he ruined by glancing behind in apprehension. Halting at the door he glowered back. "The baron directed me to ask you to dine with him shortly, should I find you not too weak to stir!"

"Send my thanks and tell him I accept."

"No doubt! Well, he'll send his men-at-arms to butcher you, if I have my will!"

Kane elaborately drew back his dirk to throw. Lystric departed.

There was a tight atmosphere of uneasiness hanging over the dinner table, and Kane noticed it despite his preoccupation with the board. He ate his first full meal in many days with careful attention, savoring each mouthful. A man who has been on short rations for many days does not bolt his food—it is a novelty to be slowly and thoroughly appreciated. At the same time he watched with interest the others gathered at the long table in the castle dining hall. Baron Troylin and his daughter ate nervously, with a forced lightheartedness that belied an underlying tenseness. Lystric the astrologer, who was also present at the high table, spent part of the time offering Kane dark looks, and the remainder watching anxiously the young man sitting next to him.

The youth Troylin had introduced as his son Henderin. Ignoring Kane's greeting, he had spent the first of the meal glaring stonily at the food set before him. Kane observed that Henderin carried no knife with which to eat, and that the two brawny attendants who stood close behind him seemed to pay an unnecessary amount of attention to their charge's every move. No comment had been offered on the situation, and Kane had discreetly raised no questions, although it was obvious that something was amiss in the household and that the baron's son seemed to be the center of the anxiety. He was a well built and well favored young man—a few years his sister's senior—with the pale blond hair of his family. He bore no signs of ill treatment, although he somehow impressed Kane as a privileged prisoner who was allowed to sit in at his captor's table.

Henderin chose to end his petulant silence by breaking into an anecdote of his father. "This meat is *burned!*" he intoned hotly. "I specifically told you to bring me nothing but *raw* flesh!"

The two retainers behind him stood poised. Breenanin halted her cup before her mouth and froze in anticipation, while Troylin nervously glanced toward Lystric. The astrologer spoke in soothing tones, "Of course—the cooks must have forgotten. I'll personally speak to them about this. But since all the rest of us are eating, why don't you have a little cooked meat too. It's still nice and red, you see—all the fire did was warm it for you."

"I said I wanted raw flesh!" Henderin exploded. "Not burned dead by the fire, but still warm and bleeding! Bring it to me!"

Lystric went on hurriedly. "But there isn't any meat left that hasn't been cooked. So why not eat just a bite . . ."

Henderin screamed an oath and hurled his plate onto the floor. Behind him the two attendants rushed in, but Lystric waved them to a halt. Several hounds had sprung from the corners of the hall and had fallen upon the scattered meat. Henderin watched enthralled as they greedily fought over the scraps. With a wild smile he snatched a large joint of meat from a tray, pulled it to him, and buried his muzzle into it. He tore the flesh in large chunks, devouring it with gusto. From time to time he gave a low growl.

For the others the meal proceeded with relative quiet.

With the business of eating completed, the dinner began to gather steam. Servants cleared away the debris and settled down to the more serious duty of keeping their master and his guest well supplied with ale. Kane prepared himself for a long evening of drinking and conversation, aware that Troylin expected him to repay the baron's hospitality by entertaining him. It appeared to be developing into a most comfortable evening. At the lower tables, the baron's retainers and men-at-arms were making a lusty chatter, serving wenches made free with the ale, and the great fire was blazing. Even Henderin was quiet, for the moment slowly drawing pictures on the table with an ale dipped finger. In the shadow of a column close by the high table a tall man toyed with a lute.

Kane had asked few questions during the meal, and to his relief neither had Troylin. The baron seemed content to accept Kane's story at face value, and merely listened with interest to his guest's anecdotes. To his delight, he found Kane an entertaining and informed conversationalist, with a fantastic variety of material to draw upon. Deeming it none of his concern, he showed no interest in Kane's business in this region.

Judging it not altogether indiscreet, Kane at length asked, "How is it that you are wintering here in Marsarovj? Even Carrasahl must be warmer and more congenial than this wilderness."

Troylin laughed depreciatively and replied readily, "Well, I get tired of civilized winters after a while. So I thought it would be a nice change to spend the winter here in the provinces. My family has maintained this old castle for years—it's really a fortified manor from the Empire days—and I thought it would make a snug, rustic spot to spend the winter. Hunting is excellent too—all year around."

He lowered his voice and added uneasily, "Also I'd hoped the atmosphere would be good for Henderin. The boy's a little unsettled, you've noticed no doubt. Lystric assures me though that this is just the thing for him."

Kane nodded and changed the subject to the matter of hunting. Marsarovj, he knew, was a province rife with subarctic game.

He became conscious of an unpleasant sensation of scrutiny after a while and looked for the source. In the shadows slouched a figure with a lute, a lean man whose eyes gleamed a startling red in the firelight.

Following Kane's gaze, Troylin caught sight of its object and called out, "Ah, Evingolis! There you are! Wondered where you were lurking tonight. Come over and give us a tune! We've been jabbering too hard to do any serious drinking." Turning to Kane he said, "This is Evingolis, the most accomplished minstrel you'll ever have the pleasure of hearing. I had the fortune of attaching him to my patronage this summer, and he's a delight to have

29

around on these winter nights." He went on to describe the many virtues of the minstrel.

The object of the baron's praise strode silently from the shadows and took a vantage point by the fire. Moving his long fingers over the lute strings with fluid grace, he sang in crystalline tones of a blind princess and her demon lover. One of the Opyros Cycle, Kane recognized, and he recalled the bizarre fate of that blighted poet. The minstrel was himself an unusual figure. He was an albino, with the characteristic pale skin, white hair and pink eyes. Kane could hazard no guess as to his nationality, having found the singer's accent unlike any he could place. In height Evingolis was several inches taller than Kane, and although he was thinly built, there was no hint of softness or weakness to him. His features were finely molded, but sharp rather than effeminate. His thin hair he wore cut short; his face cleanshaven. As he sang, his pink eyes stared into infinity—perhaps seeing the strange events of which he told. Kane noticed that Henderin watched the minstrel with rapt attention, seemingly magically charmed by the tale.

The rising lament that concluded the song died out with a keening moan from the lute. He was an artist, conceded Kane, who could not recall hearing a better performance of that difficult poem. Men shuffled their feet and made uneasy sounds in the stillness following the song. "Excellent!" commended Troylin after a pause. "You always have something new for us, don't you. Ah, how about another, Evingolis. One a bit more rousing for this cold night."

"Of course, milord," spoke the minstrel, accepting a tankard from a scurrying wench. "One moment while I sweeten my throat." He tossed off the ale and broke into a rollicking ballad of a woodsman's five daughters, which moved the baron's men to join in the bawdy chorus.

"A bit morbid in his tastes," confided Troylin, "but if you insist he can be common enough."

"Some hold that true beauty lies only in the uncommon," Kane murmured, watching the firelight's gleam in Breenanin's pale hair. She smiled, wondering if his remark was to compliment her. But Kane, sunken into brooding, noticed only that her teeth shone white and sharp against her red smile.

The baron was involved in an endless anecdote of a winter hunt he had once enjoyed, and Kane had for some time been making only a token attempt to pay attention. At the point when some stag was goring a favored hound, several of Troylin's men entered the hall, loudly stamping snow from their gear.

"Well, Tali. Back at last, I see!" Troylin greeted their leader. "What's it like out there?"

"A white hell, milord, it truly is! So cold your spit cracks in midair, now that the sky has cleared. And the snow's piled so damn high, it was almost impossible for us to push through as far as we went. Couldn't even get a sled out in that stuff. We're snowbound for certain until this crusts over solid."

"No matter," said the baron. "We've provisions here to last all winter, and there's plenty of game, I know."

Tali shook his head. "I don't know myself on that one. The area is full of wolves, for some reason. Big, mean fellows—and bold ones too! Saw maybe half a dozen at one time following us along—keeping just out of bowshot! Looked like they'd just as soon rush us, they did! Game must be scarce to bring them out in the open like that.

"And that's not all, milord! We stumbled on something really terrible out there in the snow! Came on it just as we was starting back. Party of dead men, it was, milord!" A horrified rustle went through the listeners. Tali gulped and plunged on. "Looked like eight or nine of them and horses too, but they were so torn up it was hard to say for sure. Wolves got them—ripped them to shreds! My guess is that they were attacked in the storm when they couldn't see what was happening. Must have been a really big pack to attack that many men. All armed too, they was. Course you couldn't tell much, but their gear was strange. Not like anything you see around here. Well, when we saw this, you bet we turned around! Beat it back here fast as we could! Wolves attacking armed parties—I've never heard the like!"

He tossed a gold medallion onto the table. "Saw a couple of these around the bodies."

Baron Troylin frowned. "Well, wolves can't get to us in here," he concluded. Which seemed to strike Henderin as quite amusing.

Kane examined the gold medallion with its familiar circle of elder hieroglyphics. The followers of Sataki would hound him no further.

IV. Hunters in the Snow

"Personally I think the baron is crazy to ride to the hunt after what Tali and them told us last night," observed the steward, evidently in a loquacious mood.

"Mmm?" Kane grunted noncommitally, while he tested the balance of several hunting spears.

"You didn't hear all those things they told to us afterwards. Brrr! When I think about those poor devils they found out there! Not much left but bare bones, they said! All those wolves around, and the baron still says it's a beautiful morning to hunt! I'd think after all you've been through, sir, you'd of had your fill of all that snow."

Kane selected the best spear and felt the edge of its iron head critically. "Ought to do it," he concluded. "I doubt if there'll be any problem with wolves. They probably attacked those others because of the storm. Our party is large enough, and the light of day will keep them hidden probably. And in the woods the snow's thin enough in most places so a horse won't bog down. Problem will be to run down any elk.

"Of course," he went on carefully, "I guess the game around here must be pretty sensational for the baron to drag his household all the way up here in the middle of nothing." He watched the steward fidget nervously, fighting to hold his loose tongue. "Or was there some other reason for this exile?"

It was too great a temptation. "I don't suppose the baron would care for you to know about it," the steward

32

began, looking around dramatically, "but someone's sure to tell you, and so I might as well. Since it doesn't do no harm anyway.

"Baron Troylin *had* to leave Carrasahl! That son of his, you know, him being crazy as an owl and all! Why, they were some actually talking about *burning* poor Henderin! So the baron pulled out to let things cool off. And Lystric —he's in charge of the young man, you know—said it would be good for him to get out away from things. All this is supposed to be soothing to his mind. That's why Henderin does everything nearly that the rest do—except they watch him careful—instead of being locked up like maybe he should. Lystric says he'll come back to normal easier if he leads a normal day's life, which seems to make a little sense.

"Personally though I wouldn't trust that crafty old buzzard—for all his fine talk, he's just a penny ante wizard! Wouldn't surprise me at all if some of those stunts he's tried haven't just made Henderin crazier. And everyone knows he's never held down a reputable position for long in his life—until the baron took him on as his son's physician.

"Beautiful bit of irony that! Few years back old Lystric was providing entertainment at a court banquet the baron attended. Troylin's drunk and he makes jokes about the old bastard's spiel. Lystric gets stuffy and he calls the baron an unlettered hick, a feeble minded oaf and all that —so old baron sics the dogs on him and they chase him all down one table through the food and everything. Really was funny! Course old Lystric's mad as can be, and the baron really had to eat crow to get him to take the position. Still Lystric was all the help Baron Troylin could find after what Henderin done."

"Just what is it about Henderin that made people talk about burning him? asked Kane. "Madness isn't usually treated quite that peremptorily."

The steward warmed to his subject. This was getting to the good part. He looked about again and lowered his voice impressively, "Because this wasn't just some ordinary

33

lunacy. No sir! Henderin isn't as harmless as he looks—that's why they keep so close a watch on him!

"Why, back at Carrasahl he *killed* a man, he did—one of the court guards! And that's not the worst of it! He killed him by ripping his throat out with his teeth! Was still chewing away at it when they caught him! Growling just like a wild animal worrying his prey!"

Seeing Kane's obvious interest, the steward expanded. "So they locked him up, and it was all the baron could do to get him out of the city and up here. Lystric says it's clearly possession, and he talked so clever that the baron packed him along with the rest of us in spite of their grudge.

"And I'll tell you something else! A couple days ago just as the storm was hitting, one of the servants got his the same way exactly! Something tore his throat out! Babbled something right at the end about death coming out of the storm for all of us! It plain wasn't natural, let me tell you! And I'll tell you something else too! It may have been a wolf that caught him—but there's some of us who wonder if old Lystric is telling it straight about Henderin being in his sight all the time!

"Listen, I could tell you about some other stuff going on around here of nights that don't quite ring true! No sir!"

But whatever other gossip the steward had to exhibit remained under wraps. A call from outside announced Troylin's approach. The baron was impatient to get started. Swinging the hunting spear as he brooded over the steward's disclosure, Kane hurried to the courtyard and mounted the horse his host had provided. The party, numbering over a dozen, rode out into the snow-clad forest.

Hounds raced through the snow baying joyously, within their shaggy coats oblivious to the subzero cold. Despite the crystalline coldness of the air and frozen ground, the distant sun shone through the clear sky and dazzled the hunters' eyes. Even under the trees the bright reflection from the snow was significant; beyond the forest it was overwhelming.

Kane watched sharply for wolves, squinting his cold

blue eyes against the glare, but he could see nothing of the great packs that had terrified the baron's party the day before. Tracks were uncertain, since the snow drifted continually. Still the snow bore numerous signs that Kane recognized as marks made by the passage of forest beasts. The hounds growled from time to time as they encountered the spoor of wolves, and the huntsmen kept them in line with difficulty.

On the surface the group seemed a normal hunting party. Besides Kane, the baron had brought along the minstrel Evingolis and perhaps another ten of his hunters and men-at-arms. Shouts and the usual banter passed back and forth. If any man was concerned over the grim discoveries announced by Tali last night, he gave no indication. The thrill of the hunt and daylight had wiped aside such forebodings. All carried hunting spears save the huntsmen who tended the hounds, but except for long knives and a few bows no one carried exceptional weaponry other than Kane.

Kane rode with his heavy sword strapped to his saddle in easy reach. Evingolis had laughed at this. "We're on a hunting party, wanderer, not a war party!"

Kane hadn't cared for the albino's jibe, but remembering that minstrels and jesters were expected to be impertinent, he had only shrugged. "A man of my profession finds his sword a life long companion."

"And a true colleague, no doubt!" Evingolis laughed. "I think it's rather an extension of your brawny arm, and you can't leave it behind. But your profession—what exactly is that?"

"Death," answered Kane levelly. "But I make no charge for minstrels. There isn't a coin small enough to accept as a fair payment, I find."

The others were hugely amused at the byplay between guest and minstrel. But Kane and the albino did not join in the laughter.

The hounds began baying in earnest, drowning the casual exchanges of their masters. In excitement they strained against their leashes, dragging the handlers.

"Fresh spoor!" was the shout. "Elk! Good big one from the tracks!"

"Turn them loose!" bellowed Baron Troylin. "Hot damn! Venison tonight for sure!"

Released, the hounds plummeted along the forest trail, hurtling fallen logs and plowing through drifts in their frantic haste. Exuberant howls tore the air and rang against the dark trees as they poured forth their eagerness to take their prey. Behind them galloped the hunters, no less eager than their dogs for the blood of the quarry. Shouting their own calls of encouragement they recklessly plunged after the pack—heedless of looming trees or hidden obstructions that threatened to bring horse and rider to a crashing fall.

"Come on! After them! We'll miss the kill! Watch out, you bastard! A day's wages the hounds finish him before we even get there! You're on! Remember Kane gets first throw after the baron! Hurry! It's a stag for sure! Damn you! Stump! Listen to them howl!" Perhaps the hounds were shouting much the same.

The headlong charge broke into a clearing and fell into sudden confusion. The trail had abruptly split, and the tracks plainly showed that the pack had left the clearing in two directions. "Thoem's beard!" shouted Troylin in delight. "Look! There's another one!"

From the evidence in the snow the first elk had come upon another here in the clearing. The second animal had bolted off on a different trail, and the pack had split apart to follow both spoors. "We'll get them both!" cried Troylin. "Kane! Take after that one heading west! Bunch of you go with him! Hurry, damn it! The elk'll kill the hounds with the pack split up!"

He plunged after what he judged to be the first elk. Kane and five of the baron's men broke off and galloped after the newcomer. The forest quickly swallowed the sounds of their rushing passage, leaving the clearing strangely still—but not untenanted.

There was no presentiment of disaster. Kane's quarry had been fresh and the hounds had already chased the other elk far. Thus the second stag had run far before the pack had been able to gain. However, the greater endurance of the dogs along with the lesser hindrance posed for them by the snow soon told, and with the pack hard on his heels the bull elk chose a small ravine to make his stand. Only three dogs had followed this second quarry, and they were unable to bring the great elk down. Around him they pranced, slashing at the giant, then darting back to avoid the deadly hooves and antlers. When the hunters came upon them, one hound had already been gored to death and the stag bled from a dozen tears in his mighty body. Kane cast his spear with fatal accuracy, hitting the elk in the neck. His throat transfixed, the forest monarch staggered, trumpeting in agony. The remaining hounds closed in for the kill, as two more spears stabbed into the mortally wounded elk. Shouting in triumph the hunters surrounded the body of their prey, lying red in the snow; two hurriedly dismounted and ran to pull off the crazed hounds.

At which point the wolves attacked.

They fell on the hunters swiftly, silently as a striking serpent. A pack of perhaps fifteen huge, gray killers suddenly were on them, having come up unseen from the trees behind the hunters. One second the thrill and excitement of the kill; then a shriek of terrified agony and a ravine swarming with snarling shapes! They were the great gray wolves of the northern wastes—nearly six feet long and 150 pounds of slashing, yellow-eyed death. In a rage of blood lust they attacked the startled humans, and hunters now switched roles with prey.

The first to scream died almost instantly. A giant wolf had leapt upon him, hurtling him from his saddle and onto the snow. Choking the gaping fangs with an elbow, the hunter drew his knife and gutted the beast with a desperate stroke. Yet before the beast's hold had broken in death, a second gray killer slashed in and ripped open the man's throat.

The two hunters on the ground never had a chance. One lived long enough to wrest free a spear from the elk's carcass. He spitted the first wolf to meet him, but as he tried to pull the weapon loose, two more bore him to the frozen ground and tore him apart. The other was down before he could react. But he managed to get to his hunting knife, and beneath the gory huddle of gray shapes his arm plunged in and out—long after it seemed possible for life to remain. His efforts inflicted deep gashes in several of his slayers.

The hounds closed with the wolves with the unquenchable hatred of the tamed canine for his wild brother. At least one wolf rolled away from the snarling melee with his eyes glazed in death, and several others were flung back with crushed legs and gushing wounds. But numbers and wild ferocity overwhelmed the valiant struggle of the great hounds, and their fearless defiance ended in crimson ruin.

Kane had been among the first reached by the wolves' deadly ambush. Only his fantastic reflexes and blinding speed had saved him from their initial rush. Twisting in his saddle as the first beast had sought to leap upon him from behind, his powerful hands had locked in the wolf's ruff. Kane whirled the huge creature about and flung it from him; the wolf dashed against a tree close at hand and caromed into the snow with a broken back. In a flash Kane's mighty sword arm snatched the blade whistling from its scabbard. A second killer had followed almost on the heels of the first, but Kane's draw was faster and the keen blade sheared through the beast's skull. His horse reared in panic as the others closed in, and Kane had to clamp his legs to its flanks tightly to stay on. Another wolf went down, its skull smashed by the plunging hooves.

The other two hunters were able to hold out briefly against the swirling, gray shapes. One still retained his hunting spear. His cast caught the first wolf to reach him full in the chest. Had he not attempted to bring his bow into play, he might have lived awhile longer. As he struggled to notch an arrow he was hit from two sides at once. For a moment he tried to jam his bow down the throat of one attacker, held in the saddle by the opposing pulls of the wolves on either leg. He succeeded in breaking one wolf's grip, but before he could do more, the other dragged him to the ground. A gray nightmare closed over his writhing form, and the struggles abruptly ceased. The remaining hunter buried his knife in the ribs of one wolf which leaped to drag him down, but the flailing beast had fallen back with the blade wedged in its ribs. Weaponless, the rider sought flight. However, before his horse had covered half the distance of the ravine, it had been pulled down by the slashing fangs. Beast and rider collapsed in a squirming heap of gray and crimson, one wolf crushed beneath them.

And Kane was alone with the wolves.

Half a dozen gray killers circled their prey warily. Some were crippled and bleeding, but they showed no hint of abandoning the last man. Their blood fury was completely aroused, and their savage minds were set on an unshakeable goal—to drag down the human and steep their muzzles in his blood. Kane glared back at them, lips drawn in a snarl and killer's eyes blazing with hellfire. His own insatiable lust to kill and to destroy burned incandescently within his spattered frame. For the space of several heartbeats killer looked upon killer.

Their attack was a gray blur of coordinated fury. Two wolves went for Kane, while the others attacked his steed. The wolf on his left Kane met with a blinding sword stroke that clove the beast's skull asunder. The other wolf arched through the air in a graceful, deadly leap that carried it into Kane's lap. Its fangs snapped shut spasmodically, but without aim—for its yellow eyes were already stark in death. A dagger had buried itself hilt-deep in its throat. Right-handed, Kane had thrown the weapon with unerring aim, just as the wolf had begun its leap. The wolf had died even as its fellow had fallen under Kane's sword.

The heavy carcass in his lap encumbered Kane for one deadly instant. Before he could toss it aside, another wolf buried its fangs in the horse's neck. Cursing, Kane broke free of the carcass; his sword flashed out and chopped through the wolf's neck. But the damage had been done, and with a shrill scream Kane's horse fell to the frozen ground.

Already Kane had vaulted clear of the saddle, and he landed catlike in the snow as his horse crashed to the earth in mortal agony. Only a split second did he have to get his balance, and the last three wolves were on him. He thrust out his sword; the wolf tried to twist aside and avoid the blade but was too slow. As the long blade transfixed it, another wolf leapt at Kane from the right, even as the third gathered its feet. No time to pull free his sword, Kane caught the wolf in full leap with his free hand. Swinging the beast by its foreleg, he hurled it aside and jerked his sword up. The third wolf had been injured and was just a little slow in joining its fellows' rush. Kane's rising blade caved in its side as the wolf leapt for the man's throat.

Meanwhile the second wolf had recovered its balance after landing harmlessly in the snow. Kane flashed around to meet this last adversary. The two last combatants in the death-filled ravine faced each other in deadly concentration. For an instant their two minds met in understanding, in mutual admiration of the other's sheer ferocity and awful capability. The wolf made a movement as if to turn and flee, then whirled and sprang for the man in one mighty leap of ripping fury. Kane's stroke almost missed the twisting gray blur. But not quite. And then only one living thing moved amidst the carnage.

Kane looked about him carefully, but no more wolves came into the ravine. He gulped air in great gasps and tried to remember how long the battle had lasted. Something like five minutes, he guessed—blood was streaming from the wounds of the elk yet.

He glanced at himself. By a miracle he was almost unscathed. Only a rip in his right arm where the last wolf's fangs had raked him in passing. His clothes and face were smeared with wolf blood, making him look like a crimson goblin. Quickly he retrieved and cleaned his weapons. He had to reach the others before any more wolves found him on foot. Assuming the rest of the party hadn't met a similar fate, he mused.

The entire attack seemed fantastic anyway. That the wolves had been drawn by the noise of the hunt and maddened by the kill would be a natural explanation. But unlikely. In the face of the other attacks especially. The incidents almost seemed like carefully planned campaigns. He pondered uneasily over what could inspire wolves to engage in systematic massacre of humans. The possibilities were not encouraging.

A horse's whinny cut short his musing for the moment. In the trail ahead of him stood one of the horses which had bolted at the start of the attack. The animal was still quite frightened and eyed the man nervously. It wanted human companionship in this danger ridden frozen forest, but was still extremely spooky. Kane called the horse softly, soothingly—coaxing it close enough to reach. At least the wind was toward him—if the horse caught the scent of wolf blood, he'd turn and run for sure.

But the animal with agonizing slowness came close enough to let Kane catch its rein, after several heart-stopping attempts. He swung into the saddle and gave the skittish mount its head, galloping back along the trail over which many had passed a short time ago.

After a few miles Kane heard a distant scream—a terrified plea for help. He considered a moment and decided to check it out. The cry seemed human enough, and it was definitely feminine. Kane cautiously, nonetheless hastily, guided his mount toward the cry's source, curious to learn what manner of throat produced it.

The horse caught a scent it remembered and whinnied in alarm. Kane tried to catch the scent too, but the reek of wolf on his body masked whatever it was. But from the horse's reluctance to proceed, Kane guessed it must be wolves the beast smelled. If there were wolves about, they were probably the cause of the girl's shouts. However, it seemed unlikely that the girl would still be alive to scream—which argued for an inhuman source of the disturbance. Kane was familiar with instances of would-be rescuers having been lured to their doom by following unseen cries for aid, and in view of his recent fight he felt inclined to caution.

Yet the screams sounded familiar, and acting on a hunch Kane spurred his reluctant mount forward.

Two wolves were snarling around the trunk of a large, low-hanging fir. Perched on a branch was the center of their attention—Breenanin.

Kane drew his blade, shouted and charged the lurking wolves. They gave a last glare at the treed human and broke for cover from the newcomer.

He halted under the tree and helped her from the branches; she landed in a sobbing heap in his arms. Kane tried to get a few questions in, but Breenanin only clung to him and whimpered. So he made what he hoped might sound like soothing, sympathetic sounds, and let her run down.

He had almost reached the clearing where the second elk had been come upon, when his charge stopped long enough to sniffle. "Ugh! You're a mess! Did you take a bath in elk's blood or something?"

"Or something. What in the name of the Seven Nameless were you doing out here? I seem to recall leaving you at the castle this morning."

"I wanted to go on the hunt, and Father wouldn't let me because of the stuff about wolves. Only I had to get out and see what the woods looked like after the storm, so I saddled my own horse and rode after you. The porter let me out because I've got the goods on him and anyway I said I was just going to ride around by the walls. Except I rode on after you and I thought I could catch up and Father would be too interested in the hunt to bother sending me back since I was along anyway.

"But all of a sudden this pack of wolves came after me. I knew I couldn't outrun them in the forest, so when my horse ran under that low tree back there, I slowed him enough to grab a branch and scramble off." She sniffled. "I thought my arms would pull out, but I knew I had to hang on. One of them nearly grabbed my leg before I could climb clear of them. But most of them kept chasing the horse—I guess they got him, but I didn't see—and just the two stayed to wait for me to come down. So I shouted and yelled hoping someone would come by from the hunt and hear me. And that's what you did," she concluded.

Kane was amazed at the girl's coolness. Most women would have been too panic stricken, too stupid, too weak. Yet Breenanin had survived and seemingly was relatively calm once again. It was unbelievable.

He rode into the clearing and saw with relief that Troylin and his party were waiting there. Intact and complete with elk. They shouted an exuberant greeting, then fell into mystified silence at the bloody rider along with his prize.

"Kane! What the hell!" gasped Troylin in amazement.

"Here's your daughter—safe enough," Kane said. "The rest are back with the elk. They won't be following us."

V. Tales on a Winter Evening

The hunting banquet was rather a dismal affair. These chases often had their fill of danger, and casualties of the hunt were frequently toasted to *in memoriam*. But five corpses were too many. Men drank their ale too seriously for fun, and in place of the usual raucous horseplay small groups spoke of the weird attack in quiet, anxious tones. The behavior of the wolves was decidedly unnatural, and not a few old legends were retold in the gloomy shadows of the dining hall.

At the high table the diners were in a no more festive mood. Breenanin was still shaken from her experience and did not pursue her accustomed banter with her father. The baron had been so thankful for her safety, that he had forgotten to punish her. Henderin's place was empty, and his two wardens were absent as well. The crazed youth had slipped away from his keepers that day and eluded them for several hours of frantic searching, before he was recaptured scrambling over the outer wall. He had been violent, and Lystric had been forced to place him under restraint until the spell passed. Lystric himself was no different from usual. The long-bearded astrologer sullenly gobbled his meal, while favoring the others with a baleful look.

Baron Troylin had just listened to Kane's retelling of the massacre in the ravine. He had asked him to repeat it three times now, and each time he had shaken his head at the conclusion and made the same comments about the uncanny behavior of the wolves. He was trying to fix the details in his thick head, in the vague hope that somewhere in Kane's narrative would lie the explanation for it all.

He caught sight of Evingolis, who was sitting in the shadows as usual, watching the diners while he gnawed a rib of venison. "Minstrel!" he rumbled. "This place has less life than a wake. Let's have some music to liven things a little." A raucous cheer went up from the diners in anticipation.

The albino strolled from his perch and collected his lute. Playing over the strings a moment, he raised mocking eyes to Kane and announced, "Here's a tune perhaps our guest will recognize."

His clear voice began the song, and Kane barely repressed a start. The minstrel's song was in archaic Ashertiri—a tongue Kane doubted if another man within days of travel could understand! The song was the work of the long dead and ill famed poet Clem Ginech of ancient Ashertiri, whose efforts had left those of his age uncertain whether he was a poet turned sorceror or the reverse.

Within an endless mirror of my spirit's infinite soul,
I reach back into timeless ages beginning or unbegun;
And see a crystal pattern, fluctuating panorama,
Forgotten by the gods, but unveiled to inward sight.

"Let's have something in Carrasahli!" roared a drunken soldier.

An insane elder god, in his madness sought to build,
A race of mortal creatures in the image of divine.
In foolish egomania, fatal folly, the artist had conspired
Within this mortal image godlike perfection to contain;
Blindly had forgotten that an image so conceived,
Must embody the very madness of its deluded parent.

44

Great cataclysmic toil, cyclopean effort, did he make;
To the taunting laughter of his fellows, amused to see
  a fool,
He cluttered all the earth with his blighted handiwork,
And rested in smug content with his idiot labor.

Several louts began to beat on the table in protest to
the eerie, unintelligible song.

In time this fool's creation multiplied all through the
  land,
And disgusted those before them with their drivel,
Content to live a wormlike existence for the pleasure
  of their god,
Who in his mindless conceit only giggled with his dolls.
Yet in one there rose rebellion with this crawling in
  cosmic dung—
No maggot but a serpent was this son of divinity's folly.
And in his hellish fury at the crooning lies of that
  creator,
He chose to be his own master and defied this nameless
  god,
And with his hands he slew his brother—choicest
  plaything.
Now despair racked the broken mind of this insane
  elder god,
For he saw the flaws within his cherished children
And recognized himself as the author of that image.
This rebel he cursed in rage to bleak, eternal wandering,
And gave him eyes of a killer, so all know the Mark
  of Kane.

"Damn your pale hide, minstrel!" bellowed the drunken
soldier. "I said give us something we all know!" He
lurched to his feet and stumbled over to Evingolis, in-
terrupting the ancient song. "Now let's hear something
else!" He tossed his mug of ale in the minstrel's face and
roared with laughter. His fellows joined in.

In Evingolis's face there flashed a look of white, hot
anger. He laid the lute aside and wiped his burning eyes.

Then with a movement too swift to follow, his hand lashed out and struck the soldier's laughing face. As if kicked by a horse the drunkard shot backwards onto the stone floor. He did not get up. Shocked silence caught the audience; they had considered the lean albino a weakling.

"Sonofabitch!" gasped Troylin in awe. "Shows you not to pick a fight if you can't hold your brew! Must have hit the floor on his head or something. Somebody get him out of here."

Sneering at the startled crowd, Evingolis picked up his lute and stalked out of the hall.

"Just as well!" the baron observed. "He's going to goad those guys a little too far with his superior airs one of these days—they won't stand for it in a minstrel. May not get off a lucky punch next time." He chuckled. "Quite a character, isn't he though? Sure can sing the strangest stuff I've ever heard. Make any sense of that one, Kane?"

Kane looked after the departing minstrel in calculation. "Some little," he murmured, and fell to brooding. His eyes looked into the dancing flames, and none could say what he saw there.

VI. A Man Not Man

It crouched in the shadow of the wall, watching the sleeping manor in silent hatred. The cold wind ruffled its white coat, and its panting breath raised small puffs of steam. Yet the creature felt not the cold, only conscious of a burning hunger that shrieked to be satiated. With its inhuman sight it regarded the quiet out-building which housed the baron's off duty men-at-arms; in the darkness all objects stood clearly in varying shades of light tan and brown. Within that lodge there would be soft human bodies—hairless weakling ape creatures now sleeping without care. Their tender flesh would be warm with seething blood. The creature trembled in unspeakable anticipation, lips drawn back over champing fangs.

From the nighted forest, dark shapes were loping across

the snow and silently gathering outside the gate of the enclosure. The creature felt their presence with its mind and welcomed them. Many of its brothers had answered its voiceless call. They too sensed the many hated man creatures inside the castle walls, and their feral minds rejoiced in the scenes of slaughter drawn for them by their leader.

More than thirty lean, gray forms now were waiting beyond the gate. It was enough, decided the creature. Once more its mind reached out to its brothers, impressing upon them the plan they must follow. No opposition was encountered. This was the wolf leader; they must obey his summons, must carry through his commands. It had been this way since before man first dropped from the trees and challenged the Brotherhood with his puny clubs and stones.

The creature unlocked the gate and effortlessly swung it half open. Into the courtyard the hungry wolves filed, slipping along the shadows until they reached the lodge. Behind this door slept the detested humans, wrapped in their stolen furs and besotted with burned flesh and rotted plant juices. The leader silently stole to the door, knowing it was kept unbolted so that late revelers might stagger in. Another wave of awful hunger shook through it. Now!

Its fearfully taloned hand gripped the latch. Its red eyes shone with blood lust, and an inhuman grin of triumph exposed the gleaming rows of fangs arming its sloping muzzle. The creature threw open the door and sprang within! On its heels poured the snarling pack!

The soldiers awoke from their dreams to find a nightmare of ripping fangs and flailing bodies. The creature howled its victory—over a dozen men for the slaughter! Out of the blackness the pack sprang upon the helpless sleepers. Gray forms struggled over the writhing victims, snarling and tearing into the warm flesh. Screams of death agony—of utmost horror—filled the lodge and overflowed into the night, mingling with the hideous triumph of the feasting wolves.

The screams were stilled.

Now! snarled the leader in command. Now, go! Before

the others can come! More of this will follow for us! But now, go! The wolves were loath to abandon their twitching prey. It was asking much to go. But the leader must be obeyed. Reluctantly the pack released their booty and pointed their gray muzzles to the outside.

Several humans greeted them in the courtyard—the hopeless shrieks of the dying had aroused the castle. Now the humans stopped in terror to see the crimson-splashed pack pour from the lodge behind their leader.

It was silhouetted there in the pale moonlight—a ghastly hybrid of man and wolf. Covered with white fur it was, and taller than the average human whose shape it borrowed. Cruel claws ended its toes and fingers; its arms long and legs strangely set. Atop its great shoulders was set a demon's visage—a furry head with high pointed ears and a long jaw more wolf-like than human. Its sharp tusks dripped red in the moonlight. And its bestial eyes gleamed an evil crimson with blasphemous hatred of mankind.

The soldiers drew their weapons in desperation. But they were only four, and the wolves simply overran them—bearing their victims to the earth and slashing them to tatters. A few wolves fell before the humans died. The creature threw itself in fury upon one soldier whose blade had smashed through a gray murderer. Knocking away the human's weapon, the creature pulled him to its chest in an awful hug. Ribs and vertebrae snapped, as razor fangs buried in the unprotected throat. Then the leader tossed the husk aside and raced through the gate with the pack, as now more men with torches and weapons emerged from the castle. They vanished into the forest.

A scene of hideous carnage greeted the belated rescue party. Those who entered the fatal lodge recoiled in horror at the sight of the slashed and mutilated carcasses of their comrades. In the trampled courtyard, one man yet lived.

"Wolves!" he gasped out with his final breaths. "Dozens of them! It led them in here! A demon! A werewolf! Let them in so they could murder us all! A werewolf!" He died screaming shrilly of dripping fangs.

Kane considered the man's disclosure. He had just

gotten to the scene and had not seen the retreating attackers. Questioning of the men revealed that no one had had any more than a fleeting glimpse as the wolves slipped into the forest. The servants and soldiers who had slept within the dining hall had been first to the scene, and none of them could give an intelligent story of what little they had witnessed.

In a frightened group they dared to go beyond the gate. The tracks of many wolves could be seen in the torchlight. Other tracks were present as well—a single set of almost human footprints. But no bare human foot had made them, for the steps were oddly contorted and the marks of talons reached deeply into the snow.

The worst part was when they dared to follow these uncanny tracks. For the trail of the werewolf led only part way to the woods. Then it curved around and headed back to the castle, to a point along the wall on the far side of the courtyard. Here the tracks indicated that the creature had vaulted the high wall, and on the other side the snow was too trampled to say where he had gone. But it was all too clear that the werewolf had not left the courtyard again.

"May all the gods have mercy on us!" cried someone. "One of us is a demon!"

VII. "One of us . . ."

"Not counting the women, that leaves our strength at about thirty," was Troylin's gloomy conclusion. "And out of this number, one of us is a werewolf," he pronounced, looking over the grim assemblage. It was noon of the following day. A careful search since dawn had failed to turn up any trace of the creature. Since no one had left the enclosure, the werewolf had to be still within. The castle was small—really no more than a fortified manor. A systematic search, check and recheck, of every conceivable hiding place had been carried out. It was plain then that the demonic leader of last night's attack was not present in the form described by the dying soldier and only faintly glimpsed by those first on the scene. Only one conclusion was possible. The creature was a werewolf —a demon capable of assuming human form to mingle with unsuspecting mankind. As it now was doing.

"There are several types of creatures generally referred to as 'werewolves'," explained Lystric. "One type is a human who for some reason can alter his shape into that of a wolf or semilupine hybrid. In other cases, some malevolent demon, ghost or other spirit will assume such a form—although this is merely one choice of many physical manifestations within its power." He warmed to his lecture. "Yet another type occurs when a wolf is able to assume human form. This monster is usually called the 'wolf leader' and is by far the most dangerous. While the other types represent basically solitary habits, the wolf leader is able to co-ordinate the action of many wolves in order to carry out its fiendish goals—usually wholesale slaughter of mankind. Of course, there are many finer shades and distinctions. Not to mention those harmless individuals who through some mental disorder imagine themselves to be wild beasts."

"Meaning your charge Henderin, no doubt!" snapped Tali. "Sorry, graybeard, but we're not buying your burst of fine talk and lecturing! We all know that madman's no harmless nut—we know about that poor bastard he killed in Carrasahl! Same as these other guys here! 'Demonic possession' I believe you said it was then.

"Well we think this thing has gone far enough! You've had your chance to exorcise the devil! All you've done is loaf around and use Henderin to get free meals! Well by Thoem, we've had enough stalling, and now there's going to be some action!"

"Just what do you mean by that?" thundered the baron, pounding on the table. "Just what sort of 'action' do you have in mind against my son!"

Tali retreated a bit, then supported by the opinion of his fellows, he began less belligerently, "Now, milord, we all understand how much the boy means to you. And the bunch of us has been loyal to you throughout. There was plenty who said we'd regret ever coming up to this godforsaken place with a madman along. But damn it all, we're not about to sit here and be slaughtered in our beds just because your son is too highclass to burn for his crimes!" His fellow retainers murmured assent.

"May I remind you," Troylin hissed, "that murder of an aristocrat—no matter how insane—by a commoner carries a sure penalty of crucifixion! And I assure you that anyone who tries to lay a hand on my boy I'll cut down myself!"

The crowd was getting dangerous. Tali retorted, "Well then, there's some of us who'll run that risk if we have to— better than taking our chances being snowbound with a wolfpack at the walls and a werewolf in our midst! And there's no punishment when there's no witnesses!" he added significantly.

"What are we doing!" Breenanin shouted over the ugly growls of the crowd. "You stand there talking about murdering someone who's never given any of you a just cause to complain! A month ago you would have died for Baron Troylin! Time and again I've heard you congratulate yourselves on being in the service of one of the most generous and easy going gentry in the land! And now because you're suddenly frightened, you talk of killing his only son—. whom all of you thought was a great guy before his sickness! You even talk of massacring all of us! I'd prefer letting the wolves in—they'd show more gratitude! You don't even know if Henderin had anything to do with these murders!"

The two factions glared at one another uncertainly. They were ordinary folk, a country baron and a lot of provincial retainers from a backwater kingdom. Murder and mutiny were foreign to their rustic background, but terror of the unknown and the presence of hideous death brutalized them all. The retainers must regain their accustomed security at any price; Troylin would fight to the death to preserve his son.

Kane had carefully avoided identification with either side. It was not his fight and as always his only loyalty was to himself. He needed the baron's hospitality until the way south was open. After that he cared less how they resolved the dispute. Still as long as he was here and a werewolf was haunting all in the castle, he was an interested party. And at present he did not want to get involved in mutiny—especially since strangers made bad risks as witnesses.

Tali persisted. "Well, if Henderin isn't the werewolf, there's sure a lot of evidence against him! First, we know he killed that guard like he was a wild animal, and we all know he's crazy. All the time asking for raw meat and howling nights and going berserk! Second, when the hunting party was attacked yesterday, Henderin was running around loose. Caught him coming back from the forest. Mighty strange wolves attacking armed men on horseback, while an unarmed man on foot runs around unharmed. Like he didn't need to fear them—like he was out there telling them to kill us! Ok—where is Henderin when these other attacks happen? Poor Bete gets his in the storm, bunch of travelers get theirs too—and the thing last night in the soldiers' quarters! And Henderin—oh, he's safely locked up! So we're promised. Only thing is—we've just got Lystric's word for that! And I for one don't care to believe everything that scheming old fossil has to say!"

Lystric snarled a stream of curses, and the affair came close to blows. Kane saw his chance.

"That's a most interesting point you've made." The baron eyed him in disgust, but he went on. "Let's talk about Lystric for a moment. I understand he was just a fifth-rate hack of a wizard with a smattering of occult knowledge—unable to make a go of it, until suddenly he gets this job. Sort of suspicious, don't you think? A perfectly normal, likable guy begins to act like a wolf, and this cunning old fakir announces he knows how to cure him. Nice soft position for him—but only as long as Henderin stays mad. And I understand about all Lystric's idea of treatment consists of is letting Henderin run around until he snaps out of it. Interesting way to treat demonic possession. Put it all together and it sort of sounds like Lystric has made a plush position for himself. There are several strange drugs and countless spells that can make a normal man begin to act like a wolf."

Lystric was shrieking protestations and curses by this point, too enraged to make a rebuttal. The others were listening intently.

"So Lystric thinks he's all set," continued Kane. "Once in a while Henderin gets away from him and stirs up some mischief, so the old vulture finds it necessary to claim he was under lock and key all the time. Or take it a step further. Maybe he's mad himself, and he's using Henderin as a tool to destroy us. I understand he and the baron have no cause to love one another. Magicians have curious ways of settling grudges.

"And for that matter, Lystric just might be a werewolf himself. Not the first time a sorceror lost his humanity by meddling in the black arts. With Henderin as camouflage, it would be a perfect set up to wipe us all out while we chased the wrong fox."

"So what do you suggest we do?" asked Tali, no longer as sure of himself.

"Remain calm. My point is we don't know that Henderin is really a werewolf, and Lystric has some mighty questionable connections himself with all this. So we place a guard on them both. Henderin is locked up—we just need to make sure he stays that way. At the same time put several men to watch Lystric. That way they're both harmless—and no one gets hurt. If they're innocent, we'll let them go. And since they're under surveillance, we're safe from them. No rebellion, no useless fighting. We might even see a sudden improvement in Henderin's condition."

He paused. About him his listeners were showing signs of assent. Here was a reasonable solution that both factions could accept.

"Sounds good," concluded Tali, who seemed to act as spokesman. "We'll do it then. Forgive us, milord, for our threats. Of course none of us mean any harm to you or to Henderin—if he's innocent. It's just this whole business has gotten the lot of us unhinged. We're all in a bad fix here, and not knowing whether the man next to you is a friend or a monster . . . We just lost our heads."

"I understand," assented the baron, his temper still aroused but somewhat suppressed. "Let this be the end of this nonsense and I'll let matters pass. Sure we'll put a guard on Lystric and my son—and we'll watch them. But there'll be no harm to Henderin while I'm master here!"

"All right!" Lystric hissed, forcing himself to speak slowly. "I've listened to all this stupidity as long as I can stand it. I've heard myself insulted, my motives misinterpreted, my methods criticized—and by a batch of ignorant slobs. I've been accused of all manner of nameless crimes and schemes. Now I'm to be put under guard. All right! Go ahead! Obviously I can't stop you blundering, cowardly fools from your idiotic vigilantism! So lock me up then!

"But I promise you you're barking up the wrong tree. Time will prove I'm innocent as well as my charge. And while you're guarding me the real werewolf—assuming it's not just the product of your terrified delusions—will be running around with impunity! And don't forget I'm better suited to protect you from it than anyone else among you. Who else has any training or understanding of the necromantic arts? Given time, I tell you, I can discover means to ferret out this creature in your ranks—to seek him out and destroy the beast! Didn't I earlier warn you all of the danger I had foreseen in the stars! And no one listened. Fools! Ungrateful scum the lot of you!" The astrologer's manner was not designed to win him sympathy.

"And now let me tell you something for a change. I've done some thinking on my own, and I've got some of my own suspicions! Does that surprise you? Sure! He's a scheming old charlatan, you say. Bah! What do ignorant buffoons like you know of true genius! Peasants who measure ability by material wealth! I tell you, my talents are so far beyond your mundane groveling imaginations that I waste my breath even trying to help you!

"But listen! Think on this while you smugly pass judgment upon your betters. When did all this start? When this man called Kane came riding up to our door out of the storm, that's when! And just what do you know of him? A wandering mercenary, he tells you. And you believe! Well I'm not an ignorant backwoods plowhand, and I know something of what goes on in the rest of the world!

"And there are plenty of legends and rumors and wild stories that I've encountered about a man called Kane. And none of them speaks well for him! At best he's a treacherous, murderous rogue who's figured in more plots and dark schemes than Lord Thoem and his demons ever dreamed of! And at worst the legends hint he's some sort of immortal cursed by the gods to wander the earth and bring havoc wherever he stops!"

About time to put a stop to this, Kane realized. "Ok, old man! You've had your chance to clear yourself! All you've done is insult good people and brag about your own dubious abilities! As for these dark legends and nonsense, I don't suppose you can produce any of it either. Sorry, graybeard, but the old divide and conquer ruse is a lot older even than you—and these people are too smart to be sucked in by your desperate ravings! How about it, Tali? Heard enough from him?"

"Plenty!" came the hot reply. "Come on, fellows! We'll take this old viper up to his lair and see he stays put! He can batter Henderin's ears with his garbage!"

Spluttering still, but trying to look dignified through it all, Lystric let himself be borne away to the wing of the castle where he and his charge were quartered.

The tension in the room was eased. The enemy within was dealt with to the apparent satisfaction of most. It was daylight, and plans could be made for the night to come. Guards would be posted. Doors locked. Weapons kept at hand. The bulk of the survivors departed on their own business.

"Thanks for what you did," Baron Troylin told Kane awkwardly. "For a moment I thought you'd thrown in with them. Now I see you were just leading them along, stalling for time."

"I'd hoped you wouldn't think me so ungrateful for your hospitality. But it was the best way to manipulate them."

"You seem pretty adept at that sort of thing," returned his host. "Seems there's a lot of talents you possess that speak for more than a common mercenary."

"I never said I was a *common* mercenary, though," said Kane with assumed levity.

Troylin discreetly let matters drop. Nonetheless he found himself pondering the astrologer's accusations. The name of Kane was not unfamiliar to him, now that he strained his memory. Of course, political matters other than those of Carrasahl were only obscure if interesting gossip to his way of thinking. He was a simple man, and his chief concerns were usually connected with filling the hours between waking and sleep with as much enjoyable activity as possible.

But now that he thought about it, hadn't there been a general named Kane connected with that ugly business down in Shapeli? And Kane wasn't exactly a common name. Certainly, he really did know nothing at all about his mysterious guest. He began to speculate about this red-haired stranger with the uncanny eyes.

VIII. One by One

The hour was getting on toward midnight. Most of the castle's inhabitants had sought their beds for what sleep their nerves would allow them. All were not asleep, however. Several men stood guard outside the chambers of Lystric the astrologer. These were in the northwest wing of the castle—a tower set apart from the more frequented hallways. This was convenient for both occupants: Lystric could pursue his studies in quiet, with a good view of the stars from the tower's summit, while Henderin could rave and howl as he saw fit without disturbing the others. The open area on top of the tower was used by Lystric. Immediately below this was the chamber wherein Henderin was confined; its one window was barred and overlooked a seventy-five foot drop to the courtyard, and the door which opened onto the tower stairs was thick and heavily locked. Below this was another room given over to Lystric's studies and filled with a clutter of sorcerous paraphernalia. Still below, at the base of the tower where it adjoined the main body of the castle, was the room in which Lystric slept. This chamber had two doors: one to the tower stairs which was locked, and the other which opened into the hallway at that end of the castle. This latter door was now bolted from the outside, and five armed men stood guard beside it, keeping close watch over the sleeping astrologer. No one could enter or leave the tower chambers except through that door.

A few others were still awake in the great hall. A fire was burning lustily, and those who did not feel like sleep sought its companionship. It had been agreed that for some men to stay awake through the night was an obvious precaution, as well as having guards patrol the hallways in pairs. More would have been better, but the castle's strength had been dangerously cut by the previous attacks.

So Kane sat awake beside the fire, sipping larger quantities of ale than seemed wise and moodily listening to the minstrel. The albino sat in the shadow of the beams as usual, evoking strange melodies from his lute and from time to time singing along to these rare works of departed genius. He was an unusual man, Kane mused, his performance and repertoire displaying fantastic sensitivity and skill. He wondered what made Evingolis content to attach himself to a country bumpkin like Troylin—perhaps something in the minstrel's past had barred from him the richer, more appreciative patrons of the southern nations.

Scent of delicate perfume and sparkle of pale gold hair in the warm glow. Breenanin sat down beside him in the hearth light. Kane remembered her face as it had first formed in his vision. Only a few days before was it that he had come so close to frozen death in the storm. Time had no meaning to Kane. A dozen years or as many minutes—once past both fitted into the same span of memory. Either a century ago or just that morning he had fled across the northern wastes—and for how long? It was nothing, for it was past and beyond him. His life was only a minute focus of time, an instant of the present balanced between centuries of past and an unknown duration of future existence. He felt a moment of vertigo, as his mind hung poised over time's chasm.

"I couldn't sleep with all this on my mind, so I came down to the fire where it would be cozier," she told him, feeling it necessary that she offer some reason for her presence beside him.

Kane stirred. "It's a haunted night. There's a certain tenseness in the air as before a battle. Death hovers near, and man is reluctant to sleep because he knows an eternal sleep may be his fate within a few hours more.

"Some ale to soothe your thoughts perhaps?" She nodded and Kane rose to pour a cup.

She accepted it with a slight smile, uncertain of her feelings toward the other. He was so strange—huge and brutal, every inch a machine of destruction, she sensed. Yet he was civil of speech and manner—and far more erudite than any man of her experience, other than those learned fossils and simpering dandies of the court. There were many contradictions embodied in the big stranger, nor could she hazard a guess to his nationality or even his age. He seemed so inhumanly aloof and alone. He gave her the same sort of eerie thrill that some of Evingolis's strange songs created.

"You never say another person's name when you speak to him," she commented.

Kane favored her with one of his uncanny, penetrating stares. "No," he admitted. "I don't suppose I do."

"Breenanin," she prompted softly.

"Breenanin."

In silence they shared the fire and the minstrel's song.

I saw her in winter's silent cold light
Clearly, with her warmth upon the sparkle
Of that magical, crystalline night.
And love I knew unspoken passed,
Its timeless warmth, one frozen instant,
Eternally encased in infinite amber.
But what I sensed I could not return;
The instant vanished in that crystalline storm.

In vain do I call through this dancing myriad
Of relinquished emotions, frozen fragments of time.
For the moment has passed, now lost in that swirl—
Splintered shards of time's reflection—
Reflections for the winter of my soul.

The minstrel's voice echoed into silence; his fingers
stilled the strings of his lute. Quietly he left the hall to the
two seated before the fire. In the far corner of the room,
a few half-asleep servants rolled dice.

"Where'd you get him?" broke in Kane.

Breenanin shifted in her chair. The minstrel's song had
lulled her into an almost trance-like state. "He came to us
last summer. Came up from the southlands, I suppose—
he never said anything about his past. Sort of wandered
about the court in Carrasahl for a while, then attached
himself to Father's patronage. We were glad to get him—
others offered him more money than we could. He talks
occasionally of some far away places he's been, and most
of his songs no one can understand. Guess he's just wandering about the world as his fancy suits him.

"Must be nice to go somewhere new. In Carrasahl we
don't get to travel much. Can't handle an estate from
somewhere far off, Father always says, and travel's dangerous for anyone to risk. Once we went to Enseljos to
see Winston's coronation, though."

They talked of various matters for a while—long periods
of mutual silence between their spots of conversation. At
length Kane looked over and saw that she slept. He was
reluctant to disturb her, but at the same time he knew she
should not be left alone in the great hall with death abroad
in the night. So he lifted her in his arms and carried her
up the wide stairs to her room on the balcony across that
end of the hall.

She stirred in her sleep, but did not awaken. A half-
smile was on her thin lips, and her fine teeth were white
against her pale skin. She was soft and warm in her fur
robe. Kane felt an emotion stir within him as he carried
her that he had not experienced in long years. It might
have been love, but then he could not remember.

Returning to the hall, he sat before the fire again. But the spell had been broken. Now he felt strangely restless, sick of brooding over dead memories in the firelight. After another cup of ale, Kane arose, fastened on his sword, and announced to the few remaining servants that he would walk around to see how things went with the others.

The hallways were long and dark, their silence only faintly broken by Kane's soft tread. He walked the cold stones slowly, hand near swordhilt and keen eyes searching every shadow. There was an almost tangible aura of fear abroad in the torchlit corridors, and death crouched invisibly in each spot of darkness. The spirits of those horribly murdered danced about him, laughing and gibbering in his ears, pointing derisive fingers at the lone man who in his conceit thought to avert their hideous fate. The numbing cold of the winter soaked through the stones along with the blackness of its night. The feeble torches were useless in dispelling either its cold or its gloom.

Faint winds from nowhere, damp ghost breath, played upon the hairs of Kane's neck. Sudden scurrying sounds haunted his steps, causing him to whirl about and stare along the corridor through which he had just passed—then reel about once more as the wraith-like movements teased him. There was nothing to be seen. Even when Kane stopped long minutes to listen, or walked back again over the same stones. Nothing even for his eyes to discover. He realized his nerves were getting the better of him, and fought to control himself—for he knew he must not become dull and insensitive on this haunted night. Because sometime a shadow might hold a less intangible menace.

He stopped suddenly, looking everywhere about him with painful concentration. Then he bent over quickly and touched a finger to the spot, knowing even as he did it that the smear was fresh blood. He strained his eyes against the uneven torchlight. Normal vision would perhaps have missed it, but Kane could see the faint trickle of blood trailing along the stones. Sword in hand, he followed the shining path—every sense strained to alert him of ambush.

The trail halted before the door of an unused bedchamber. Kane remembered checking through the chamber during the morning search. They had found nothing, and had left the door securely locked. Now the door was still closed, but unlocked. A smear of blood marked the jamb.

Kane considered only a moment. He could bring more men, but the creature, if inside, could then escape and mingle with those who came to assist him. He could shout for aid, but that would take awhile to arrive, and the werewolf would be alerted of his presence. A sudden attack seemed best. Kane had considerable confidence in the deadliness of his mighty sword arm.

He kicked the door open and lunged into the room, swirling his sword in a shining arc of death.

He whirled once quickly, saw nothing to attack immediately, then jumped back with the wall to his back and carefully examined the room. The werewolf was nowhere to be seen among the slightly dusty furnishings. But it had been there. At least it was unlikely that the four corpses had entered the room on their own.

They were the broken bodies of four of the guards who were supposed to patrol the hallways. They were freshly killed—still warm, Kane discovered. Of three the necks had been broken; the fourth had his throat torn out. A crude attempt had been made to sop up the blood, but enough had trickled through to leave a trail to the room. The creature was cunning, Kane realized. It had silently killed these guards—probably leaping upon them from behind after they passed the door. It had tried to kill them bloodlessly so as not to give evidence of their fate. Evidently on one the werewolf had been forced to use its fangs, and it had not been able to stop the telltale bleeding completely.

The question now was what to do. How did the werewolf's presence here relate to Lystric and Henderin? Kane decided to check this out. He was close to that wing of the castle anyway, and those guards would be his nearest source of help. He would investigate the situation at that end, and if clear summon their aid to hunt down the were-wolf before it realized its presence had been detected.

Warily, as fast as he dared, Kane rushed to the tower chambers. The five guards still sat in front of the door. At least they had not been overpowered, he thought with relief.

The first thing that struck him was that he had not been challenged. They couldn't all be asleep, surely!

They were not. They were all quite dead. There was not a single mark on any body—at least that a cursory check could disclose. They sat or sprawled about the door in vaguely lifelike attitudes—probably arranged that way, Kane decided. An empty ale pitcher lay beside one of them, and Kane sniffed it cautiously. There was no scent of poison that he could distinguish, but there were many that bore no taint. Poison seemed the only logical answer to these five silent, unmarked deaths.

Still determined to see it through, Kane stepped to the door. It was unlocked, as he had expected. A peephole was agape through which the guards had watched the interior. Looking through, Kane could see nothing lurking within.

He once more kicked in the door and hurled himself into the room, following his earlier procedure. Nothing moved. Lystric was in one corner, half under a table.

Kane examined the astrologer. Whatever his schemes or abilities, he would exercise them no more. Lystric's head was all but torn from his body, and hungry fangs had ripped away most of the soft flesh of his arms and legs. The werewolf had not been able to contain its unspeakable appetite all night.

Nerves prickling, Kane slowly rose from the mangled ruin of a man. Perhaps the answer would lie in Henderin's chamber upstairs. Sword ready for instant action, he tiptoed to the door leading to the tower stairs. The door was still locked, whatever that might portend. Kane carefully manipulated the bolt.

A sudden scratch of claws on stone warned him! Kane jumped from his attention to the bolt, whipping around with blade swishing!

The werewolf glared at him balefully, its bloody tusks gnashing hideously! A low snarl rumbled in the creature's throat. Taller than Kane it stood, and under its white fur rippled bands of steel-like muscle.

Before Kane had a chance to do more than recognize the beast's awful presence, it sprang for him! Putting all his tremendous strength behind his stroke, Kane smashed his blade full against the lunging werewolf!

Had his attacker been a man, the blade would have sundered him to the waist. But from the werewolf's shoulder the sword bounded back as if it had struck slightly resilient iron! The sound was a dull thunk, and no other evidence was there that the blow had landed—the werewolf's spring was not even slackened! Yet Kane's arm ached to the marrow with the force of the resounding blow, and his sword bounded from numb fingers!

In a split second the creature was on him, fangs slavering, fetid breath in his face and taloned hands clutching for his throat! Kane had no chance to dodge! The snarling force of the creature's lunge smashed him onto the floor! His head cracked against the stones, and consciousness mercifully left him, as those burning eyes bored into his mind!

Sometime later he regained consciousness. Kane rolled to his knees weakly. His head was in agony and his mouth was full of blood. Then with a start he realized two things. One, that for some reason he was still alive. And secondly, he was no longer by the tower stairs, but lying beside Lystric's corpse. In disgust he recognized that the blood in his mouth was not his own!

He spat in revulsion and groggily stood up, staggering to the doorway.

"Don't move another step! I'll skewer you for sure!"

Kane saw, with sudden awareness of his situation, that Evingolis was standing in the doorway—a crossbow aimed at the other's heart.

Running feet and shouts sounded from the hallway.

"Well, Kane," said the minstrel in awe, "you played it cleverly. I'll admit I never thought you'd be the werewolf!"

IX. Impasse

The surprising thing was that they had not killed him immediately. Kane's fast tongue was some help in postponing matters, but he suspected Breenanin had been more effective. The baron had not completely forgotten that Kane had rescued his daughter from almost certain death.

Evingolis had spelled it out, point by point. The first death had occurred right before Kane had ridden out the storm. A search after the storm had disclosed the mutilated remains of another band of travelers—abroad in the blizzard with Kane. During the hunt it had been Kane's party that the wolves had attacked, and only Kane had been witness—himself miraculously unscathed. And when the werewolf and its pack murdered the soldiers in their lodge, Kane had not come upon the scene until late. Finally, this last attack had come while Kane had prowled the hallways alone. And when Evingolis had discovered him, he was crouched beside the torn body of the old astrologer—a man who had claimed to have damning knowledge of this mysterious stranger.

But they had not killed him yet. Instead they had taken Kane and thrown him in a cell in the castle's cellars. Now a thick wooden door fastened by a stout bar stood between Kane and three menacing guards. Through a narrow grilled aperture in the door, Baron Troylin regarded his prisoner.

"You know you're making a mistake in this," offered Kane.

"I suppose you killed Lystric because you knew he'd unmask you. And to think you even had me suspecting that poor man!"

"Damn your thick skull! That old fool couldn't count his fingers and get a correct answer! I told you I found him like that before the werewolf knocked me senseless by the stairs!"

"Strikes me as a bit odd this werewolf didn't kill you—

even went to the trouble to drag you across the room. Didn't know such a thing had that much restraint."

Kane pounded his fist on the wall in frustration. "It may be a monster, but the creature's as cunning as any man. Looks like it hoped to frame me and throw the rest of you off the scent."

Troylin snorted in disbelief. "Speaking of framing, that's a nice job you did on my son. Guess you figured to make it look like he'd broken loose and slain the lot! Only we caught you before you could finish preparations—had to stop for a meal, I guess! Too bad you didn't arrange for Henderin to escape first. You might have had us all believing it was him!"

"You're just so damned anxious to clear that son of yours, you'll grasp at anything else that presents itself! Why wasn't I a werewolf when Evingolis found me? Why didn't I kill him and escape? How'd I get this crack on the skull? Why did I rescue your daughter from the wolves?"

"Oh, I'll agree there's a few things that don't seem to check out. That's the only reason you're still alive—which you won't be if you try to break out of here! Most of them would be just as happy to see you burning right now, only I figure I owe you at least a chance.

"So we'll just watch you a few days—Henderin too, just to be safe. If the creature strikes again, we'll be sorry for doubting you."

"More than likely you'll be dead—and me with you! And what if nothing more happens?"

The baron shook his head grimly. "Guess then we'll just have to build a fire for you to sit in."

Kane cursed in frustration as the baron departed. The yokels would do just that, and Troylin would consider Henderin cleared of guilt. Meanwhile if the werewolf still were at large, which seemed an absolute certainty, the idiots would drop their guard and let him roam at will. He sat down in disgust, enjoying the agony of his battered skull.

After several hours of watching vermin crawl through the straw, Kane heard a fierce growl. He jumped to the door and saw one of the baron's hounds bristling before the entrance.

"Stay back, milady! He's on guard and he'll bite your pretty leg sure's the world if you go any nearer!"

"Then call him off! I want to talk to Kane!" It was Breenanin.

"The baron said no one was to talk to Kane except him." Some coins tinkled. "Well, guess you can see him just for a moment. Make it short though! Don't want to make trouble. Come here, Slasher! Easy boy! Cut that growling now! Hear me!"

Breenanin's frightened face appeared before the spy-hole. "Oh Kane!" she cried. "I was sure they'd kill you!"

"About what I figured," he replied. "Thanks for pulling for me with your father. I'm afraid though that they're convinced I'm their werewolf, and either way things don't look too bright for me."

She looked at him in consternation. "Well, I know you can't be a monster! Not after you saved me from those dreadful wolves! Anyway, you're too gentle to be a monster!"

Kane started. No one had accused him of gentleness in some time.

"They're wrong, I know! And time will prove it to them!" She stopped uncertainly. "But the only way they'll know you're innocent will be for the werewolf to kill again . . ." She trailed off, unsure where this left her. It seemed horrible to hope for more deaths, but if the creature stayed hidden, then this man whom she believed she loved would die hideously in the flames.

"The werewolf is still here, you can be sure of that. But whether it'll attack again soon, who can say. It's true that steel can't hurt them, though! I should have cut the beast in half by all logic, but my blade rebounded without a mark. Uncanny sensation—it was all solid flesh when it hit me, but my sword was turned back as if I'd struck stone. Left my whole arm numb from the impact.

"They say only a few things can kill a werewolf, outside of more potent sorcery. Fire, of course. Silver is said to be the only metal to pierce its magic invulnerability.

66

Outright physical combat can hurt one, too. I've read of wolves tearing them in rare battles for leadership of a pack. If you have anything silver to use for a weapon, you might keep it near you. If the baron would only listen to me, he should cast some silver points for arrows or spears."

"I'll try to talk him into it," Breenanin answered brightly. "And I've got a little silver bladed dagger that I wear for hunts. Not much of a weapon really—just a lady's toy—but I'll keep it under my pillow."

The guard muttered anxiously, "Hey, come on now, milady! If the baron finds you here of all people, he'll damn sure flay me! Cut things short!"

"I've got to run now," she told him wistfully. "I'll see what I can do. Don't worry!" She ducked from the aperture and left the dreary cellar.

Kane listened to the watchdog's snarl, and an uneasy thought recurred to him. Where had Breenanin been during these murderous attacks? Something about her presence in that tree and the wolves' half-hearted attempts to reach her had been nagging the back of his mind for some time.

He shook the thoughts away. Again only guesses and circumstances! Any man here could be shown guilty by that course! Troylin, Evingolis, Tali—any of the baron's men. And she was but a girl!

But wasn't the she-wolf fully as dangerous as the male?

X. Fangs in the Night

When the light of the full moon shone whitely through the bars of his window, Henderin knew it was time. Most of the furniture of his room was in shambles—smashed during his rages. Now he rose from the nest of litter he had collected in one corner; he assumed a crouched stance and began to shuffle stealthily about the debris-strewn chamber, a low growl in his throat. It was hard to think at times, but he fixed the details of what he must do into his disordered brain. Excitement over what must happen tonight ran riot through his senses, and he delighted in prowling around, listening for sounds of his guards, savoring the thrill of the adventure.

All was silent. Henderin slipped to his window and looked down over the courtyard below. Nothing moved. Satisfied that none watched, Henderin pulled at the stone at the base of the window ledge, grunting with the strain. As he knew it would, the stone tore free of its setting, for the crude mortar which held it in place had been carefully weakened. He placed the heavy stone on the floor of the room, then turned to the iron bars. With the stone removed, the bars set exposed in their sockets, which had been cut into adjoining faces of the inside and outside stones of the ledge. Henderin easily worked the bars out of their half sockets below and slid them down from their upper attachment to the wall.

The way cleared, he swung onto the ledge and carefully lowered his body over the edge. Now was the difficult part, but one which he knew he could carry out. The wall was built of rough-cut stones, whose edges jutted outward unevenly. The tireless hand of the elements had eroded enough of the grainy mortar to provide an appreciable crevice between the rough stones. These furnished a precarious hold at best, but to one of Henderin's strength and agility it was sufficient purchase to climb down the wall and drop into the empty courtyard. And furthermore, Henderin obeyed secret urgings beyond all denial—he could not fail.

With a bark of triumph he dropped the last few feet. It had been a faultless escape. Laughing softly, Henderin vanished into the shadows of the courtyard. There was much yet to accomplish.

The castle slept uneasily. Death had struck relentlessly among its inhabitants. Even now, when the creature who held them all in cold terror must be securely locked and guarded, a fearful doubt yet gnawed at their hearts. But still man must have sleep. So they trusted to locks and guards and slumbered fitfully—this pitiful remnant of the castle's household.

And in the silent hallways, death stalked. No human eyes had seen it slip across the snow strewn courtyard and in the shadow of the gate softly draw back the bar. Only the dead eyes of Gregig the porter—he had slept at his post a final time—watched the long, gray shapes slink through the opening in an endless line of red death. No one saw as this silent pack of blood-mad wolves followed its leader through a small, unguarded door in the castle's rear.

Nails clicking softly on the dusty stone, the deadly horde padded across the unfrequented storage room and penetrated the heart of the castle.

The hounds were first to scent the presence of their natural enemies, and they greeted the pack with fierce snarls. Thus the men who patiently stood guard outside Henderin's empty chamber looked upon death.

For one startled moment they were frozen in horror as the howling wolves and their nightmare leader raced through the hall toward them. Then they shouted the alarm and drew their swords for a desperate last stand. The shouts of the doomed retainers added to the snarls of the lunging wave of gray fury—and the combatants swirled in a howling, milling melee!

This time the wolves faced not helpless sleepers or unsuspecting victims. The retainers were well armed and mad with the hopelessness of their position. Dripping swords hewed into the onrushing ranks, smashing through one furred devil after another. The hounds battled gamely beside their masters, equally determined to meet death with as many of their hated enemy as possible. The stones ran slippery with blood, as the halls resounded with shrieks and howls of agony.

But the wolves were too many, and their awesome leader made them invincible. In unspeakable fury the werewolf leapt among the struggling figures and seized one of the soldiers. Ignoring the human's desperate sword-thrusts, it hurled its helpless prey against the stone floor, smashing his skull with the impact. Already the hounds had gone down under an avalanche of slashing fangs, and the remaining humans now tottered before the pack.

Blood spurting from frightful wounds, they continued to hack wildly at their slayers, even as the pack pulled them down to mangled extinction.

Then the hallway was still, but for the death throes of a few wolves. For an instant the pack stood panting, tasting the warm salt of their victims' lifeblood. Already sounds could be heard as the others responded to the alarm. The werewolf raised a chilling howl of maddened power, then led its pack dashing down the hallways to find the rest of these terrified weaklings, whose stupid pride it was to be man.

Sounds of the battle above them penetrated even to the cellar room where Kane was imprisoned. The guards dropped their dice and listened. "What the hell is that!" gasped Tali in shocked amazement. Kane jumped to the door to see what was happening.

Someone threw open the door at the head of the stairs and shouted down, "Come on! Hurry! Wolves! The castle's full of wolves! Hurry or they'll kill us all!"

The guards rose up in panic. Snatching their weapons they ran up the stairs to join their rallying comrades.

"Wait! Damn you! Wait!" Kane bellowed futilely. "Come back and let me out of here! Come back! Thro'ellet take you all!" He shouted after the last man had disappeared up the stairs, but it was useless. Either out of panic or distrust they had left him here. In disgust he envisioned the fight in the upper floors of the castle and its probable end. Bitterly he pictured himself sitting here helpless while the werewolf and its pack came to finish the prisoner trapped in his cell.

Kane strained to see the fastening of the door through the spyhole. He knew it was secured by a heavy wooden bar, for as they had thrown him in, he had automatically examined the fixtures of his cell. In the short glance he had had, it had seemed that the iron fastenings that protruded from the stones of the wall, and upon which the bar rested, would be the weakest point. With this in mind he backed off across the cell, then hurled his over 300 pounds of bone and corded muscle against the unhinged side of the door.

He ricocheted painfully from the bruising impact. The door held solid. Making another attempt, he again tried the door. It seemed to rattle slightly more loosely. Perhaps the iron fastening was pulling away from its setting in the stone. But the jarring crashes against the unyielding door were dealing him brutal punishment. Altering his strategy, Kane launched himself in a flying kick at the spot where the bar reached across the door to the bracket. With startling agility for his bulk, Kane landed lightly after the blow. He knew the fantastic power such a kick could deliver when properly executed.

He lashed out again. And again. Teeth set in determination, he battered the door of his prison relentlessly. The iron bracket would give sometime, he was certain. But how much time was left to him, he could not guess.

Within her chamber Breenanin listened in terror to the fierce struggle outside her door. She had awakened with these sounds in her ears—the shouts of the castle's defenders and the enraged snarling of the wolves. The death cries of man and beast. She tried to imagine how the battle was turning, but from her chamber she could tell little. And the scenes offered by her terrified imagination drove her to hysteria.

On Kane's warning she had provided herself with a silver dagger, although the weapon seemed laughably inadequate. In addition she had tied a silver chain across the fastenings of both her door and the shutters of her windows. She had little faith in their efficacy, but it had been something she could do.

The fight now seemed to be moving to another quarter, for its clamor was growing dim. What could be happening out there? she wondered. From what she had heard, evidently a great pack of wolves had invaded the castle.

A sudden rattle on the stones outside one of her windows caught her attention! In abject horror Breenanin riveted her eyes on the shutters. From without now came unmistakable sounds of something scraping and clambering upon the ledge!

A heavy blow smote the shutters, caving them back dangerously! Petrified with terror, Breenanin watched the fastenings with awful fascination. Another blow! And one more! With a brittle crack, the lock splintered and the silver chain snapped apart!

And through the wreckage of the shutters leapt— Henderin!

Her brother was almost unrecognizable. His fingers were torn and bleeding; his clothing disordered. There was stark madness in his rolling eyes, and his teeth gnashed wildly. Blood ran upon his face and spotted his chest.

He dropped to the floor in a crouch. With a bizarre blend of titter and growl, he began to stalk his fear-sickened sister!

Breaking from the spell of dread that bound her, Breenanin uttered a soul-tearing shriek and bounded across the room for the door. Behind her Henderin shambled, mouthing insane slobbering noises.

In panic she fumbled with the bolt of the door, pulling loose the silver chain. Gasping, she freed the bolt and shot it back! She swung wide the door!

And looked into the face of gore-splattered nightmare!

Howling in hideous glee the werewolf lunged from the crimson tiled hallway through the gaping doorway! For the moment it had chosen to allow its pack to fend for itself against the crumbling ranks of the castle's defenders. Its red eyes brimming with unspeakable lust, the slavering demon stretched forth its talons for the terror stricken object of its desire.

Breenanin recoiled in absolute horror as the hulking abomination stalked across the room toward her. Henderin was forgotten in the face of this inhuman beast of scarlet streaked white that now crept toward her in dreadful certainty of its prey. In a moment the werewolf had her trapped in one corner of the bed chamber. The creature slowed, a snarl of fiendish laughter in its throat; it clashed together the awful fangs of its long muzzle, savoring to the fullest the piteous terror of its victim. In despair

Breenanin hurled an urn at her attacker, but the werewolf disdained even to dodge, and the vessel smashed into fragments against its hairy chest. It moved toward her confidently.

"No!" shrieked a voice that had been stripped of its humanity. "No! You can't have her! You said she would be mine!"

The werewolf halted and flung a contemptuous snarl across its shoulder to the frantic Henderin. The insane youth was gnashing his teeth and jumping about in the frenzy of his rage. Ignoring the frothing madman, the creature returned to the focus of its dark appetite.

In a silent blur Henderin pounced upon the werewolf's back! Driving his knees into the creature's spine, Henderin dashed it to the floor; even as they toppled he locked his arms about its neck and dug his teeth into the flesh of its nape. Caught off guard by the human's strike, werewolf and madman rolled to the floor before Breenanin's feet. Henderin was a powerful man, and his strength was doubled by the surge of his insane rage. Pressing his advantage, he forced the creature's snout into the stones, while continuing to crush his knees into its spine.

Reacting in the fury of its pain, the werewolf raked its assailant with its claws, at last securing a grip on the human. With a burst of strength it ripped the writhing youth from its back and hurled him across the floor. Henderin landed heavily, but rolled to his feet in time to meet the monster's charge.

For a moment they lashed punishing blows at each other, neither of them able to secure a hold on his opponent. Then they flung themselves together in a clawing, gnashing embrace of deadly hatred; they struggled viciously for several heartbeats, and fell in a tangle on the floor. Over and over they rolled, as each sought to remain on top.

Freed from her corner, Breenanin shook off her paralysis of fear and darted across the room for her bed. Flight did not register with her—for the werewolf seemed inescapable. But she remembered Kane's advice now, and in a frenzy she sought underneath the bedclothing. She felt a surge of hope as her small hand closed about the cold hilt of the silver dagger. Drawing the white, bladed weapon free, she turned to the thrashing combatants!

Henderin had neither the strength nor the means to press home the initial advantage of his sudden attack. Only luck and his berserk strength had made it possible for him to hold out this long. But now the werewolf was astride his struggling body. Locking its long arms about its victim's chest, the monster squeezed him in a crushing embrace of death. Even as the ribs cracked rottenly, its razor-like fangs tore through Henderin's failing guard and sank into the human's neck! Ultimate blackness closed upon the youth's tormented mind, as human muscle and bone proved unequal to the test. Overcome with blood-lust, his slayer greedily gulped down the gushing flow from the ruined throat of its victim.

Seeing her chance, Breenanin rushed upon the momentarily pre-occupied werewolf. Her lithe arm raised high; then she drove the silver blade with all the desperation of her fear and loathing into the creature's unprotected left shoulder! It sensed the danger at the last moment and tried to avoid the blow, but too late! Only slightly off its target, the keen blade sheared through inhuman flesh and glanced along the scapula!

Had the dagger been as long as a real weapon, the stab would have been a mortal wound. Instead, the werewolf howled in unaccustomed agony and sprang to its feet. Only barely did Breenanin succeed in maintaining her desperate grasp on the dagger's hilt, as the werewolf wrenched itself free in its lunge.

Its pale fur now matted with its own blood, the werewolf whirled to face its small assailant. Fury was in its eyes, but as Breenanin raised her dagger to strike again, something like panic also appeared. The dread held by the creature for the silver weapon was out of all proportion to a human's judgment. But the inhuman mind recognized a threat to its existence—a threat that held all the more terror because of its unfamiliarity. Wounded and uncertain, the werewolf decided to try a safer strategy.

Snarling defiance it sprang to the open window and leapt from the room to the courtyard thirty feet below.

Sick and shaken from her hideous ordeal, Breenanin slumped to the floor, moaning incoherent sobs. In her shocked state of mind she knew only that the ravening demon had left her—beyond this she could not understand. Weakly she dragged herself to the torn corpse of her brother. She realized dimly that his intervention had preserved her from an abominable fate, and with this came the recognition that this importunity had cost the life of her brother.

Forgetting his madness and the crimes perpetrated under its cloak, she fell upon Henderin's mangled body and sobbed hysterically. She did not even hear the shuffling footsteps that pushed through the doorway behind her.

Baron Troylin staggered drunkenly into the room, his mind fogged with pain and horror. Behind him tottered two of his retainers, similarly weakened from numerous wounds. Troylin seemed to regard his shuddering daughter without recognizing her. "All dead," he intoned dully. "All dead but us. The werewolf even smashed in the door where the women were hidden and let his pack loose on them." No one listened to Troylin, not even himself. Only his mind numbly recounted the events of the past half hour.

"Wolves everywhere. Those awful bloody fangs. Snapping. Leaping at you from all sides. Once you're down they just tear you to ribbons. Somehow we stopped them. Their leader left them. Werewolf gone we could hold out against the rest. Kill the devils. So damn many though. Drove them off somehow. Finally they stopped coming. Don't know if they're all dead too, or just run off. But we're all that are left."

He stopped his mumbling and stared dumbly at his daughter. Slowly his eyes began to focus. He saw her stretched beside the scarlet stained body of . . . Recognition dawned. Screaming an oath he raced to his son's side and flung his daughter away.

"Henderin!" His soul broke under the shriek of anguish. "Henderin! My son! Not you too!" He collapsed in the hysteria of his grief.

Breenanin recovered somewhat. Her father and his men had returned. She was safe with them. Hesitantly she laid a hand on his heaving shoulders. "Father," she stammered.

His face snapped upward to gaze at her. In his eyes the light of madness burned. The baron had been a simple, straightforward man. During the nights of fear he had lived under strains unimaginable to his worldly mind. And under the relentless terror and slaughter of this final battle with the wolves, he had seen the comfortable world that he knew fall to crimson destruction. Death had brushed by him everywhere, and now he looked upon the mutilated corpse of his son, his most beloved possession. With the crushing weight of grief and horror, his mind had broken.

Now he stared at his daughter's bloodstained nightdress. She recoiled before the soulless gaze of a stranger. "You!" shrieked the baron shrilly. "You!" He clutched the silver dagger which Breenanin had dropped and lurched to his feet. "You killed him! You're the werewolf! You killed them all!"

Mouthing insane curses, Troylin grasped his terrified daughter. The silver blade flashed downward! A gasping shriek of agony. Sound of a soft form falling to the floor. White hands strained as they plucked ineffectually at the pain.

Stillness.

He gazed at her fallen form. Death eased the lines of fear and pain. Below her left breast a spreading crimson over her white gown, pale flesh. Red on white. Tumbling images through his mind. Red on white over and over. Days nights of red on white. So much red. So much white. And the end?

A harsh snarl behind him broke off his kaleidoscopic thoughts. Troylin ran to the doorway. The werewolf had returned.

One retainer was already dying, his throat ripped open from the savage fangs that had struck without warning. While they had stood there gaping at their master's madness, death had stolen upon them from behind. Troylin watched in the agony of disbelief as the werewolf brushed aside the other's frantic sword thrusts and crushed his neck in its taloned hands. The creature was unkillable then!

It turned at last to the baron, scarlet fury blazing in its eyes. Unarmed, he backed away in horror, pitiful pleas slobbering from nerveless lips. The creature advanced relentlessly, arms outstretched and a low growl in its throat. Something pushed against the baron's back. It was the balcony railing! he could retreat no farther!

With a howl the werewolf lunged for him! It raised the screaming man high above its head. Then it threw him from the balcony, arcing him high over the great hall. With a sickening crunch, the baron's body bounced upon the stone floor, but half a step from his place at the high table.

And as life leaked from his smashed skull, a flash of sanity returned to the human. In that moment Baron Troylin knew that the end to the kaleidoscope was death.

One final kick and the cell door flew open; the stubborn iron bracket had at last been torn from its socket. Breathing heavily from the exertion, Kane limped from the cell. Around him all was silent. No wolves met his sight.

Carefully he ran up the stairs from the cellar and peered along the empty corridors. Again nothing. Silently he slipped down the hallways, heading for the main part of the castle. As he had no weapon, he moved with extreme caution, knowing that his chances were slim should he encounter the pack. But nothing challenged his progress, other than an occasional cluster of dead. From the many human and wolf carcasses he met, it was clear that within the castle had been fought a vicious battle.

His keen ears caught the sound quickly, and he smiled grimly as he recognized it. Silently he followed it to its source. He entered the great hall.

Evingolis sat in his accustomed corner, his long fingers once more drawing haunting notes from the lute. The two regarded one another in the stillness of the darkened hall.

Kane broke the quiet. "So it was you. I was a fool not

to have realized it before! I had suspicions—but I felt the same way toward too many others."

The minstrel continued to play, favoring his left arm slightly. "They seldom realize until it's too late," he began. "No one expects violence of a minstrel—an albino, at that. Over and over it's happened. I prepare the trap, and while they're falling one by one, the survivors fight among themselves with fear and suspicion. Break down trust, and men are helpless. And no one suspects the minstrel. Always it goes that way."

"Always?"

"Perhaps. The pattern repeats itself. Variations fall within the frame. Usually it happens as it did here. I wander into a new place, play around the area, pick up information until I find an arrangement that I can manipulate.

"And once I succeed in isolating a group of men into a situation that I control, my pack and I wreak our vengeance! For it is your race, Kane, that dared to leave its home in the trees to challenge the Brotherhood! Man and his weapons and his traitor hounds! Man who seeks to banish the Brotherhood to the wastelands! Man who declares his stifling cities to be civilization—a society superior to the wild freedom of the pack!

"Perhaps the day shall come when man and his cities shall be destroyed by the plagues, the famines, the wars his idiocy perpetuates. And then shall the Brotherhood once again run free! But until then there will be those in your smug flock who will pay the penalty for the insolence of your race! These shall know the wrath of the Brotherhood!

"Here it was rather simple. I found out in Carrasahl that Baron Troylin owned this conveniently isolated estate; then it was just a matter of discovering how to get him here. Easy enough. A spell on his son causes him to run berserk, a scandal results, and the baron is forced to retire. This way I not only could use Henderin for a scapegoat, but under the spell I could also control his actions. He was useful at times—and so was old Lystric. The fool gladly took credit for any suggestions I offered—even to bring Henderin up here.

"So I have a sizable party of humans isolated from their fellows. Next step is to cut off escape. The storm I summoned took care of that part. I almost had you on two occasions that night, but you eluded me each time. Then it was simply a matter of slowly cutting down their strength until an outright attack could destroy the remnant. My strategy should be obvious to you by now. At first I arranged for my wolves to split the hunt by driving a second elk across your path, then they ambushed your half. They should have killed you then, but again I underestimated you."

"Then you know who I am," said Kane, "—and what I am."

The minstrel laughed softly. "Yes, I know about you— and I've guessed a lot more. As I've wandered I've cut across your trail occasionally—it seems neither of us stays in one place very long! And I've heard a good many stories about a wanderer named Kane. The old legends and sagas haven't forgotten you either. Even that old fool Lystric had some suspicions of the truth about you."

He laughed again. Kane remembered the panting laughter of the wolf—soft, tongue lolling. "I even saw you once in my youth—over a century ago now, in old Lynortis. You were scheming your way into the court, I recall. The city was destroyed not long after that—by treachery within, the tale was.

"So your presence here had me worried after I realized who you were. But I soon found a use for you as an added diversion. You played into my hands last night in Lystric's chamber. I spared you then in order to make it appear as if you were the werewolf everyone so desperately feared. If they killed you as I had intended, then you would be taken care of, and the rest would relax their vigilance. Instead they let you live, split their strength to guard both you and Henderin, and were still careless.

"Tonight I had Henderin escape again, planning to use him for a diversion while I let my pack inside the castle. As it happened I didn't need him for that—the guard at the gate slept until the moment Henderin killed him. Later when I discovered Breenanin had barred her cham-

ber with silver, I used him to break in and drive her out.
The fool attacked me then, and I had to kill him before
I had intended. The bitch had spirit though! She stabbed
me with a little dagger, and I left to circle around.

"Meanwhile Troylin had been able to fight off my wolves
in my absence. But I came on him outside her room and
finished them."

Kane surveyed the destruction about him, the smashed
figure on the floor. "And Breenanin?" he asked, wondering that he felt concern.

Evingolis snarled. "That gross fool killed her himself!
The idiot must have thought she was to blame for all my
work. Killed her with her own dagger!" Kane winced.
"Really makes me furious—I had some interesting plans
for the girl! She's still warm and I suppose I can still
have some fun—but it isn't the same as when her struggling heart forces hot red spurts over your muzzle!"

He laughed again, running a long tongue over his lips
in memory of unspeakable pleasures. "What's wrong,
Kane? I know you aren't squeamish about such things.
No, I think you really felt something for that girl. Love?
You don't even know what the word means! Kane—
doomed with the curse of eternal wandering—in love with
a mortal girl! A flower who would be faded and gone
before you could even understand! Her lifetime a day
of yours! By this time you've surely seen this happen
enough to understand the absurdity of it! No, I know what
it was! She loved you—and you were simply stunned to
receive anything other than false love artificially induced
by your cunning manipulations—and more often by far,
to receive only fear and hatred! And you were so moved
with the novelty you tried to discover tenderness in that
stone you call your heart! Ah, Kane! You've grown soft
headed in your dotage!"

Kane stared silently at the taunting minstrel. In his eyes
the cold flames of death were leaping.

"Yes, it is a rare jest! And here the two of us stand—
two human shapes in a hall of death. Human in shape
only, for the humans all lie dead! Kane—you're as far
apart from this carrion in your own way as I am in mine!

Two immortals, it seems, and both of us leave only death and destruction in our wake! I wonder, Kane! The wretch I killed at the first of my storm—from beyond death he made a prophecy that out of the storm would come a man not man who would bring death to all! I wonder though—which of us did he mean!"

The albino laid aside his lute, still chuckling wolfishly. "Well Kane, this has been a most interesting game. I salute you. You have led an extraordinary career, to use an absurd understatement. I admire you. Perhaps I understand you. And you of all men are the first to command my respect.

"I will derive immense pleasure from killing you!" He arose.

Kane had been prepared for the change, but he had not expected its abruptness. One instant the minstrel stood laughing before him—there was a split-second blur, as if Kane's eyes had momentarily gone out of focus—then a snarling hulk of white furred death was leaping for him!

That ruined one chance, cursed Kane, who had hoped to launch his attack while the creature was in the throes of transformation. As Evingolis hurtled toward him, Kane grasped the table which separated them, and heaving with all his fantastic strength he hurled the massive structure full against the rushing beast. The werewolf went under in a crashing tangle of splintering furnishings. For a moment it had to free itself from the wreckage; in that second's hesitation Kane dashed for the stairs at the end of the hall. From the minstrel's story, the silver dagger should still be impaled in Breenanin's lifeless form, growing cold in her chamber. Kane knew his chance of reaching it was slight, but it would be a weapon against the werewolf if he could get to it.

He pounded up the stairs. Howling in rage, Evingolis tore clear of the wreckage and hurtled after Kane. Kane had a slight lead and he moved with all his great speed, but before he had reached the top stair his awesome pursuer had nearly overtaken him. Snatching claws raked his boot. Kane made the top and tried desperately to reach the door of Breenanin's room. Halfway there and he knew he would never make it—another few steps and the werewolf would be on him!

Kane suddenly leapt into the air, pivoted in midflight, and lashed out with his boot into the chest of the werewolf. The power of his blow knocked the creature backward, grunting in surprise and pain. The dagger was beyond reach. Kane knew his only chance would be to kill his assailant with sheer physical force. But man against demon seemed hopelessly mismatched. Yet Kane was not an ordinary man.

As Evingolis tottered from the surprise kick of the human, Kane hurled himself against the werewolf! Driven with the brutal power of his thick legs, Kane's massive body caught Evingolis off balance and sent him reeling backward over the brink of the stairs. Wrapped in a deadly embrace, man and demon plummeted down the long stairway, rolling over and over, crashing agonizingly against the steps and wall! With a surge of strength Kane gained a brief contact with the spinning stairway and used the purchase to push their fall over the edge. Splintering the railing, the locked combatants plunged off into space ten feet above the stone floor under them! Kane wrenched himself atop the snarling werewolf just before they smashed onto the floor.

The force of the fall flung them apart. Evingolis's furry body had cushioned Kane's fall, and he rolled away with only severe bruises from the tumble. Leaping to his feet he faced his enemy again. The fall would have crushed a human antagonist, but Evingolis appeared only to be even more enraged. Still he seemed to be a little stunned and staggered as he rose to meet Kane.

Once again Kane rushed the werewolf, hoping to hit him before he could recover. But the creature leapt aside, catching Kane in a loose grip, and threw him across the floor. Kane skidded over the stones, breaking his fall, and he was able to catch himself just as Evingolis sprang for him. With lightning speed Kane pulled up his legs, and with his back on the floor he caught the lunging beast on the chest and hurled him on over his body. The werewolf landed heavily, but was again on his feet with Kane.

The two circled warily, watching for the other to offer an opening. Evingolis was amazed with the human's strength and speed—and the punishment he had taken was considerable. Painfully throbbing and bleeding once more, the dagger wound was handicapping him. Raw fury coursed through his demon brain. He must kill this human —must tear out his life. Kane was badly battered as well, but his hellish blood lust was fully aroused. No fear did he experience—only the insane desire to kill and destroy. Silently they waited for the other to make a mistake.

Evingolis's impatience to kill his human foe spurred him to break the impasse. Confident in his inhuman strength and razorlike weapons, the werewolf sprang! Kane knew to leap back would only leave him exposed to the followup of the creature's attack. Again he did the unexpected. Ducking down, Kane let his opponent's clutching arms pass over him; then he hurled himself at the creature's throat!

Kane's powerful hands gripped the werewolf's furry throat, holding those gnashing tusks away from his straining flesh. Evingolis wrapped his long arms about the human's body, striving to crush his spine in this deadly embrace. They rocked back and forth in the gloom of the hall, two titanic figures straining with unbelievable strength to overpower the other. The pressure on Kane's ribs was unbearable, but his powerful muscles knotted to resist the awesome strength of the werewolf's embrace. All the while Kane tightened his strangler's grip about the thick throat of the demon.

Evingolis began to feel the consuming need for breath. He relentlessly tightened his crushing hold on Kane's trunk, trying to snap the human's back and thereby break his stranglehold. But the wound in his shoulder kept him from getting full use of one arm, and the werewolf had never encountered such massive strength and endurance in a human before. He champed his fangs futilely, unable to reach the human; clawing Kane's back with his fearsome talons, he fought the need for air. He could feel ribs starting to buckle under his tightening arms!

The pain from his back and ribs was a white hot agony now, but Kane continued to lock his hands about Evingolis's throat. He knew his only chance would be to outlast his opponent, even though the awful pressure made it almost impossible to force air into his own lungs. Sudenly the werewolf loosed his vice-like grip! Evingolis must have air; frantically he tried to break Kane's grip, snapping his slavering fangs and ripping wildly with his clawed hands!

They fell to the floor then. Kane landed atop the werewolf, and immediately he sought to pinion the punishing arms, whose talons now sought his face. Hunching forward on Evingolis's chest, Kane succeeded in pinning his shoulders with his knees. The creature writhed in great spasms, his limbs flailing desperately!

Then the wild struggles of the werewolf grew weaker. Its inhuman vitality was failing under the attack of a more powerful one. With glazing vision Evingolis stared into the cold blue eyes of Kane and recognized the death that flamed within. Under Kane's deadly hands suddenly grated the dull crunch of snapping vertebrae.

"Thus died Abel!" hissed Kane, slowly forcing his fingers to relax their deathhold.

There came that same abrupt blur over Evingolis's body, and Kane found himself clutching the broken neck of an albino wolf.

Epilogue

It was early morning, and a solitary horse and rider stood in the snow. Searching the outbuildings, Kane had come upon his own horse, overlooked by the wolves, and now well rested and fed. Painfully he had saddled him and put together a pack of provisions for another long ride. Kane had suffered several cracked and bruised ribs, along with numerous deep gashes and scratches from the werewolf's claws, but he dressed his wounds as well as he could and mounted, determined not to spend another night in the dead castle.

As he watched, the flames of the burning castle rose high into the air. Another floor had fallen in, and soon the stone walls would stand completely gutted. Kane had fired the structure before he left, making a giant funeral pyre for human and wolf alike. In those flames was now being destroyed the corpse of Evingolis as well; the minstrel would sing his songs and cast his webs no more.

Somewhere in those flames was being consumed another who would sing no more. Kane had wrapped her in her white fur cloak and laid her gently on her bed, before setting ablaze the pyre. Perhaps Breenanin had found peace, if death were peace. Kane could never experience either. Still he had for a moment experienced something with her—some emotion that he had forgotten he ever had known. Even in memory, he could not identify the sensation.

Kane shivered, suddenly realizing how cold it was.

He urged his mount southward. The snow was thickly crusted and bore him easily. But for spots.

Cold Light

he assault on the ogres' stronghold had been brutal, reflected Gaethaa as he wearily looked over the ruins. Pulling off his silver-trimmed helmet, he ran a bleeding hand over his grimy face, pushing the sweat-soaked blond locks from his eyes. He squinted through the smoke that made red the sun. Inside the fortress walls all was one chaotic turmoil of smashed and burning buildings, seige engines—bodies of both his men and the ogres' retainers.

He pushed a corpse from an overturned cart and sprawled onto the vacated space. Wincing against the pain as he sucked in a deep breath—some bruised ribs there at best, but the cuirass had turned the sword—Gaethaa permitted himself the tired exultation befitting a man who has brilliantly conceived and executed a difficult task, one fully as honorable as it was dangerous.

Credit must be given to many others, to be certain. Had it not been for the genius of the young Tranodeli wizard, Cereb Ak-Cetee, the sorcerous flames that guarded the ogres' walls would not have been extinguished, nor their impenetrable obsidian gate blasted into splintered rubble. Mollyl had been magnificent as he led the first wave through the smouldering gap and into the full fury of the ogres' minions. And the Red Three had very nearly succeeded in overwhelming his soldiers, even with the failure of their spells and the rout of their servants. Many had been smashed and torn under the huge weapons of the seemingly invincible ogre brothers. Then Gesell, the middle brother, fell from the poisoned arrow which Anmuspi the Archer threaded through the visor of his helmet. And Omsell, the oldest, was grievously wounded from a swordthrust of the dying Malander, and as the ogre fell to his knees, Gaethaa himself had struck his hideous head from his shoulders. That left only Dasell, who had been knocked senseless when he tried to leap in escape from the fortress walls. Gaethaa had ordered him bound, and now the ogre's twelve-foot body swung in grotesque dance, as it dangled from a gibbet overlooking the valley that he and his brothers had so long held in terror.

Alidore approached him through the haze, his broken arm now roughly bandaged. You did that when you blocked Omsell's axe from splitting me, thought Gaethaa, and vowed to make his lieutenant a generous gift from his personal portion of the booty, although such bravery was truly a knight's duty to his lord.

"We've got it all about mopped up, milord." Alidore had started to salute with his other hand, but decided it would look foolish. "Looks like we've rounded together everyone still alive inside. Not too pretty—the Red Three must have ordered all captives slaughtered when it was obvious that we were about to break through the wall. So that leaves us with maybe twenty survivors that we're holding for your orders—the last of their soldiers and servants."

"Kill them."

Alidore paused, reluctant to dispute his leader. "Milord, most of them swear they were forced to serve the ogres. They either obeyed their commands or were eaten like the others."

A cold note crept into Gaethaa's voice and his face was hard. "Most are probably lying. The others deserve worse, for they stooped to save their own lives by becoming tools for the enslavement and destruction of their fellow men. No, Alidore, mercy is commendable to be sure, but when you seek to destroy an absolute evil, you must destroy it absolutely. Show mercy in expunging a blight, and you only leave seeds to spread it anew. Kill them all."

Alidore turned to give the order, but Mollyl had been listening and was already loping across the court to see it carried out. He would enjoy that, Alidore thought in distaste, then dismissed the Pellinite from his thoughts. He addressed Gaethaa sincerely.

"Milord, you have done a really magnificent thing here today! For years this land has lived in abject terror of the Red Three. Most of the countryside has been stripped bare by them, and no one can say how many captives have ended their lives as food on the ogres' table! With their death the area can return to life once more—its people can farm the lands and sell their wares in peace, and travellers can enter the valleys and pass without danger. And here—as before when I have followed you on your missions—you will accept nothing from the people but their gratitude!"

Gaethaa smiled tiredly and waved him to silence. "Please, Alidore! Save eulogies for my death. I can't bear them now. Many have died to help me in my crusade, otherwise I could have done nothing. They are the ones who deserve your praise.

"No," and his voice was dreamy, "my only desire is to destroy these agents of evil. It is my goal in life, and I ask nothing in return."

Admiration glowed on Alidore's battle-weary face. "And now that the Red Three are destroyed, what is to be our next mission?"

Gaethaa's voice was inspired. "As my next mission I will seek out and destroy one of the most dangerous agents of evil that history or legend knows. Tomorrow I will ride out for the death of a man called Kane!"

I. Where Death Has Lain

At times the awesome curse of immortality weighed on Kane beyond all endurance. Then he was overcome with long periods of black despair, during which he withdrew entirely from the world and spent his days in gloomy brooding. In such dark depression he would remain indefinitely, his mind wandering through the centuries it had watched, while within there cried unanswered a longing for peace. Ultimately some new diversion, some chance of fate, some abrupt reversal of spirit, would cut through his hopeless despair and send him forth once again into the world of men. Then cold despair would melt before the black heat of his defiance against the ancient god who had cursed him.

It happened that such a mood had seized Kane when he came to Sebbei. He had just fled the deserts of Lomarn, where his bandits had for a few months been plundering rich caravans and laying waste to the scattered oasis towns. An ingenious trap had cut down most of Kane's forces, and he had fled westward into the ghost land of Demornte. Here his enemies would not follow, for the plague which had annihilated this nation was still held in utmost dread, and although it had struck this desert locked land nearly two decades before, still no one entered and no one left silent Demornte.

Dead Demornte. Demornte whose towns lie empty, whose farms are slowly returning to forest. Demornte where death has lain and life will no more linger. Land of death where only shadows move in empty cities, where the living are but a handful to the countless dead. Demornte where ghosts stalk silent streets in step with the living, where the living walk side by side with their ghosts. And a man must look closely to tell one from the other.

When the great deserts of Lartroxia West and Lomarn to the east had been carved from the earth, some freak of nature had spared Demornte. Here, shouldered between two mighty deserts, green land had held out against scorched sand, and a considerable region of gently rolling hills and cool lakes had sheltered thousands of inhabitants under its low forests. It had been as a giant oasis, Demornte, and its people had lived pleasantly, working their many small farms and trading with the great caravans that crossed the deserts from east and west.

The plague had ridden with one such caravan, a plague such as these lands had never seen. Perhaps in the faraway land from which it had come, the people had formed a resistance to the disease. But here in fertile Demornte it sped like the wind throughout the green land, and thousands burned in its fevered delirium, screaming for water they could not swallow.

Desert locked Demornte. The plague could not cross the sands, so its fury fell fully on this peaceful world. And when it had run its course at last, peace returned to Demornte. The land became one vast tomb and knew the quiet of the tomb, for rarely were there enough survivors to bury the dead. Demornte, where ghosts stalk silent streets in step with the living, where the living walk side by side with their ghosts. And a man must look closely to tell one from the other.

Some few the plague had spared. Most of these gathered in Sebbei, the old capital, and here a few hundred dragged out their days where before 10,000 had bustled about their daily tasks. In Sebbei the remnants of a nation gathered together to await death.

To Sebbei Kane came seeking peace. A deathless man in a land of the dead, he was drawn by the quiet peace of the city. Along overgrown roads his horse had carried him, past farms where the forest was ineluctably obliterating all signs of man's labors. He had ridden through debris strewn streets of deserted towns, watched only by empty windows and yawning doorways. Often he passed piles of bleached bones—pitiful relics of humanity—and sometimes a skeleton seemed to wink and smile knowingly, or rattle its bones in greeting. Welcome redhaired stranger! Welcome you with eyes of death! Welcome man who rides under a curse! Will you stay with us? Why do you ride by so fast?

But Kane only stopped when he came to Sebbei. Through gates left open—for who would enter? who would leave?—his horse plodded, past rows of empty buildings and down silent streets. But the streets were kept reasonably clear, and an occasional house showed occupants—sad faces that stared at him with little curiosity. None challenged him; no one asked him any question. This was Sebbei, where one lived amidst death, where one waited only for death. Sebbei with its few inhabitants living in its silent shell—mice rustling through a giant's skeleton. To Kane Sebbei seemed far more eerie than those towns peopled solely by the dead through which he had ridden.

At the town's one operating tavern he had halted. Assailed for a moment by the uncanny lifelessness of the city, he paused in his saddle and licked his cold lips with tongue dry from travel. Over his right shoulder protruded the hilt of the long sword he wore slung across his back, and its scabbard rattled when he shook the tightness from his corded muscles. Lightly he slid from the saddle and entered the tavern, gazing speculatively at the incurious eyes that greeted him. Eyes so dull, so lifeless, they seemed clouded with corpselike glaze.

I am Kane, he had told those who drank there. His voice had echoed loudly, for in Sebbei they speak in hushed whispers. I have grown tired in crossing this desert, and I plan to stay here in your land for a time, he had explained. A few had nodded and the rest returned to their thoughts. Kane shrugged and began to ask questions of some of the townsmen, who listlessly gave him the answers he sought.

At length someone pointed out a faded old man who sat at a table in one corner, his back straight but his face broken. Here was one called Gavein, who served as Lord Mayor of Sebbei—a somewhat ironic dignity, for his duties were few in this town of ghosts, and prestige only a half-hearted echo of tradition. Gavein regarded Kane without comprehension when he attempted to explain his wishes to the mayor, but after a moment he seemed to awaken from his reverie. There are many empty houses, he told Kane. Take whatever you require—there are palaces or hovels, as you please. Most of our city has remained untenanted all these years since the plague, and only ghosts will take issue with your occupancy. Food you may purchase here at our market, or raise what you desire. Our needs are few these days, so you may soon grow tired of our monotonous fare. This tavern furnishes our amusements, if you feel inclined to such things. Stay with us then for as long as your spirit desires. Do as you wish, for no man will pry into your affairs. We are a dying people here in Sebbei. Our visitors are rare and few stay for long. Our thoughts and manner are our own, and we care not what chance brings you among us. It is our wish only to be left alone with our thoughts. We in turn leave you with yours. And Gavein tugged the worn folds of his cloak closer about his thin shoulders and returned to his dreams.

So Kane wandered through the deserted streets of Sebbei, watched by only an occasional pair of clouded eyes from the few inhabited dwellings. At length he took residence in an old merchant's villa, where the rich furnishings appealed to his taste for luxury, and whose neglected gardens along a small lake promised solace to his anguished spirit.

But he lived there not alone, for often there came to him a strange girl named Rehhaile, whom many called a sorceress. Only Rehhaile among those of Sebbei showed more than distracted aloofness to the stranger who had stopped in their city. An outsider herself, Rehhaile spent long hours in Kane's company, and she ministered to him in many ways.

Thus came Kane to Sebbei in Demornte. Demornte where death has lain, and life will not linger.

II. Death Returns to Demornte

Death came again to Demornte. Nine gaunt horses beat their hooves with hollow echo through the silent streets of Demornte, past the overgrown fields, past the empty, staring houses, past the mocking smiles of skeletons. Death had returned to Demornte flying varied standards—idealism, sadism, duty, vengeance, adventure. New banners, but it was death that marched beneath them, and the omniscient eyes of the deserted houses, of the laughing skulls recognized death and welcomed it home.

Only nine men. Many had started, seasoned mercenaries hired with Gaethaa's wealth, adventurers drawn by the boldness of the mission, men of hate with festered scores to settle with Kane. But the way had been hard, and some had fallen on the trail, others had deserted when they thought more about the man whom they were seeking. At Omlipttei outlaws had mistaken them for a troop of the Lomarni guard; their ambush had slain many. And when they at last had reached Demornte, many had not trusted the triple spell which Cereb Ak-Cetee swore would protect them from the dreaded plague. They had tried to desert; Gaethaa had pronounced them traitors and thus servants of evil, and he had ordered all deserters executed. The fight had been short and vicious, for these were hardened warriors. At the end there were left only Gaethaa and eight of his men to ride to Sebbei, where Cereb Ak-Cetee's magic had shown Kane to be staying.

We are enough, said Gaethaa. We must not give this demon a chance to escape his doom. And so they had followed him into the ghostland of Demornte.

Gaethaa—called also Gaethaa the Crusader, the Good, the Avenger—had fallen heir to extensive baronial estates in Kamathae. As a boy he had spent most of his time in the company of his family's men-at-arms. He had grown to despise the pampered luxury and wasteful existence of his class, and to yearn for adventures like those the men talked of by the fires. At manhood he had resolved to use his wealth to fight the battles of the oppressed, to seek out and destroy the creatures of evil who preyed upon mankind. He was a fanatic in the cause of good, and once he had recognized a center of evil, he trampled over every obstacle that would hinder him from burning it clean. For several years he had marched forth against petty tyrants, evil wizards, robber barons, outlaw packs, and monsters human and inhuman. Always he had vanquished evil in the name of good, shackled chaos with law. And now he rode against Kane, a name that had always fascinated him, but which he had half regarded as legendary, until he began to realize the truth that lay in the fantastic tales of this man. Kane would be a magnificent challenge for Gaethaa the Crusader.

Alidore had followed him from the first. A younger son of impoverished Lartroxian gentry, he had left home early and had passed through Kamathae when Gaethaa was organizing his first mission. Gaethaa's idealism was mirrored in Alidore, and the young man had joined him with unfailing enthusiasm. Through all of Gaethaa's campaigns he had followed faithfully and fought bravely against all odds. Now he was Gaethaa's lieutenant and most trusted friend. Alidore would follow wherever his lord should lead and fight beside him with the same unfaltering zeal of idealism.

Cereb Ak-Cetee was a young wizard from the plains of Tranodeli. He looked like a gawking hayseed choirboy in his silken mage's cloak, but he was very far from harmless. Cereb needed wealth and experience before he could pursue his training to the not inconsiderable height of his ambitions. Gaethaa had noted the sorceror's skill in penetrating defenses and ferreting out fugitives, and he paid Cereb handsomely for his services.

Next in rank—although Cereb's position was ambiguous came Mollyl from the ill-famed island of Pellin in the Thovnosian Empire. Mollyl was a dark man who smiled only when another screamed in agony. His total lack of fear—perhaps he lost it in the exultation of killing—made him indispensable to Gaethaa in battle. Mollyl took

Gaethaa's wealth, but he would probably follow him without pay, so long as his lord offered him new fields of delight.

Also from the Thovnosian Empire, but from the island of Josten, came Jan. Ten years ago when Kane's pirate fleet had terrorized the island empire, Jan had seen his family butchered, and Kane himself had chopped off his right hand when Jan had tried to fight back against the raiders. Since then Jan had laced a padded base to the stump of his wrist, and from the base he could affix either a blunt hook or one with needle tip and razor-sharp inner curve. He had joined Gaethaa for vengeance.

Although aging, Anmuspi the Archer still boasted he could thread an axehead at hundred paces. Few who had seen the mercenary shoot would care to call his boast. Anmuspi's luck had run out in Nostoblet in Lartroxia South. A palace revolution had failed, his employers were crucified, and Anmuspi was put on the slave block. Gaethaa had bought him after hearing the auctioneer proclaim his skill as an archer. For Anmuspi it meant only another shift in employers, and he followed Gaethaa's every command faithfully. For Anmuspi right and wrong were not his to question; obedience was his code.

Dron Missa was a footloose adventurer from far Waldann. His people were a warrior race, and even among them Missa excelled as a swordsman. Gaethaa promised him adventure, so Dron Missa had exuberantly come along for the ride.

Two others sought vengeance. One was Bell, a peasant from the Myceum Mountains. Bell was fully as stupid as he was brutal and powerful. Five years before Kane had sacrificed two of Bell's sisters as part of an ill-fated sorcerous experiment. Bell never tired of telling people what he planned to do to Kane someday.

Sed tho'Dosso listened carefully to Bell's descriptions of torture, for like Jan and Bell he had a score to settle with Kane. Several months previous when Kane had been organizing the desert raiders of Lomarn, Sed tho'Dosso had offered resistance on the grounds that he should lead since his band was the largest. Kane had peremptorily smashed Sed tho'Dosso's forces and had left the bandit chieftain staked in the sun to die. By a freak chance he had escaped death, and when he heard of Gaethaa's mission in crossing the Lomarn, Sed tho'Dosso eagerly joined him.

So they rode through Demornte, each man silent with his own thoughts. Death rode nine gaunt horses through the familiar streets of Demornte, and dead Demornte bade Death welcome.

III. Ripples and Shadows

The moon cast pale light upon Rehhaile's slender body, as she watched Kane moodily toss stones into the lake beneath their perch. Goose pimples rose on her tanned skin, and she wriggled over the velvet moss of the bank to press her shivering form against his. His body was warm, though his mind was distant, and she rested her head against his shoulder in contentment.

Rehhaile did not share the gloomy apathy, the bitter despair of her people. She loved the sunlight while the others generally kept to their shops and houses. As a result her lean figure was tanned an even brown that matched her unbound hair, and there was a strong hint of freckles across her face. Her features were somewhat boldly shaped, although not to the point of losing femininity. Her breasts were small and firm, her hips slim— making her appear a few years younger than her twenty years.

Bunching her long fingers over the massive muscles of Kane's shoulders and back, she began to massage them, trying to shape the knotted muscles to the pattern of the ripples on the lake. Kane seemed to ignore her, but she reached out with her mind and sensed that she was drawing him into lazy arousal.

For Rehhaile was blind, her wide eyes altogether sightless. Her mother had died from the plague while Rehhaile yet lay in her womb. Her father had sworn that death should not take all from him, and a physician had quickly torn her from the dead womb. Both father and physician died of the plague within the week, but somehow Rehhaile had survived while all about her Demornte was seared by the plague. Someone had taken care of her, for Demornte was a land of motherless children and childless mothers. Later she made a living by whatever way she could, for the most part hanging around Sebbei's sole tavern.

But Rehhaile had been blind since birth. And yet she had in place of sight an infinitely more precious power of vision. Her macabre birth, a genetic mutation, some whim of the gods—the reason was unknowable and unimportant. She was given a psychic talent that provided a far more wondrous sense of perception than any human eyes could afford.

Rehhaile could reach out to link her own mind with another. Through this psychic contact she could share the other person's perception of his surroundings, in effect see through another's eyes, hear through his ears, feel through his fingers. And along with this sharing of sensory impulses, Rehhaile could actually sense the feelings of another mind—not so much read the thoughts, but experience for herself the myriad emotions that drift through the corridors of the mind. Her incredible talent to see into another human mind established Rehhaile as a sorceress in the eyes of the townspeople of Sebbei, and in their despair they accepted this without concern or curiosity.

Because she could perceive the emotional turmoil of others, Rehhaile shared the distress of that soul she touched. If there was pain, she tried to soothe it in whatever way she could. For the people of Demornte nothing could be done. Theirs was an inconceivable, inconsolable grief, and their emotions were a burned out wasteland that could never be healed. The people of Sebbei largely ignored Rehhaile just as they ignored everything except their bitter memories. Rehhaile lived with them because there was nothing else she could do. And in sharing their thoughts, she shared their joyless depression, a steeping in gloom that almost overwhelmed her own soul.

The rare travellers whom chance brought to Sebbei

were a marvel to her. She bathed in the exotic colors of their thoughts, finding a universe of unimagined interest and vitality even in the mind of a stray camel driver. She often tried to persuade these strangers to take her along with them across the desert, but inevitably the knowledge of Rehhaile's witch powers would turn them cold to her appeal.

Then Kane had come to Sebbei, and she had experienced worlds of sensation unlike any she had ever imagined a human mind could hold. Kane had been a whirling labyrinth to Rehhaile. Most of his emotions were altogether alien to her, and many frightened her with their strangeness. But she had recognized the awful need for rest that screamed within him—the unaswerable longing for peace. So she had gone to him to minister to his agony in the arts that only she knew, and through the months of companionship they had known, it seemed to Rehhaile that the pain had somewhat dimmed within Kane.

She tugged a shock of red hair playfully. "Hey! What do you see down there in the pool?"

His mind was cold, far away. "Ripples on the water like the passing of years. Man enters life and there is a splash. His life sends out ripples—small ripples for a little man, huge waves for a great man—waves that overwhelm the tiny ripples, wash them away or remold them. But in the end it is all the same, for the ripples go out into the lake of life and soon die away, to leave the lake smooth for new lives or stones."

She scratched lightly with her nails. "Make that up just now?"

"No. I heard that analogy from the sage Monpelloni whom I studied under in Churtannts." Rehhaile did not know that Churtannts had lain in ruins for over a century. "Only I don't fit the frame he proposed here. I'm something marooned on the surface of existence. Instead of a short splash, I keep floating there, struggling about and making an endless succession of waves."

"I can see you there. Like an old bat fallen in and flopping about the pool." She dug her nails in deeper. "Come back to me, Kane! Don't you love me?"

He rolled over so abruptly she nearly slipped off the bank. His cold blue eyes bored into her blind face. Those eyes—how they frightened her with the promise of death that lurked within! But now Rehhaile thought she sensed an even more haunted glare.

"No, Rehhaile!" He said with slow intensity. "Can't you understand! Your life is only a brief ripple across the pool, and mine is a constant flow of waves into infinity! Your ripple is only noted in passing and swept aside!"

She shivered with a coldness not of the wind.

"And do you love me?" he returned.

"No!" she answered him softly. "For you there can be no love. I can only pity you and try to soothe that which can never be healed."

"I think you begin to understand," Kane said with a bitter laugh. Then soon they lay together under the pale moon. And about them the ghosts of dead Demornte slipped by unheeded.

IV. The Crusader in Sebbei

"Their faces are as empty as the skulls we've passed!" commented Dron Missa, craning his long neck to stare down a seated townsman who stolidly watched them ride by. "Bunch of fish faces! I've eaten baked fish that had more intelligence in their boiled eyes than these cretins."

"Thought they ate only flesh in Waldann—raw flesh at that," scoffed Cereb Ak-Cetee.

Missa laughed unappreciatively. "Nothing wrong with raw flesh. Tastes good with a little salt. Once ate a squirrel raw on a bet—whiskers to tail with the thing still kicking. I've hated the little furry bastards ever since."

"How about keeping your mind on finding that tavern," interrupted Gaethaa caustically. His nerves had been on edge since entering Sebbei. Ruined cities were no novelty to him. But the utter lack of curiosity shown by the people was unnerving. Their indifference upon seeing a band of heavily armed stranges ride into their city was unsettling—and something of a subtle insult.

The first person they encountered in this city of ghosts had been a disheveled fat man with a yellow streaked beard. He was sitting loosely before a stagnant fountain near the unguarded city gates. With a vapid expression he had watched their approach, then scurried off giggling when Alidore stopped to question him. It was not an auspicious welcome.

Several others that they met had turned away or closed their doors when hailed, and Gaethaa had grimly recalled the stories heard while crossing the Lomarn that in Sebbei there dwelled only ghosts and madmen. Still it seemed evident now that they would confront no organized opposition from the townspeople. This would make their mission one of more direct attack—Gaethaa had been prepared to use more subtle tactics should it have developed that Kane had established himself as ruler of the dead city.

Finally, persistent questioning of those they met indicated that someone named Gavein, who held the office of Lord Mayor, was more or less responsible for central authority in Sebbei. This Gavein could likely be found at Jethrann's tavern. Directions to Jethrann's tavern had been given with the provincial assumption that a stranger knew his way through the city to begin with. Sebbei was an old city, laid out in chaotic growth, and its narrow streets were disturbingly labyrinthian.

After several wrong turns and unenlightening inquiries, they came upon a brown haired girl seated under a tree. She seemed to be asleep, for she failed to notice them until the riders drew close. Then her head snapped toward their approach, face wild in an uncanny wide-eyed look of fright.

"By Thoem—at least here's somebody that doesn't have both feet in the grave!" smiled Dron Missa appreciatively. "Hey, Miss! Care to help some bone dry travellers find a cool place to rest? We're looking for a tavern—Jethrann's place."

The girl rose to her feet and began to back away from

them, her face oddly contorted in fear. Gaethaa spoke quietly in reassuring tones, explaining that he and his men were strangers passing through Sebbei, that they . . .

She turned from them and broke into a run. As she dashed from the shade, sunlight caught the flash of tanned limbs beneath her short dress of green trimmed brown suede. Hooves struck the earth in faster rhythm. Mocking laughter overtook her. Defiance edging her squeal of fright, the girl was jerked from the street by a bronzed arm and swung onto a saddle.

Mollyl laughed as he pinioned her lashing arms against her side. "Cut it, sweetheart!" he grinned. "Young girl like you must be real lonely here with all these dried up old scarecrows! Is that why you shy away when you see a real man, sweetheart? Maybe I could teach you the right way to say hello to a stranger."

"All right, Mollyl! We don't want to frighten her any more than we have already!" Gaethaa growled. "Stop squirming, child! We're only trying to get directions to Jethrann's tavern. Please forgive my men's lapse of breeding—we meant no harm to you. Now can you please tell us the way?"

Fear still lined her features, but her struggles grew less. Helplessly she perched on the saddle edge, crushed against Mollyl's hard chest. "It isn't far," she answered haltingly. "Keep on down this street maybe half a mile. You can begin to see the market square on down to your left then. The tavern is on the square."

"My thanks, child," Gaethaa returned. "We were on the right track at least. Guess our preconception of a market square doesn't fit this ghost town."

The girl wriggled hopefully, seeking to slip away. The expression of unaccountable fear still marred her face. Cereb Ak-Cetee grunted curiously and leaned toward her, peering at her face. Frowning in puzzlement he moved his long fingers before her eyes. She drew away with a shudder when his hand brushed her flesh. The wizard examined her speculatively.

Gaethaa spoke in command, and Mollyl reluctantly permitted his captive to slip to the ground. Shaking herself as

104

if to shed some taint, the girl stepped back, still staring at them in dread fascination. Abruptly she whirled and disappeared into an alley.

"She's blind," observed Cereb Ak-Cetee as they rode away. "Did you notice? No focus. Her eyes are sightless."

"What do you mean—blind?" Alidore exploded. "She damn well acted like she could see good enough. Had a strange look to her eyes, granted. But she can't have been blind."

"I said she was blind," the wizard persisted tight lipped. "I'm not at all sure how she perceives things, but I know enough to recognize blind eyes when they present themselves to me."

"Yeah—Ok!" Alidore answered in dismissal. He was not about to provoke the wizard's petulance.

"Hey, Bell!" Dron Missa whispered. "Cereb says we just took directions from a blind girl. Doesn't that ring a bell even in your thick skull?"

"You're funny, Missa," Bell rumbled. "Real funny. Yeah, you're a scream. You ought to become a jester. You'd be good. You're really a riot."

Alidore wondered how long it would take Dron Missa to push Bell too far—or vice versa. The Waldann's sword arm was among the deadliest Alidore had witnessed, but Bell could tear him into quarters if he ever got the drop on him.

"That's it!" Jan pointed with his hook. "Hell, man! I can smell that wine from across the square!"

"Good!" Gaethaa exclaimed. "And this part of town is as stagnant as the rest of the place. Doesn't look like there's any kind of organized force here, but we can't be sure what Kane will have done. Looks like he's just lying low so far though. So we'll play it by ear until we know the set up. Stroll on into the tavern just like we were on our way across Demornte and stopped to rest. Alidore and I will start stalking with this Gavein—assuming he's here—and sound him out. Then we'll take it from there. But no mention of Kane by any of you until I make the move. And easy on the wine—things might happen fast."

Tethering their mounts before the three-storied stone

structure, Gaethaa and his band entered the open doorway. Inside the air was cool, albeit somewhat stale. A small number of men stood at the bar and sat at small tables occupied with their drinks. Low-voiced conversation broke off as the riders sauntered across the smoky room to the bar—a conspicuous entrance even had strangers been commonplace in Sebbei. Still the townspeople returned to their incurious aloofness once the initial stir had settled, and the murmur of quiet voices began again.

Jethrann, the scar-faced innkeeper, took their coin with an empty smile and brought them wine. In response to Gaethaa's guarded inquiry he indicated the Lord Mayor, who sat alone and half asleep at his usual table.

Wiping the wine from his mustache, Gaethaa carried his mug across to Gavein's table, followed by Alidore who brought along the bottle. "Mind if I join you?" he asked.

Gavein shrugged. "Suit yourself."

"Have a drink with us?" suggested Alidore, already filling the mayor's empty mug.

"Thoughtful of you," Gavein observed. "Bunch of well armed toughs comes stomping into the place when we see maybe a dozen strangers in a year, and right away they want to share a bottle with the mayor. Maybe mercenaries are better mannered now than in the old days, but I doubt it. So thanks for the drink, and what do you want?"

"My name is Gaethaa," he introduced himself, deciding to come directly to the point. This gambit fizzled when Gavein made no show of recognition at the name. But Gaethaa was not a vain man, and he realized that it was unlikely tales of his exploits had penetrated empty Demornte.

He shifted to another approach. "I see my name is not known here in Sebbei—but then there are many names known far wider than Gaethaa. Take the name *Kane* for instance—there's a man whose fame has reached across our world. I seem to have heard that Kane came through Demornte once—perhaps you've met him?"

"I know a man of that name," Gavein admitted.

Gaethaa caught Alidore's eyes significantly. "Perhaps this isn't the same man. The Kane I have in mind is a giant of a man—stands about six feet and is built like he had the muscles of three strong men stretched upon a single frame. He has sort of a coarse face, has red hair and often a short beard. Generally carries his sword slung across his back in the Carsultyal fashion. Left-handed— although he's a deadly swordsman with either arm. His eyes though—people remember his eyes. Has blue eyes with some sort of insane menace in their gaze . . ."

"We're talking about the same Kane," Gavein grudgingly acknowledged. "What about him?"

Gaethaa forced himself to speak noncommittally. "So Kane is in Sebbei, is he?"

The mayor considered his wine cup. "Yeah, Kane's here in our city—Thoem knows why he stays. Lives out in the Nandai's old villa. Keeps to himself—Rehhaile's the only one who sees much of him. You some friend of his?"

Gaethaa laughed and rose to his feet. His men along the bar wavered hands near weapon hilts at the movement, but halted when they saw the eager triumph lighting the Crusader's long face. "No—Kane is no friend of mine! Far from it!" he intoned loudly. The townspeople gaped at him in startled amazement.

"In the world outside your ghostland men know me as Gaethaa the Avenger!" he announced. "I have made it my mission in life to hunt down and destroy the agents of evil who bring death and deprivation to the helpless! Too long has evil held sway over our lives—too long have the creatures of evil run unchecked among mankind! Evil has ruled the lives of men with the consuming might of merciless force—and mankind has had to bow to its terror or else be destroyed! But I have sworn to destroy the servants of evil wherever they hold mankind in thrall! I have time and again done battle with the forces of evil, and each time I have triumphed and destroyed with the greater strength of good! Order has mastered chaos— because I have fought evil on its own ground, and with the superior power of good I have conquered! Conquered because I have had the courage to confront evil face to face—because I have turned against evil the very violence with which it holds mankind under its heel—because I have met force with force and destroyed brute power with brute power!"

Gaethaa's face was bathed in demonic transfiguration as he breathed fierce sincerity into his explosive diatribe. His listeners watched him with the awestricken attention commanded by saints and madmen, and even here in Demornte none dared to break into the spell of ferocious fanaticism he spun for them.

Seeming to recollect himself, Gaethaa paused in his harangue and gestured toward his men. "These are my followers," he explained hoarsely. "A small army at the moment, but they're picked fighters and every man a seasoned and fearless warrior! Many have followed my command through other hard fought campaigns, and all have endured sufficient hardships and danger just in winning through to Sebbei to put old sagas to shame! For I have come to Sebbei with my men to seek out this creature who calls himself Kane! I am here to deliver your city from Kane!"

Gavein shrugged uneasily, uncertain how all this was going to involve him and his townspeople. "But Kane does nothing to us here in Sebbei. He keeps to himself in a villa at the edge of our city, as I've said. We don't even see him except when he comes by from time to time to buy provisions. Why don't you take your quarrel elsewhere?"

Gaethaa was aghast. Stunned by the mayor's indifference, he turned to Alidore to see if madness had claimed all present. Alidore cleared his throat and suggested in Kamathaen, "It may well be, milord, that we underestimated the parochial isolation of these people. Incredible as it seems, I don't think they have any idea who Kane might be. Why else would they have permitted him to remain in their city?"

Once more assured, the Avenger addressed his nervous audience. "Obviously then you people don't realize what manner of fiend is living here in your city! It seems incredible in view of his dark history that he hasn't already turned on you—Tloluvin only knows what demonic scheme he has in mind for you and your land! I've pitted myself against some utterly ruthless black hearted monsters in human guise in the past, but this Kane could be the most evil man ever to walk the earth! His crimes are so numerous, so colossal in infamy that most people believe Kane nothing more than wild legend! I once thought him legendary myself—until in my far searching crusade against the forces of evil, I began to cut across his blood stained trail too often for me to doubt his existence among us!

"Legends—there are countless legends if you travel far enough to hear them! It's astonishing how far back these tales go in man's history. A lot of these things may well be spurious or latter day reinterpretations, but there are enough common themes to make me give serious consideration to many points. These legends tell that Kane is immortal—further that he was one of the first true men! They say Kane rebelled against his creator—some forgotten god who had attempted to create in mankind a perfect race modeled according to his own warped ideal. This god had failed many times before he finally created a golden race that he kept in a sheltered paradise for his own amusement. It's not clear how, but evidently Kane provoked this golden race of men to revolt from their paradise existence—even killed his own brother when he tried to prevent this. Kane's defiance and murderous violence resulted in the destruction of the golden age, with the subsequent scattering of humanity across the ancient earth. Kane himself was doomed by this god with the curse of immortality! A curse of eternal wandering, never to know peace, haunted by the spectre of the violence he introduced to mankind—marked an outcast from humanity by the brand of his eyes, a killer's eyes! Only through violence such as he engendered can he die, but throughout the centuries no man has been able to destroy Kane in this his own element!

"Well, that's the gist of the oldest legends, and of course you can't tell where to draw the line with these old tales. But there are too many other legends and sagas over the centuries in which the name of Kane appears to lay this entirely to chance or to recurrent poetic theme! A few facts appear certain. Kane has lived for at least a few centuries—he is not the first agent of evil endowed with preternatural longevity by any means—and during this time he has brought nothing but death and destruction wherever he has wandered! Catastrophic violence seems to slither behind him like a shadow! And Kane has generally been the author of this bloodshed and ruin! He has engaged in the most hideous acts of black sorcery—the wizards of Carsultyal even drove him from their land in abhorrence at one time! He has been a pirate, a bandit, an assassin—committed countless numbers of violent deeds! He has gathered and led gigantic armies and navies against peaceful lands for purpose of conquest and pillage! He has ruled nations as the blackest of tyrants. He has been involved with—often instigated—numberless conspiracies to overthrow lawful governments! His name has become a byword for treachery over the centuries!

"I'm not just rehashing a bunch of fantastic legends for you to hear! Men who are with me today will attest to his guilt—they have seen Kane's insane deeds with their own eyes!" It was essential to Gaethaa that Gavein and his people recognize the justice of his mission—fully appreciate the infamy of Kane. "Talk to them! Just ask either Jan or Mollyl there what the name of Kane means to their fellows in the Thovnosian Empire! Ask Bell what Kane did to the people of his native Myceum Mountains! Ask Sed tho'Dosso to describe for you the murderous attacks Kane and his bandits made upon caravans crossing the Lomarn here at your doorsteps only a few months ago! I've talked enough now—go on and question these men!"

Gaethaa looked about him, earnest eyes seeking the faces of the townspeople—faces that turned away in frightened confusion. Finally Gavein essayed to speak, blinking at the Avenger as if hoping he and his men would suddenly fade off into the late afternoon shadows. His response gave Gaethaa his greatest shock of the long, trying day.

"Please! I don't really care to hear your tales of ancient

legends and black evil run rampant in the world beyond our land. We of Demornte have quite enough to consider in our own sorrows. You speak to us of murder and destruction—but we have watched the death of our entire land and its people. Kane's crimes mean nothing to us here; we care nothing and ask nothing of the outside world. What happens or has happened there does not concern us."

The paleness of his face made his lips a red wound. Checking his hand that longed to seize sword hilt, Gaethaa thundered incredulously, "Do you mean to say that you intend to protect Kane!"

Gavein looked at him with a touch of almost pity in his tired face. "You misunderstand. We care nothing of your quarrel. If it is between you and Kane, then go to him with it. The two of you settle it according to whatever laws seem best to you. In Sebbei we ask only to be left alone with our sorrow. As regards your 'mission,' we will neither help you nor hinder you in any manner whatsoever. It's your fight—do what you wish. But leave us alone!"

Shaking his head in astonishment, Gaethaa turned to Alidore for counsel. "They're obsessed, you know!" he exclaimed in sick pity. "The whole land is like this it seems. So obsessed with this one thing that they've lost all perspective! I don't think a man here really understands anything I've tried to tell them!"

"I'll agree it looks hopeless for them. At any rate they'll pose no threat to us," Alidore observed. "Kane's backed himself into a corner this time, and it appears that he has only himself to turn to for help. Ask the old man to tell us where Kane's villa is."

"And get lost again?" Gaethaa growled. "Got a better idea. We'll let him lead us there in person."

Invited to accompany them, Gavein protested that it was not his affair. But when Bell and Sed tho'Dosso eagerly stepped toward him at Gaethaa's nod, the Lord Mayor gloomily rose to his feet and was escorted into the street outside.

V. To Trap a Tiger in His Lair

Rehhaile frantically hurried through the narrow streets of Sebbei, her mind still crawling with fear and loathing. The shock of confronting Gaethaa and his men had been brutal, and her concern for Kane was obscured by the pall of revulsion she had felt on touching their thoughts. Her soul felt outraged at the contact. Never had she experienced such a barrage of depraved, bestial images and cravings. Kane's mind was altogether alien to her, and she took care never to reach too deep within its tortuous depths. But among the thoughts of Gaethaa's band outright cruelty reveled alongside demented lusting, and Rehhaile's mind still cringed in memory, sick and soiled by the touch.

She ran along recklessly, stumbling in her haste, avoiding jarring collision time and again by the closest margins. To her sightless mind the twisting alleys of Sebbei assumed a bewildering pattern of clarity and darkness. Wherever possible Rehhaile cast out her mind to draw sight from another. At fortunate moments she made contact with one of the townspeople who was in the vicinity and through whose eyes she could see a portion of the course she followed. But in deserted Sebbei such chance encounters were too few, and more often Rehhaile found her path blotted out in darkness. Where there were no other's eyes through which she could see, she attempted to make a detour by reaching out to touch another nearby mind and follow a circuitous route along this region of light. But this wasted too many invaluable minutes, and Rehhaile was forced to plunge into the darkened segments of the labyrinth frequently—there to rely on shadowy hints from distant minds, or to feel her way along blindly. Although she knew the streets of Sebbei well, these passages of absolute blindness placed deadly obstacles in her search for Kane.

As she had felt certain she would, Rehhaile found Kane

at the abandoned Nandai villa. Gasping for breath she ran through the walled gardens, her remaining steps made certain as Kane watched her disheveled approach. Kane had been half asleep, moodily contemplating the late afternoon sun from the shade of a densely laced roof of floral vine. A nearly drained amphora of thin Demornte wine leaned beside him, still damp from the cool waters of the lake. Alongside rested a bowl of strawberry domes.

"Hello, Rehhaile," he greeted her thickly, rising to his feet at the panic that lined her face. "Hey, what the hell's the matter? Somebody chasing you?"

"Kane!" Exhaustion forced her words out in strangled bursts. "Kane! You're in danger here! There're some men in Sebbei! They've come to kill you! They've been searching for you for weeks! They know you're in Sebbei! They'll be coming here to kill you as soon as they find out where you are! They'll be here any minute! They're going to kill you!"

Desperately Kane fought to command his semi-drunken faculties. "'Men in Sebbei looking for me!" he exploded. "How many? Who are they? How are they armed? How do you know they're on my trail?"

Rehhaile poured out an incoherent account of her accostal by Gaethaa and his men, babbling frenziedly of strange men with harsh minds and thoughts of violence and death. Her words were disjointed, attempting to convey sensations for which language failed to accommodate— but Kane immediately understood the imminent danger of his position. Cursing bitterly the monumental carelessness into which his despair had lulled him, Kane questioned her sharply for details. She followed him into the villa as he dashed about buckling on his sword and searching for an extra quiver of bolts for his crossbow.

"Kane—what are you going to do?" Rehhaile moaned. "Are you going to try to stand them off from the villa?"

Kane's boot caught the edge of a bench, and he reeled away clumsily, slapping at his shin and snarling angrily. "I'm not sure what I'll do! Nine seasoned professionals make tough odds in an open fight! And they must be damned good to have trailed me to Sebbei—Tloluvin

113

knows why, although that's beside the point at the moment! If I wait for them here, they can bottle me up like a bear in his cave! I can run for it, but if they've followed me this far, there's no reason to hope they won't hunt me down elsewhere in Demornte or the desert beyond!"

With practiced hands Kane worked the action of his crossbow. He felt grim satisfaction that he had permitted no rust or dirt to collect on his weapons—at least he had not fallen altogether under the spell of dead Demornte! "The best chance is going to be for me to get out of this villa, but to stay here in Sebbei. I can use the empty buildings for cover, and strike back at them on my own terms! These bastards won't be the first hunters to make the mistake of daring their prey within its lair!"

He started for the garden gate, when Rehhaile abruptly cried out a warning. "Kane! Get back! Those men are almost here! You'll never make it to cover!"

"That tears it!" growled Kane. Wheeling about he darted back into the villa—cursing vehemently in several languages. Quickly he gained the second floor of the dwelling and glanced through a window in the direction Rehhaile indicated. The sun cast long shadows away from the group of riders who stood near the edge of Sebbei watching the villa expectantly.

"You can see them now," Rehhaile observed.

"Yeah, I see them!" Kane rasped. "And they seem to know just where to find me! Is that Gavein with them? Wonder what's holding them back now!"

At the outskirts of Sebbei Gaethaa halted with his men to consider the villa before them. The inner wall of Sebbei stood behind them. Beyond the old wall extended a periphery of newer structures—shops, inns, estates of the wealthy—a scattered suburban area outside the dirt, noise and stench of the crowded old city, but still within the confines of Sebbei's widely flung outer wall. Only now the outer wall guarded a ghost city from nonexistent raiders, and the forest was seeking to reclaim the outer city unchallenged by any hand.

The old Nandai villa had been situated somewhat apart from neighboring structures. It stood against a small lake on one side, a lake which curved back upon the inner wall in one direction and extended toward the low outer wall in the other. Rotted piers tenanted by half-sunken vessels reached out across its quiet surface, and the lake shore was overgrown with tall reeds and low shrubs. The overgrown gardens encircled the old villa, and outside the garden wall there had once been tilled fields. These fields were now in weeds with a sparse growth of young palms and pine trees, but there was little or no cover afforded here, and the villa was in effect surrounded by a clearing.

"No chance of riding up on him unobserved," Alidore commented.

Gaethaa grunted acknowledgment. Turning to Cereb Ak-Cetee, he asked, "Gavein still swears he knows of no protective magic that Kane has invoked to guard his lair. How about it?"

The wizard absent-mindedly picked at his nose and stared at the villa. "Well, there's no immediate evidence that we'll be dealing with sorcery here. I think we've caught Kane totally off guard. Give you odds we could ride in on him right now and take him."

Mollyl looked at Gavein knowingly and whispered something to Jan, who laughed and stropped his gleaming hook across his leather pants. "Now, Gavein," Mollyl grinned, "I just know you're telling us the truth about old Kane living out here all alone and all. But Jan here thinks maybe you might be holding back something on us— maybe that Kane keeps some men around as bodyguards, or maybe Kane has some little sorcerous devices waiting for his enemies. You sure you got your story straight, Gavein? You're not going to let Jan change your mind for you now, are you?" Gavein shuddered, eying the razor-edged hook in fascination.

"Cut it out, Mollyl," Gaethaa commanded. "I believe him. These people are too gutless to lie to us.

"Cereb, make damn sure Kane doesn't have anything in store for us we aren't expecting! The black hearted devil didn't live this long on the strength of his reputation alone. Others have been destroyed by Kane when they thought he was helpless, and I'm not about to believe we'll walk in and find him snoring away on a pile of empty wine jugs!"

The wizard slipped to the ground and began to remove a number of items from his voluminous packs. "Let you know for certain in a minute. But we'll end up wasting our advantage of surprise at this rate."

"Kane has no reason to expect us," Alidore pointed out.

"No, we don't look too suspicious, do we now." Cereb Ak-Cetee shrugged and bent to his work. His movements were certain, and his slender fingers arranged his paraphernalia with professional confidence. For all his youth, the Tranodeli was well on his way to becoming a powerful wizard. In his own mind, Cereb had decided to seek tutelage from one of the old Carsultyal masters after he had gained the experience and wealth of a few more of Gaethaa's missions.

Carefully he filled a copper bowl with water from a canteen, poured a few droplets of oily fluid from three vials, then dusted the opalescent surface with tiny pinches of powdered substance from other containers taken from his kit. He squatted over the bowl, his bony knees poking tightly against his robe, and began to chant into the bowl, but its surface remained clouded. Abruptly a tiny mote of red fire seemed to dance upon the center of the bowl. The surface shimmered faintly for a moment, then vaporized with a rush of thick fumes. The red flame lingered sullenly for a second, then winked out.

Dusting his hands on his cloak, Cereb straightened and began to collect his accoutrements. "As I said, nothing," he explained. "Any forces of magic connected with the villa before us would have been reflected on the surface of my bowl. As you observed, the only response was a flicker of crimson. This I interpret as representing Kane himself, who if all tales are true has sufficient sorcerous influences about him to elicit a reflection."

He chuckled affably. "I'd say we've caught Kane completely by surprise. They claim he's a good enough wizard in his own right, but so far as I know Kane's never made a sorceror's pact with any god or demon. That means he has no powers to turn to for immediate assistance. Without some form of patron deity to call upon, a sorceror—no matter how adept he may be—requires a lot of time, effort and materials to cast any sort of effective spell. Black magic isn't some cheap charlatan's trick you can perform with a finger snap and a puff of smoke, after all. Well, Kane hasn't had any time, and I doubt if he has any sorcerous materials at hand either. He's all yours, Milord Gaethaa."

"Well done, Cereb," Gaethaa returned with a thin smile. "We'll put your words to a test then. All right men, we'll play it like Kane doesn't know we're searching for him yet. The road to the outer wall leads straight past the entrance to the villa. We'll ride along it like we were headed on out of Sebbei minding our own business. Then once we get abreast of the villa, we'll rush the place. With luck he won't suspect anything until that moment. The garden gate will pose no problem, and once through, Mollyl, Jan, Bell take the front with me; Sed and Missa take the back with Alidore; Anmuspi and Cereb hold back to see if he gets past us. Cereb, I'm counting on you to be alert for any sorcerous defenses. Gavein, you can go now. So act nonchalant then, and let's get him!"

Released, Gavein gloomily watched them ride away toward the villa. He ran damp fingers across his throat, as if to convince himself it was yet intact, then shuffled back through the streets of Sebbei muttering under his breath.

Gaethaa led his men at a slow pace along the road, offering only casual attention to the villa they approached. Dron Missa argued with Mollyl over an imaginary dice game, and Jan loudly complained that both men had cheated him of his share of the pot.

They drew closer to the villa. Still there appeared no threatening movement from inside. Yet it seemed impossible that Kane was not watching their approach. Did he suspect?

At about two-hundred yards there sounded a sudden deadly hiss! Bell screamed and fell back on his saddle, reddened fingers clutching at the crossbow bolt that had abruptly sprouted from his left shoulder! His horse reared in alarm at the scent of fear and pain.

So Kane had been waiting! Gaethaa whirled in his saddle to shout an order, and a second bolt screamed through the space he had just turned from! Alarmed at the accuracy and speed of Kane's marksmanship, Gaethaa again realized there was no cover for them until they could reach the villa.

"Get back!" he bellowed, as his men started to spread apart to ride in low. "Get back out of range! Hurry!"

A third bolt glanced across the back of Alidore's mail as the men wheeled on his command. Alidore cursed and bent low over his horse's neck. Luckily the shaft had struck him as he was turning and merely glanced on past him. Even at this range a direct hit from a powerful crossbow would slice through chain mail such as he wore. A fourth bolt narrowly missed Dron Missa before they galloped beyond range.

Bell held his saddle until they returned to the shelter of a grove of palms. There he slumped to the earth and sat against a palm trunk while Sed tho'Dosso examined the wound.

"Can't be fatal if he can still cuss like that," Missa offered thoughtfully. A few inches off the heart, but not bad for the range. Why call us back here, milord?"

Gaethaa scowled at the villa in reappraisal. "Don't want to risk any further casualties. Too little cover around the place, damn it! Fast as he was firing, Kane must be working the cocking lever by hand. He'd be sure to get off a few more shots before we reached him, and at the range he hit Bell he must be as good a marksman as they claim! Damn near finished a few others of us anyway—he waited till we were well in his range before attacking! Not worth the risk to rush him now. We'll have darkness shortly. So we'll hit him again when the light's too poor for archery, but still too bright for Kane to slip away—if we watch carefully!"

"That's cutting it close," Alidore commented.

"Don't tell me what I already know!" Gaethaa retorted. "Anmuspi! Think you can get a fire arrow in where it can smoke him out? If we drive him from the villa, then Kane will be the one caught in the open!"

The archer smiled deliberately, his lined face asymmetrical with the sword scar that flashed white in rare moments of anger. "Roof of that place is timber, of course. I can ride a bit closer and pepper it with as many fire arrows as you want. It's an easy target that size, and I'll still be out of Kane's range. No crossbow can shoot as far as a heavy horn bow—unless you count those stupid-looking contraptions that take five minutes for a strong man to wind to a cock."

"Great! We'll burn him out then!" Gaethaa declared.

So Anmuspi the Archer rode back toward the villa. Dismounting beside a clump of young palms, he kindled a small fire and wrapped the ends of several shafts with resinous material. Lighting these from the fire, Anmuspi stepped into the open to draw his bow. He sank his first arrow into the roof of the villa, and his second shot struck about two feet from the other. They burned dismally, evidently unable to fire the timbers. The third arrow was snuffed out in flight and fell without effect upon the roof.

"Try for a window, Anmuspi!" Alidore called.

The archer nodded and shifted his target. Without apparent effort, he fired two more arrows through one window and embedded another in the wall beside the opening. This time he was rewarded with billows of smoke from within. Dron Missa applauded loudly.

Anmuspi was drawing a seventh arrow then, when a crossbow bolt tore straight through his heart. Released, the last arrow shot into the sky and made a burning arc through the gathering night before it plunged into the lake.

"Damn!" exclaimed Gaethaa in amazement, staring at the archer's body on the ground. "There died a good man! Chalk up one more point on Kane's tally—he'll make an accounting soon!"

"Looks like he's put the fire out too," observed Alidore glumly after a pause. "See—the smoke has just about cleared away. Bell will live, but he's useless for the moment. That leaves seven of us to deal with Kane now, milord."

"Seven to rush him, it seems," Gaethaa mused. "Still

that looks like our best strategy. Once it gets a little darker we'll charge the villa. Spread out and move fast in the bad light—all of us ought to make it to him. One man isn't going to prevail against seven like us. Kane may get a few of us before he's taken, but take him we will!"

Cereb Ak-Cetee had been rubbing his narrow jaw in thought for several minutes. Now he smiled like a schoolboy with the solution to an examination question and announced brightly, "It may be that Kane will offer us no further resistance, milord. I know of one spell that has a fair chance of drawing his fangs, and I should have enough time to cast it before the light grows too dim to keep watch!"

"You picked a fine time to remember it, wizard!" Alidore exploded. "What kept you from mentioning this spell earlier!"

"Just remember that you're Gaethaa's lieutenant, Alidore, and leave the science of magic to me!" Cereb snarled. "In simple words for simple minds to grasp, I'll remind you that sorcery has its laws and limitations. As you know, I've made no pact as yet with any patron god—if I had I wouldn't be wasting my time riding around with your sort!

"Without direct demonic aid, I have to resort to the pure science of sorcery. That means in general that I require lengthy and arduous preparations to weave any powerful spell. The fact that I have no bit of hair, piece of nail, any fragment of Kane's body—not even an item intimate to his person for that matter—to serve as a focus for my magic eliminates most possibilities for any sort of really potent spell. I've never even seen Kane, and we're no more than reasonably certain that he's the man inside the old villa. Add to this the fact that Kane is himself a sorceror of considerable ability—a man who can probably block most of my spells through his own knowledge. Now then, tell me where that leaves me!"

"All right! I apologize," conceded Alidore with little grace. "So where does that leave us? What do you have in mind?"

Cereb Ak-Cetee went on with a sneer in his eyes. "I

know a fairly simple spell to induce stupor. I can diffuse it to include anyone within the villa, which will seriously weaken its influence. And Kane may bear some counter-charm against such minor sorceries for all I know. In fact, he can probably resist its effects to an extent purely through force of will, granting he's had extensive occult training. But regardless of whether he can resist it or not, unless he's completely protected the spell is going to slow him down considerably, even if it doesn't lay him out altogether. I didn't mention this spell earlier, because I had assumed he would be too great an adept to fall under its influence. Now I'm not so sure—I doubt if he's made any sort of preparations to guard against attack, in fact. Anyway the spell can soon be cast, and if it doesn't work we're no worse off than before."

"Cast your spell, Cereb," Gaethaa ordered eagerly. "If it can silence that crossbow and nothing more, it can drop Kane right into my hands!"

Kane watched the spot where his attackers had taken cover carefully, the closing darkness limiting his vision far less than for another man. "They seem to have given up the fire arrow idea for now. Guess that means a concerted attack before long. Anyway we seem to have all the fires put out."

He caressed the crossbow stock appreciatively. Kane had had it crafted according to his design, and he prized it highly. "There's a good weapon, though I doubt if many men could draw it with nothing more than this lever. Still the thing takes too long to cock and fire—though that last shot proved its worth once again. Thoem! If I just had that archer's bow, I could pick off every last one of them before they could cross the clearing!"

He addressed Rehhaile. "What are they doing now?"

Rehhaile's face was tight with concern under the soot—she had helped Kane put out the fires—working through the vision his eyes had given the scene. Cautiously she reached out with her mind to link with the attackers. Avoiding the touch of those whose contact so distressed her, she felt for Alidore. At that distance she could appreciate only dimly the sensory impulses his mind emanated.

"It's hard to say, Kane. The one you shot first is still moving. They don't seem to be getting ready to charge just yet. Some are watching us, and the others are watching someone who seems to be working at something on the ground—I can't tell what. Kane—he's the one that scared me worst—the one who knew I was blind! I think he must be a sorcerer from bits of their thoughts. I could never touch that demented mind of his again!"

"A sorceror! As if a simple attack by a band of professionals wasn't enough!" Kane swore. "I wonder though —I've heard of some madman called Gaethaa the Avenger who travels with a wizard in his band. A savior of the oppressed, they call him. Maybe this is Gaethaa then who's gone to all the trouble to trail me here—he's fanatical enough to pull the stunt from all I hear! Thought he usually kept a small army with him though."

Anxiously he gauged the amount of daylight left. "Suppose there's no chance they'll let it grow dark enough for us to make a break. They'll rush as soon as it's too dark for me to pick them off in the open. Break through the garden without any problem and be at the door. I'll try to take them one by one in the entrance hall—maybe get a few shots off first. No, they'll expect that and enter in groups from both sides to surround me. Damn! Wish I knew what that wizard or whatever they have can do! Rehhaile, can you maybe try to enter his mind long enough to . . ."

Rehhaile cried out in terror. "Kane! Something's wrong! I can't stay awake! Kane! I feel like I . . ." Her frightened voice trailed off. Like a collapsing puppet, she slumped to the floor. Arms pushed out to hold back the lethargy gave way brokenly, dropping her body to the planks with a soft thump. A tremor shook her as she struggled to rise, then her face fell back, unconsciousness preserving a mask of fear.

Kane struggled to keep to his feet! Blackness slashed through his mind, and his limbs were cased in lead! His strength slipping from him, Kane grimly recognized the cold touch of a spell of paralysis! A simple spell, but one for which he was totally unprotected. No time even to work the counterspell that almost any third-rate conjurer could command.

Desperately he fought the spell. It was a weak one, or he too would lie stretched out on the floor. Still he knew he was helpless to fight off an attack unless he could break free. Sweat dripping from his frame, Kane forced wooden muscles to move limbs of stone. There was a chance for him if he could only move outside the spell's range.

He tottered to the stairway, commanding his body to resist the spell with every atom of his will. On the first step he lost balance and slid drunkenly down the entire flight, rolling to a painful stop at the bottom. Setting his teeth in a death head grin, Kane crawled to the rear door. Already he could hear the hoofbeats of his enemies closing in for the kill. Somehow he pushed through the doorway and kicked it closed behind him. The lake offered an avenue of escape—or a death trap if he could not swim. Still it was his only chance.

Staggering, lurching, crawling, writhing on his belly— frantically Kane forced his body to cross the twilit garden. The sound of riders was closer now, and Kane had no way of knowing whether they had spotted him in the semi-darkness. Hunching forward, he gained the bank of the lake at last. Now he could hear them pounding against the front gate. A final few yards remained. Kane rolled weakly down the slope of the bank and slid off into the lake.

He floundered for a moment, trying to reach deeper water. The cool water closed over his body, and the weight of the sword on his back drew him down. Grimly holding his breath, Kane kicked against the bottom in an effort to get farther from shore. If the water were deep enough, he hoped to be able to float. But although Kane was a strong swimmer, he knew his massive bulk permitted him to float with difficulty in the best of circumstances.

His breath was growing short. With a major effort he wrenched his head above the surface to draw a gasping breath. He had progressed a good many yards from shore, he saw with relief, and as yet his attackers were too busy breaking into the villa to search for him in the lake.

The spell seemed to be lifting! Each movement seemed easier now; no longer did blackness seek so ineluctably to overwhelm his consciousness. The water, the distance he had moved from its focus had stolen power from the spell. The wizard must have ceased to send it against the villa now that his fellows were within. Whatever the reasons, Kane felt his strength begin to return to him.

With silent, powerful strokes Kane swam away underwater across the darkened lake. Behind him his baffled enemies were angrily searching through the silent villa and its gardens for their prey. But it would be too late to act by the time they realized how their quarry had escaped.

VI. Sword of Cold Light

Gaethaa had been furious once it was obvious that Kane had somehow escaped him. A careful search of the villa had turned up no one other than Rehhaile, still unconscious from the wizard's spell. A search of the gardens had disclosed a trail such as a crawling man might make that led into the lake. Reconstructing Kane's probable actions, Gaethaa had ordered his men to circle the lake shore. But by this time darkness had settled, and it was a hopeless task to search along the overgrown shoreline. Of Kane there was no sign.

In baffled disgust they finally returned to Jethrann's tavern in Sebbei. Rehhaile they bound and brought with them, for Gaethaa had hopes of learning something of value from her.

"Maybe he drowned," Dron Missa offered. "If Cereb's spell was so efficacious, he shouldn't have been able to swim. But then he shouldn't have been able to crawl off either."

"Don't make any bets on it," Gaethaa growled. The Avenger frowned and tugged at his mustache in frustration. "Missa! Damn it all—stop the racket! I'm trying to think!"

Dron Missa started and laid aside his dirk. He had been nervously tapping the horn handle against the table.

"What now?" Jan wanted to know.

"Good question," Gaethaa cursed. "We do nothing now—nothing we can do until morning! By then Kane will be half way across Demornte, no doubt! And for the moment we can't stop him. All we can do is patch up Bell and try to pick up Kane's trail when it gets light.

"Well, what's the story with this girl we captured?" he asked, as Alidore took a seat beside him.

"Got kind of a crazy story on her, but they all say about the same," Alidore explained. "Her name's Rehhaile, and she's the one Gavein mentioned earlier as spending a lot of time with Kane. Seems she's his mistress, although I gather she's pretty much anybody's who wants her. Lived in Sebbei all her life—family died in the plague—and makes a living anyway she can. Seemed fascinated with Kane when he showed up, so she's been living with him mostly since then.

"The townspeople consider her to be a sort of witch. They say she's been blind since birth—and that bears out —but she seems to have some type of second sight. It's claimed she can look into your mind and see through your eyes so to speak. They say she can read your thoughts— can tell exactly what your feelings are and what you're thinking. I tried her and the story seems to be true."

Gaethaa nodded solemnly. "A witch with psychic powers. Cereb has been telling me of such—he noticed her from the first. Just the sort of creature to be in league with Kane! Obviously she sensed our intentions when we met her on the street and ran off to warn Kane while we were wasting time here with Gavein. Damn the luck!"

"What are you going to do with her?" Jan persisted.

"I'll decide what to do with her tomorrow. She may be of some use to us yet, so we'll hold her for now. As an accomplice of that devil, she deserves death."

"No objections to our having some fun then?" murmured Mollyl, winking at Jan.

"She cost us our quarry," Gaethaa said coldly. "But don't you guys rough her up so she won't be of use to me later. Doesn't look like she knows anything important about Kane, but maybe there'll be something."

"Even if we must execute her," Alidore protested, "is it right for the men to rape her? This seems like pointless torture."

"Can't rape a whore, Alidore!" laughed Dron Missa, joining the other men in a squabble over seniority.

After the others moved away, Alidore remained at the table beside Gaethaa, a frown still troubling his tanned face. His wine cup stood before him untasted. An occasional twitch flickered along the square line of his jaw, as if there were words that must be uttered, but that he kept to himself.

Gaethaa noticed his lieutenant's mood and turned to him in concern. The Kamathaen lord prized Alidore's comradeship highly. He had admired the Lartroxian youth's tough courage and intelligent zeal when Alidore had first joined his band nearly two years ago. Alidore had been in his late teens then, and Gaethaa, about a dozen years his senior, had grown to consider him a younger brother. He knew he could count on Alidore to stand beside him in any battle and he relied on his counsel in deciding many points of strategy. While most of his followers over the years rode behind his banner for gold, adventure, revenge or other personal motivations, Gaethaa recognized that Alidore more than any of the others was drawn by the same idealism he felt. His present mood puzzled Gaethaa.

"All right, Alidore," he said quietly. "What is it? Something has been gnawing away at you for a good while now. I've watched it building up inside you bit by bit. Out with it—what's bothering you? You know you don't need to hold it back from me if you don't feel right about the way something is going."

Alidore bit his lip and raised his wine cup, not yet meeting Gaethaa's eyes. "It's nothing worth . . . It's vague . . ." he began uneasily. "Just something that's been getting to me more and more as it keeps showing up. I don't know, maybe I'm getting battle fatigue after too

126

many campaigns. I just notice it more. Nothing definite I like to bring up, but . . ."

Gaethaa watched him anxiously, knowing that in time his lieutenant would speak his mind. This much reticence was out of character for him.

"It's this girl Rehhaile . . ."

"Rehhaile?" Gaethaa's hawk-like face twisted in surprise. "Rehhaile? What's there about the witch that bothers you?"

"Well, it's not just her, it's a lot of things that keep hanging in my mind. She's an example is all," Alidore continued. "The mutiny we had at the border of Demornte. The execution of the prisoners when we destroyed the Red Three. The way we took the town apart last year in Burwhet when we took on Olidi and his gang of raiders. Those men you let Mollyl torture to tell us where Recom Launt would attack next. The hostages you let him butcher when you refused to lift the seige of his fortress. . . ."

"The alternative was to withdraw—to turn tail and let that murderous robber baron regain his stranglehold on the trade routes. And I had to know when and where to strike for that first battle with him. The lives of his henchmen and of some hostages were unimportant weighed against the greater good I accomplished there by destroying Launt and permitting thousands to cross his domain in peace. Perhaps the men were a bit out of hand in Burwhet, but regardless of the destruction we caused there, Olidi and every last one of his cutthroats died in the fighting. Burwhet could rebuild and prosper with that gang of renegade bandits finally scoured from the land. Those weren't prisoners we executed—they were accomplices of the Red Three and tainted with the ogres' inhuman crimes. As for the men who turned traitor to me in the shadow of Demornte, any man who's ever carried a sword in his lord's army knows that mutiny is punishable by death. No leader could ever command respect and discipline of his men if he ignored blatant desertion. We've been through this before, Alidore.

"This sorceress Rehhaile—in view of her youth and

ignorance I could have overlooked her living with Kane. But she deliberately gave him warning of our presence here, and for that crime she must pay the price. If we had taken Kane by complete surprise—as it seems likely now we would have—our mission here would be completed. Anmuspi might well be alive still, although it's foolish to think we could have taken Kane without some casualties. Foolish to speculate over what should have happened anyway."

A woman's moan of pain broke from the upstairs of the tavern, accompanied by thick laughter.

Alidore winced. "Why not give her a clean death then? Why torture her like this?"

"She's a wanton—you told me as much yourself." Gaethaa shrugged. "She's not getting anything such a woman isn't used to. Besides the men need a break— they've ridden long and hard without any sport. Let them have their fun—I'll deal with Rehhaile tomorrow maybe."

Alidore still seemed troubled. "It's all logical when you explain it. I'm not implying we've ever stooped to senseless brutality, of course. I don't know, maybe my backbone's getting soft. It seems like there could be a little room for mercy. . . ."

Drawing a hand across his high forehead to push back the blond locks that drifted down, Gaethaa drew a deep breath and leaned back in his chair. His blue-gray eyes grew bitter in memory. "Sure, mercy. Remember the time years ago when Reanist talked me into sparing that girl we found chained in the sorceror's tower? The people of the region protested, but Reanist had an eye for beauty and insisted she was only a prisoner. That night her kisses killed Reanist and five other good men before my sword ended her inhuman thirst, and even Cereb Ak-Cetee wasn't certain what manner of demon we had harbored. Or earlier when we spared Tirli-Selan's family, then had to return later and fight a far more costly battle when we learned that they were bloodier despots than their uncle.

"Alidore, it doesn't work out like you'd hope for it to. I've let too many men die from blood poisoning still begging my surgeon not to amputate all of a gangrenous limb.

Poison spreads. A tiny cancer will ultimately corrupt and destroy the strongest organism. Let a fragment of evil evade your exorcism, and it will inevitably flourish to cause even more death and suffering to humanity. False mercy is worse than ill-advised in my struggle against the forces of evil. Its consequences can completely pervert and destroy all the goals for which I fight."

Gaethaa's face grew pale with emotion. His eyes glowed with vision, and sweat glistened over his forehead. A tremor passed through his clenched hands, as his voice shook with intensity.

"I am called Gaethaa the Crusader, and the name is one I hope to be worthy of always. I have made my life a crusade against evil, and it is a crusade that will end only when the last spark of life fails me. When I was a child I listened to the great sagas told by my father's soldiers around the fires—and I listened to the darker tales they whispered of the strange lands where forces of evil held power over all who dwelt therein. Even then I vowed to myself that when I became a man I would not waste my life among the perfumed sycophants of Kamathaen nobility. I turned my back on indolent court life, and chose instead a life of riding against the cold wind with a war cry on my lips and a sword raised in my hand. I worked from childhood to prepare myself for this life. For tutors I drew upon the best tacticians available to teach me military strategy; my training at arms was at the hands of masters of their chosen weapon. I learned to read and converse in a dozen languages, and the wisest scholars of our age instructed me in logic and philosophy —for I knew it was not sufficient that I learn to wield a sword untempered by reason, nor allow other men to be my ears and tongue.

"Alidore, I have seen the cold light of good! The cold light shed by truth, righteousness, justice. The cold light that dispels the darkness of evil! The universe is structured on these two forces—the power of good shining as a beacon of cold, clear light against the smothering blackness of evil! And as surely as sunlight drives away the night, the cold light of good annihilates the darkness of evil!

"And I have vowed to serve the cold light! To destroy with a sword of cold light the shadow of evil that darkens our world! Darkness is vanquished by light, and the forces of evil fall before the powers of good! But in the battle of light against darkness there can be no intermediate shades—no twilight powers! Those who do not follow the cold light are children of darkness, and they must and shall be destroyed by the cold, clear light of good!

"And if my crusade at times strikes you as without mercy, it is because there can be no mercy, no uncertainty in this struggle! The cold light shall burn away the darkness of evil, even if a thousand must die to drive back the shadows! Their suffering is a petty price to pay for the ultimate victory!"

Totally swept up in the spell of Gaethaa's exhortation, Alidore listened with mind awhirl—uncertain at times whether he served a saint or madman.

Gaethaa had been silent for several minutes before Alidore broke from his near trance. "I'm sorry to have sounded unworthy of the confidence you place in me, milord," he spoke dazedly, not certain how the Crusader had interpreted his misgivings.

A quiet smile crossed Gaethaa's face, and he rose to brush his fist against his lieutenant's shoulder. "Why are you apologizing, Alidore? Your concern is understandable, and mercy is an invaluable principle when it is called for. Your feelings are misplaced, that's all, and I hope I've done a little toward clearing away the confusion in your mind. You need to remember that we're only a badly outnumbered few aligned in a cosmic struggle between diametrically opposed forces. Softness in this struggle isn't mercy, but unforgivable stupidity.

"Look, it's getting late, and we'll be up and after Kane as soon as there's daylight outside. I'm going to get some sleep now, and why don't you turn in yourself. You're exhausted now, and a lot of things will be clearer to you in the morning."

Alidore watched his leader depart. Things were a lot

clearer after listening to Gaethaa, he realized. Still he did not feel like turning in. A strange restlessness still haunted him, and he sat up mulling over his thoughts and slowly sipping his wine. Sleep did not come, perhaps because every time his eyes started to close he caught the sound of choked cries from the room above.

At length when the others lost interest, Alidore went to Rehhaille also.

It was near dawn when Alidore left Rehhaile and started to pull shirt and trousers over his lean body. She was not asleep, but turned toward him on the bed, her uncanny blind eyes red from tears. There were many sullen purple bruises marring her tan skin, and her back was crossed with livid welts. Compared with other women whom Mollyl had amused himself with, she hadn't been badly messed up, Alidore thought.

She looked so forlorn there on the rumpled bed, and Alidore felt remorse for what they had done to her. She hadn't been like a whore at all—there had been no hardness, no professionalism. In a way it had made him feel like he had raped one who loved him, and Alidore couldn't shake the awful feeling of betrayal.

Rehhaile ran a tongue over swollen lips, sensing his guilt. "Don't feel too bad. You were kinder than the others at least." Alidore muttered something and offered her a cup of wine. "What is to happen to me now?" she asked, and he felt uncomfortable and told her noncommittally that this was for Gaethaa to decide. Weakly she sat up and touched her bruised abdomen tenderly, a whimper hovering on her lips. "Why are you doing this to me?"

Alidore looked away. He could tell her that she deserved no better because she had chosen to align herself with evil, but somehow the words seemed unreal now. "You did a foolish thing when you helped Kane escape. In doing so you have thwarted the cause of justice, and punishment must be carried out."

"Was raping me an act of justice? Do you think I deserve what is being done to me?" Rehhaile responded illogically.

Alidore was fumbling for a reply, when a shriek echoed from the stables!

VII. A Wounded Tiger

Kane had not fled Sebbei.

Regaining his strength, he had crossed the small lake in the darkness. Reaching the inner wall of the city, Kane had lain hidden among the tall reeds while Gaethaa and his men floundered about in a futile search for him. Silently he had watched from the shadows as Gaethaa returned to Sebbei. With noiseless step he had followed his enemies back to Jethrann's tavern.

Like a phantom he had stalked them through the ghostly streets of Sebbei, and in his killer's eyes there gleamed the cold fires of death. For Kane had no thought of fleeing from his pursuers. Their attack had made a fool of him— nearly succeeding because of the apathy into which he had drifted. Now only blood would shake the fury that drove him after those who hunted him.

Crouched in the darkness outside the tavern, Kane watched and listened, striving to learn more of his assailants. Among them Sed tho'Dosso was the only man he recognized. But once he heard spoken the name *Gaethaa,* Kane understood the reason for the attack.

Gaethaa the Avenger—so the Kamathaen lord had at last determined to include Kane in his crusade. Kane worked to recall all the scraps of information he had come across concerning Gaethaa. The prospect was not pleasing. Gaethaa was a dangerous opponent—a man of tenacious courage who was reputedly a deadly warrior as well as brilliant strategist. His mercenaries were one of the best private armies in the civilized world, it was said. From their numbers they must have had a few setbacks in finding him though, Kane mused.

Eight men—all professional fighters—plus the unknown factor represented in the wizard. The wizard would be that young Tranodeli he had heard a little about—one of the Cetee clan whose talents had run toward sorcery. And he was supposed to be as brilliant a mind to study the black arts since the strange fall of Carsultyal. The odds were clearly too great for direct attack. The game would have to be played by more subtle rules.

And so Kane waited in the darkness, waited for a chance to kill, and to his ears there came at times a girl's cry of pain.

Toward the approach of dawn Kane crept into the shelter of the tavern stable. He had hoped for a chance to attack Gaethaa's band while they slept, but several of the men had been up throughout the night—not so much standing guard as raising hell. Abandoning the idea, Kane stealthily climbed into the darkened loft to wait for events to unfold. Evidently Gaethaa's confidence in his own power was sufficient that he assumed Kane would spend the night hours in full flight. Lurking in his very shadow was as safe a position as any. Besides the night was cold, and Kane was still damp and caked with mud from the lake. Shivering from the chill, he helped himself to a pile of horse blankets and snuggled into the straw of the loft. There were fleas crawling through the blankets, but they were warm.

In the last quiet moments before dawn his vigilance was rewarded. A man now stumbled through the door—Sed tho'Dosso, Kane recognized with grim delight. The desert bandit had been awake most of the night, and now he sleepily cursed Gaethaa for sending him to look after the horses. With groggy movements he passed from stall to stall, checking to see that each mount had all the grain and water it required. Completing his rounds, Sed rested his lantern on a barrel and sullenly contemplated the pile of saddles and equipment that would have to be harnessed to the horses before long. There was time enough for a nap, he decided. With a groan he sank down against a stall and closed his eyes.

Kane watched the Lomarni bandit chieftain intently. Here was an excellent chance to rid himself of one of his enemies, but there were a few problems. Kane still carried his sword and dagger, but neither weapon was useful

133

at the moment. With Sed tho'Dosso below him, he would have to descend the loft ladder to reach him—and that meant too much noise to hope to take the other unawares. In his huddled position, the bandit presented a difficult target for a dagger throw. There was no chance for a quick, clean kill, and Kane knew he would have to strike silently. At the first shout of danger, Gaethaa's men would come swarming over the stable, and Kane would again be trapped.

Slowly Kane slipped free of the blankets. A coil of rope lay at hand in the loft, suggesting a possibility. Cautiously he crawled across the loft, watching the sleeping bandit for the first sign of alarm. The loft was laid with thick beams, and they held his weight without creaking. Still the boards were widely spaced, and a thin trickle of dust and straw sifted down from the loft as he passed. The stream was not noticeable in the darkness, but as it drifted closer to Sed tho'Dosso, there was danger that he might feel the dust brushing his face.

The desert man snored softly. Gingerly Kane rose to his feet and reached for the rope. The sky was starting to gray, but the loft was still hidden in shadow. At any moment another of the Crusader's men might enter the stable to help Sed with the horses, and Kane knew his time was running out. A chance entrance, a flash of lantern light, and he would be silhouetted against the rafters.

Quickly he worked one end of the rope into a sliding noose. Playing the hemp through his hands, he coiled it into a throwing lariat that he felt he could count on. Poising himself on the open edge of the loft, Kane looked down at the sleeping bandit. Grimly he readied the noose in his hands.

"Sed! Sed tho'Dosso!" he called softly. "Wake up, Sed!"

With a guilty start the Lomarni roused himself. Still groggy, he raised his head and looked about him stupidly. "Huh?"

Kane cast his lariat the instant Sed lifted his head. Perfectly aimed, the noose dropped over the bandit's head, and with a jerk Kane snugged it tight against his neck.

Sed had time for one thin shriek as terror slashed through the curtain of sleep, then the biting noose cut off his breath! Even as his frenzied fingers tore at the choking coil, the Lomarni was violently yanked from the stable floor and swung into the air!

Kane swore in anger, the muscles bunched along his shoulders and back as he hauled the bandit free of the earth. His cast had been on target, but he had meant to draw tight the noose before his startled victim could cry out. Now a warning had been sounded. Helplessly twisting like a fly in a spider's web, the wiry desert man kicked and contorted in Kane's grasp.

Holding the writhing bandit chieftain suspended with one hand, Kane hurriedly tossed the free end of the rope over a rafter. Then he seized the loose end and leapt from the loft. Sed tho'Dosso jerked and shot relentlessly toward the roof, as Kane's greater weight bore his end downward to the floor. Lightly he landed and knotted the rope over a stall. The entire episode had taken seconds.

Eyes bulging horribly, Sed tho'Dosso watched his laughing enemy wave a derisive farewell as he stepped through the rear door to vanish into the dawn.

Seconds later Gaethaa and his men pounded into the stable. They glared about without comprehension until Jan pointed his hook upward, and then they cut him down. But the Lomarni's neck was broken, and even as his lips formed the name "Kane," his body shuddered in death.

"Kane!" shouted Gaethaa in exultation. "Then he came back! By Thoem! I was a fool to think that he would flee us! Like a wounded tiger, he's turned on his hunters! Well, he's the fool this time, because now we don't have to ride off after his trail! We have him trapped!

"How about it Cereb—can you flush him out for me?"

The wizard tossed his bony shoulders beneath his cloak. "Just watch," he replied lazily.

Shortly thereafter Kane was not overly surprised to see the walls of Sebbei suddenly burst into blue flame. From his vantage point on the flat roof of an empty house, he watched the fires blaze with undiminished heat, despite the fact that they were fed by nothing visible, and that within them the wall stood undisturbed. But anything living would be instantly consumed he knew, for he recognized the spell.

He drew back his lips in a savage grin. Yes, it was a powerful spell, one which he had no hope of breaking in his present position. He was trapped in Sebbei. But then, he had no intention of fleeing the city until the game was played out. Gaethaa probably sensed this now, so perhaps he and his pet wizard had something in mind that might shake his resolve.

Something had to be done about the sorceror, and Kane searched through his fantastic stores of black knowledge for something that he could use to retaliate. Finally in utter frustration he realized that his opponent was certain to be protected against any spell available to him under present circumstances. Gaethaa would keep his wizard well guarded from physical danger as well. An arrow might do it, and Kane again regretted the loss of his crossbow. So far the only serviceable long range weapon he had found in the deserted buildings was a thick spear—designed only for stabbing and short casts.

Disgusted, Kane slipped away to see why his enemies had not yet followed.

In the square before the tavern he found them. Fascinated, Gaethaa and his men observed while Cereb Ak-Cetee performed a long incantation over an intricately designed pentagram. Abruptly the incense-choked air within the pentacle wavered, and then within the smoke crouched a demon with checkered, reptilian scales—summoned from some unguessable plane.

Pleased with the success of his invocation, Cereb's flushed face broke into a boyish grin. Trapped within the pentagram, the demon glowered back wrathfully and champed its reeking fangs. Suddenly its hunched shoulders heaved and the demon's crusted talons ripped out for the wizard—only to strike crimson sparks as they encountered the magic barrier! Cereb Ak-Cetee chuckled at the monster's howl of agonized rage. "Fight all you want to, slave! The pentagram will hold you fast until

I grant you release! And that I won't do until you first swear to perform a service for me!"

The demon spat out a mockery of human speech. "You have summoned the wrong servant then! In my sphere I hold only very minor powers. Release me now, and summon one greater than I to do your bidding!"

"Modest, aren't you now. No—I'm not about to call any of your brothers! A bigger fish might prove too strong for my net to hold. You can do what I require of you well enough though. We have a man who hides from us here, and I command you to bring him to us. He's trapped here—I've enclosed the town within a ring of fire. And my spell will make it possible for you to move within the ring of fire, despite the disparity of your universe and this one. All you need do is ferret him out, and to help you we've procured this . . ."

"Watch out!" shouted Jan. "It's Kane! Making a rush!"

They all whirled at the shout to see Kane dashing toward them with spear poised!

"Cover Cereb!" Gaethaa ordered. "We've got . . ."

And Kane hurled the spear! Wobbling, the clumsy missile curved across the square—easily dodged even in the short space. But Kane had not thrown at the sorceror, nor at any of the men; such an effort would have been wasted at this range. Instead he cast the spear for the pentagram!

The iron spearpoint skittered upon the packed ground and ripped into the earth, cutting through the border of the pentagram!

The demon howled in unearthly laughter as it catapulted from its shattered prison! Cereb Ak-Cetee uttered one great scream of inexpressible horror as the vengeful creature swept him up in its awful embrace! "Now who commands his slave!" roared the demon in triumph.

Shuddering roar as the cosmic portal swung open, then shut—cutting off hopeless shriek and mocking laughter in mid-peal! Then only a trailing puff of sulfurous mist marked the spot where wizard and demon had disappeared.

Nor—when they at last broke from their shock to look —was there any sign of Kane.

VIII. To Destroy the Servant of Evil

Glumly Gaethaa considered the fate of his wizard. So now it was just the six of them against Kane.

"The flame barrier has fallen, milord," Alidore observed. The spell had broken with the wizard's death.

Gaethaa pensively scratched his long jaw. "Doesn't matter. Pretty obvious by now that Kane means to finish the chase right here. Looks like Kane has lived up to his legend—easily the most deadly and resourceful agent of evil I've set out to destroy." There was grim satisfaction in his face.

He turned for the tavern, and his men followed willingly. Dron Missa rummaged around frantically for an unopened flask of wine among the wreckage of last night; a delighted cry marked his success.

"Question is, how do we find him in all this maze," continued Gaethaa. "Damn it! Quit fighting over that wine and let me think! Jan—tell that spineless host of ours to bring up some more on the double! After what we've just seen, a drink is damn well called for!" He frowned and pulled at his mustache in thought.

Mollyl glanced towards Rehhaile, who slumped bound against a pillar. "Kane seemed hot for the bitch there. Maybe if we took her outside and started to tickle her a bit, Kane would make a rush to get her. If she can't tell us anything, she'd still be good bait."

Gaethaa considered the suggestion carefully, staring blankly at Rehhaile, mindless of the girl's terror. "Could be," he concluded.

A sick feeling was growing in Alidore's stomach. Witch, whore, whatever her crimes might be—it was too much to turn this girl over to Mollyl's twisted amusements. "Milord," he said hastily, "it seems altogether unlikely to me that a demon like Kane would give a second thought to the sufferings of another person—regardless of the fact she saved his life with her warning. Mollyl's suggestion would only give Kane valuable time either to escape or hatch further schemes."

Gaethaa nodded at his logic, and Alidore felt unreasonably relieved. And in noting the expression of gratitude flashed him by Rehhaile, he missed the glare of hatred on Mollyl's face.

"Nothing for it but a house to house search," concluded Gaethaa. He rose to his feet. "Only six of us. That means we'll need the help of the townspeople.

"Gavein! I want you to call together all available men who can carry a weapon! We'll initiate a systematic sweep of the town until we can uncover that devil!"

His face was tired beyond human endurance, but his rusty voice rasped in weary determination. "Please, milord. I have already told you that we of Sebbei will have nothing to do with your fight with this Kane. We wish only . . ."

"I know—only to sit around and slowly die. Thoem! You people take longer to die than anyone has a right to! Well, you can go on with your merry little moldering lives as soon as we finish with Kane! Until then I'll demand that your people give me full co-operation!"

Gavein set his stubbled jaw. "Demand all you want then. But no one in Sebbei will bother to obey your ranting!"

Gaethaa uttered a curse of baffled anger. "Mollyl! You and Jan talk to this fool outside where they can all see we mean business! If I have to bully them into helping us look for Kane I will! It's plain this bunch of gutless slugs won't lift a hand against us!"

With a thin smile Mollyl grabbed the scrawny mayor, while Jan painstakingly rescrewed the hook to the stump of his wrist. "Gaethaa—you can't be going to torture this man because he refuses to help us!" Alidore protested.

The Crusader's face was grave. "Regrettable I know, Alidore. But desperate measures are called for. I am prepared to sacrifice any number of lives to destroy this madman Kane—because in the end many more lives will be spared from his monstrous schemes! Anyway, in refusing to help, Gavein and his people are giving direct aid to the cause of evil! They've brought this all upon themselves!" He stalked resolutely from the room.

"Stay here with the bitch if you're squeamish," suggested Mollyl with a smile. "Jan, you and Bell give me a hand. Go call the people together, Missa."

Alidore frowned irritably and started to follow, but Rehhaile called his name. So he stopped, mind in indecisive turmoil, and hesitantly approached their captive. From the square outside came a howl of agony and an inspired laugh.

"Is that what's going to happen to me?" she asked him.

He felt a sharp nausea of unreasonable guilt. "I'll see that you'll feel no pain," he declared, then cursed his callousness as he saw her frightened tears. Damn! He had no business permitting personal feelings to intrude on a clear-cut matter like this. What difference did the fate of this devil's whore make to him? She mattered nothing weighed against the rightfulness of their mission. Uneasily Alidore realized that despite her guilt, her own fate meant a great deal to Rehhaile.

He drew his knife. "Look. You don't really belong in this mess. Your crimes aren't that important to us." He mumbled on clumsily, unable to say anything that did not sound foolish in his own ears, still unable to shut up. The knife sliced her bonds as he talked.

Unsteadily she rose to her feet. "You're letting me go," she said needlessly.

Alidore gave a tight lipped nod. "I can slip you through the rear door—I can see everyone else is out front." She shuddered, her face frightened and pale. Alidore thought of her uncanny second sight and realized she could sense every detail of the beating going on outside.

"Get away from them!" she whispered fiercely. "You don't belong with them! In your soul there is still some human feeling! All but burned out!"

"What do you mean!" Alidore protested. "These men are my fellow soldiers on a mission of good! We may be forced to resort to savage methods, but our goal is to help mankind! I'd die for Gaethaa willingly! He's the greatest man of this age!"

She laughed then—or maybe it was a sob. Alidore could not be certain. Her sightless face held him as she spat back in scornful pity. "Do you call me blind, Alidore! Gaethaa a great man! A Crusader battling the forces of evil! While Kane has lived here he has harmed no one. Since you came yesterday, your great man and your fellow soldiers have terrorized the town, raped me and threatened worse, demolished this tavern, bullied Gavein—and now you're beating him to death to force the people of Sebbei to obey commands meaningless to them!"

Alidore protested hotly. "But it's for the good of all! The man we're after is one of the most villainous . . ."

"Are you so much better then? Is Gaethaa a saint who has brought all this upon us? Are men like Mollyl, Jan, Bell and the others heroes? Perverted killers! Animals! Mercenaries who kill for profit and pleasure!

"Alidore! Please leave them now!"

"Get out of here! Right now!" he snarled. "I'll not desert Gaethaa!" His mind a whirl of confusion, he buried his head in his arms upon the table. Her steps moved away hurriedly, but he no longer listened.

A thousand years passed before Gaethaa called him, and he dazedly went outside. "Well, the old fool's dead!" the Crusader snapped in annoyance. "Completely useless too. These walking dead men only ran off when we tried to show them a lesson! Locked in their houses! They'll all die in their shadows before breaking out of their apathy! Never mind though! Their cowardice makes them worthless to us. We'll find Kane ourselves one way or another!"

Hoping that Rehhaile would have time to reach some place of safety before the others noticed her absence, Alidore joined Gaethaa in the square. The twisted body of Gavein lay sprawled in the dust, a patch of dampness growing in the late morning sunlight. His veins should have contained only dust, Alidore mused, avoiding the ruined face that tilted upward toward the sky. Jan caught his eye and grinned, fastidiously polishing his hook across his thigh.

"Shall I bring out the girl?" Mollyl smiled, his pale face a tight mask. "Anything's worth trying now."

Gaethaa shrugged. "Might as well. We'll stake her out in the sun and leave her. It might draw Kane's attention and keep him close by, even if he won't risk getting to her."

Alidore casually watched as Mollyl and Bell entered the tavern. No longer did he have second thoughts on his decision to release her. He almost smiled at the angry shout from within, as Mollyl discovered her escape.

"Hey, she's gone!" Mollyl bellowed from the doorway. "Her bonds were cut! Damn you, Alidore! You turned the witch loose!"

Bristling in defense of himself, Alidore snarled back, "The hell I did! She was tied up when I left her a minute ago! One of the townspeople must have done it! Maybe Kane came back! Hell, there's broken glass all over the tavern—she might have cut herself free while you were playing with Gavein!"

"All right! Let it pass! She's gone!" Gaethaa shouted to halt the dispute. He looked at his lieutenant narrowly, but decided it was not worth an inquest. Maybe Alidore would be less moody now.

"She wasn't of any real use to us anyway," he continued. "If she's with Kane now, that's fine for us. She'll only hinder his movements, and the two should be ten times easier to find than Kane alone.

"We'll divide our forces and start searching from house to house. That will make it three to one when we find Kane, and I'd rather the odds were greater after what we've learned of him. Still it's the best we can do. If we stuck together, we'd only chase around in circles through this ghost town. And if we spread out any more he might pick us off one by one. So don't underestimate our quarry. Remember he has untold centuries of cunning to direct his every move. When you find him don't give him a chance. Call for the rest of us when you get close to him, and be ready for anything.

"Ok then. Mollyl and Jan come with me—we'll start

to the west from the square. Alidore, you take Missa and Bell and search east. Good hunting!"

Dron Missa critically eyed Bell, whose left shoulder was wrapped in thick bandages. "Too bad you can't trade that sling for a hook like Jan's," he commented. "Then you'd maybe be worth something in a fight."

Bell's coarse face grew scarlet in anger. "Anytime you want to find out, kid! Anytime—you don't even need to ask! I'll push in your smirking little face just as sure with my right arm as with both! Want to try it right now?"

"All right! Save it for Kane when we find him!" Alidore ordered.

Eyes alert for the first sign of danger, the hunters strode across the square and into the silent streets. Somewhere in this city of ghosts lurked the man they had come to destroy. This mission that had already cost so much hardship and death must soon be completed.

"By the way, Alidore," Dron Missa whispered as they moved away. "That was a good move with Rehhaile."

Alidore looked at the Waldann curiously, then answered his grin.

IX. Death in the Shadows

Kane edged along the rooftop cautiously, keeping in view the three men who walked through the street below. The morning had faded into afternoon, and now the shadows again were stretching out across the empty streets. Soon they would reach all the way across, then the shadows would soften and begin to creep over the entire city. And darkness would return to Sebbei.

Kane was waiting for the night. Throughout the day he had assiduously avoided his pursuers, moving always just a little ahead of their search. This way he could keep them in view at all times, and thereby preclude a chance confrontation. He had considerable confidence in his own prowess, but he recognized that his opponents were hardened fighters as well. At present it seemed pointless to meet his enemies on their own terms. Three of them might well hold him at bay long enough for the others to arrive. Kane did not care to be caught in a trap again.

So he waited for darkness to come. Night would be to his advantage, and in the interim Gaethaa and his men could grow exhausted and careless.

The roof was hot. Exposed on the glossy slate surface, Kane was reminded most emphatically that it was a desert sun shining down over Demornte. The tiles stung his bare flesh as he crept over them—slabs of green- and gray-hued black, whose relative darkness Kane could judge from the heat that met his touch. Sweat trickled across his body, leaving damp patches wherever he rested, making his hands slip against the slate as he climbed the sloping roof.

It was easier to steal through the streets, keeping to the alleys and slipping through the empty buildings. The few townspeople that Kane encountered slunk away from him with faces averted, all but squeezing shut their eyes to avoid any contact with him. So did they creep away from his pursuers, Kane had observed, scuttling for their burrows when the strangers demanded information of them. They would not betray him, Kane felt assured. They only stood wretchedly by while his hunters searched suspiciously through their shops and houses, or pointed blindly when impatient threats demanded an indication of Kane's hiding place. At length Gaethaa's men too dismissed the townspeople as participants or even witnesses in this hunt.

But Kane made it a point to leave the maze of narrow streets and empty buildings at frequent intervals. Their cover masked his enemies' movements as well as his own, and such apparent sanctuary could too easily become a cul-de-sac. Climbing along the rooftops he could follow their progress and alter his own course as their movements dictated.

A rustling scrape alerted him, and he spun about with knife poised. It was a long, gray lizard, crawling across the tiles away from him. The reptile halted, settled against the sun steeped slates, and regarded the human with a glassy, inscrutable stare. Kane licked his dry lips, tasting salt, and wiped his sticky face with a grimy arm. His sword belt chafed his back, and sweat dripped across his chest to soak the harness. He had rolled the sleeves and opened the front of his shirt, but his leather vest and pants offset any help this afforded toward cooling him off. With darkness the air would soon grow chill again.

The inner wall of Sebbei was growing close again, so the search had now completed half of its second circuit—once already Gaethaa's men had worked their way from the square to the wall and back again, and now they had returned to the wall a second time. Tempers were as burning hot as the slate tiles he rested upon, and Kane caught shreds of argument that he probably had left the old city altogether. Vigilance had relaxed as frustration piled up, and Kane decided it was an opportune point for him to strike.

Kane had always been careful to stay well ahead of his pursuers while he climbed across the rooftops. His boots made a soft scuffling upon the slates no matter how gingerly he moved about. In each group of searchers, one man always held an arrow ready to draw, and no building was entered until they made a close scrutiny for evidence of their quarry lurking somewhere above them. Now as he saw them approaching the empty apartment house on whose roof he lay hidden, Kane held his position.

Huddled against the stone cornice, he watched through a chink in the blocks as the three halted before the structure and looked it over. Alidore stood back with an arrow nocked and ready, his eyes scanning the building front for any sign of danger. Swords drawn, Dron Missa and Bell entered the tenement ahead of him. Once they called out to him, Alidore hurriedly stepped inside as well.

His ear pressed to the roof, Kane could hear an occasional faint crash from within, as they carried out the tedious business of examining each room of the crumbling apartment. There was no access to the roof from within, so Kane knew they could not reach him at the moment. This particular tenement had obviously been in disrepair even before the plague, and the intervening years were not far short of bringing it to total ruin. Earlier in the day

Kane had almost lost his balance when a cornice stone had shifted beneath his weight, and the decrepit state of the entire building front had suggested a possibility.

Now while his enemies searched through the rotting apartments, Kane busily attacked the cornice with his knife. The dagger point dug into the crumbling mortar as if it were mud. A growing pile of grit and dirt spread about his knees as he worked, hoping that the soft grating of metal on stone would not be heard below.

The sound of voices reached the street again, and Kane sheathed his blade quickly. Rising to his feet he tried to peer through the cracks to see when the men would step out into the street. Luck was still with him—they had not attempted the rotted stairs leading from the tenement's rear exit. But his vision was limited by the position, so the best he could do would be to estimate by the sound of their voices the approximate moment they would walk beneath the cornice.

It was time to take the risk. If his timing were off this might prove catastrophic. His feet set against the slates, Kane braced his shoulder against the cornice and slowly heaved, hoping that the entire building front would not collapse as well. The cornice resisted his pressure at first, so he threw against it the full strength of his massive frame. With a sudden treacherous release of tension, the stone facade buckled outward and collapsed! Thrown off balance, Kane waved his arms wildly and tottered on the brink, about to topple after the plummeting stonework!

The three were just emerging from the doorway in chagrin, when Dron Missa felt a trickle of grit sift past his face. "Look out!" he howled, his fighter's reflexes reacting faster than thought to the cold breath of death he sensed. With the blinding agility of an acrobat, Missa sprang into the street and rolled in a somersault across to the opposite side! Still in the doorway, Alidore leapt back into the hallway at the Waldann's cry of warning!

Bell's dull mind was slower to react. Not comprehending the cause for Missa's shout, he wasted a scant second to glare upward. His eyes had barely time to register the terror that started within him as Bell saw the wall of

146

rock hurtling down upon him! His scream had scarcely reached his lips before it was swallowed in the thunderous shock of the facade slamming against the street!

Alidore glanced in horror at the scarlet splotched heap of rubble strewn before the doorway. Only the barest fragment of time had separated him from such a death.

"There he is!" shouted Missa, recovering from the shock in time to see Kane regain his balance and dart back from the roof's edge. "Quick, Alidore! Bring the bow! Kane's on the roof!"

Scrambling over the roofing tiles like an ape, Kane dashed for the neighboring building. Not so distant shouts were answering the alarm in the street below, and Kane had no desire to be caught in the open. Another building stood adjacent to the tenement. Kane threw himself upward to clear the few feet discrepancy between the two structures and started across the steeper sloping roof.

A tile broke loose under his feet halfway up, and Kane skidded dizzily downward, hands clawing to secure a grip! But there was no purchase! Helpless to halt his slide, Kane floundered over the edge and dropped back to the tenement roof. His heart racing, Kane leapt up and began his climb again, thankful that his fall had been only a few feet rather than all the way to the street below. An arrow grazed past to shatter a tile under his fingers. Then Kane gained the crest of the roof and slid down the other side, protected for the moment.

This side abutted upon a building one floor less in height. Catching the gutter as he reached the edge, he lowered himself over the side and dropped lightly to this next rooftop. Angry shouts sounded closer now as his pursuers sought to close in, but Kane felt more confident. A stairway at the far end of this structure led him down to an alley in back.

On reaching the alley, he pushed through a door in an opposite building and vanished before Gaethaa's men could circle from the other street. While they frenziedly sought to retrace his movements, Kane ducked through several empty buildings and finally re-emerged some distance away. The darkening streets cloaked his escape.

The twilight deepened and was swallowed by the night. Across dead Demornte settled the blackness of the tomb. No lights shone in the empty towns and abandoned homes, and a velvet curtain was drawn over the plague scarred corpse of the stricken land. Starlight and gibbous moon looked down on dead Demornte, their soft illumination no more than shading the night to gray. Their glow was like candles burning at a wake, sculpturing the face of the deceased with stark angles and shadowed hollows. Among the bones of a nation crept the creatures of night, stepping solemnly as mourners through the spectral silence.

In Sebbei only a few houses showed light, and this through cracks in bolted shutters and doors. For death again stalked the streets of Sebbei, and even in their despair the townspeople trembled at the familiar sound of his step. In the darkened streets even the phantoms who nightly walked the stones seemed aware that death had returned to Demornte, and the wraiths melted into the silent shadows, abandoning the night to the spectre of death with his bared sword.

Half a dozen torches blazed yellow in the deserted streets, driving back the shadows as they passed. Grim-faced men cast suspicious eyes over each segment of nighted city laid bare by the torch flames. Warily they searched for some new evidence of their quarry's presence.

Determined to put an end to this deadly match of cat and mouse, Gaethaa grouped his remaining men together and ordered an all night search. Now by torchlight he and his band relentlessly pushed through the city of ghosts, stalking their prey through the now familiar streets and deserted buildings. If this was to be a contest of endurance, Gaethaa meant to give his enemy no chance to rest. Not even Kane could hold up against the strain of ceaseless skulking from place to place, never gaining more than a few steps on his pursuers. And if Kane's role as fox were any less taxing than that of hound, the hounds outnumbered him and could hunt in shifts if need be. Eventually Kane would grow weary and then careless. They would trap him and learn how well an exhausted fox could fight as the pack closed in to kill.

"Hell, I'll lay you odds Kane's clear out of Sebbei right now!" Jan growled, his surly temper worn thin from the hours of tedious search. "Probably sleeping somewhere out beyond the wall—while we're here wearing ruts down the streets. He'd be a fool to stay here inside the walls dodging us all night."

"That's true enough—assuming Kane is running from us," Dron Missa pointed out, an unaccustomed note of unease in his voice. "But that isn't the case here. It seems to me Kane is stalking us just as we're hunting him. We've thought we were hounds chasing down a fox, but I think it's more realistic to consider this a tiger hunt. I was on one once far south of here, and I remember the crawling sense of danger that haunted each step through that shadowy jungle. We were stalking the beast in his own element, and no one had convinced the tiger that he was supposed to be the quarry. Three of us died in the shadows before we finally brought him down."

"Well, it's obvious enough by now that Kane isn't exactly in full flight," Gaethaa broke in brusquely. "We've known that ever since he followed us back to the tavern and murdered Sed tho'Dosso. He's still with us—staying just out of sight like a cobra, waiting for a chance to strike at us. But his boldness will be his undoing eventually —we'll wear him out before he does us. So keep your eyes open, damn it! Remember he's waiting desperately for us to give him an opening!"

Doggedly the Avenger and his men concentrated on their search. Alidore worked his way close to Dron Missa and studied the normally flippant Waldann. "What's the trouble, Missa?" he asked quietly. "I don't recall seeing you in so gloomy a mood before. Is this place getting to you?"

The other man glanced at him edgily, somewhat ashamed at broadcasting his ill ease. "I'm all right. Been a long day, that's all." He paused, "No, that's not all of it. Kane, this place, these people . . . Something's getting to me. My nerves are all sort of . . . Well, like on that tiger hunt—right before that striped devil came bounding out of the brush and tore apart the guy three steps back of me. Only I've got the same feeling worse this time . . . thinking maybe I'll be the one the tiger picks to spring upon this time . . ."

His voice trailed off uncertainly. Then he smiled and punched at Alidore's shoulder, his old smile returning. "Look—don't let me pass my bad nerves on to you. I'll be in fine form once we drive Kane out into the open. This monotonous game of poking through a ghost town trying to flush a cobra is not my style, that's all. Give me an open fight, and I'll shake off my depression soon enough."

"Hell, I'm not worried about your nerves, Missa," Alidore assured him. "All of us are on edge by now—who wouldn't be! Kane is feeling it worse than we are though, and my guess is he'll either make a stand or break and run before much longer. Dawn can't be more than a few hours off."

Death waited in the shadows.

Stealthily Kane raised the heavy trapdoor. Its dry hinges rasped in loud complaint, and Kane uneasily peered about the darkened warehouse. Satisfied that no one was near enough to catch the sound, he grimly inspected the dank smelling subcellar below, then replaced the trap over the opening. Whether the old tunnel still lay open was impossible to say without light, but at least the trapdoor would open for him. Silence. His pursuers had not yet reached the warehouse, although their torches had been drawing close to the seemingly abandoned structure when last Kane had looked outside.

The warehouse was a looming structure of unyielding stone walls, stoutly built to protect costly merchandise from thieves and the elements alike. It stood somewhat apart from neighboring buildings, with only a short open space intervening between its rear wall and the inner wall of the old city. At some time in the past, evidently before the outer wall had been raised, the merchant owners had found it expedient to drive a tunnel beneath the city walls —and thereby link the warehouse with the cellars of another establishment located a short distance beyond the inner city. In those days caravans with trade goods had stopped by the outlying inn to rest and partake of pleasures offered there. It had been profitable to bring certain goods directly to the warehouse from the inn by way of the tunnel, an artifice which avoided the needless expense of custom duties, as well as suspicious eyes of city officials who might scruple over legal ownership of some items.

The tunnel had fallen into disuse in later times, abandoned altogether after the plague. Kane had discovered it one day while prowling through the deserted city in search of nothing in particular. Despite its advanced state of disrepair, curiosity drove Kane to risk one trip through the tunnel with its rotting timber braces and settling walls. Now he remembered the old warehouse with its smugglers' tunnel, and centered upon this he had planned a rather dangerous attack upon his pursuers—a trap that could strike either way.

As Gaethaa and his men drew close to the deserted warehouse, Kane moved on ahead of them, certain that they would again enter to search among the dust laden stacks and bales. There was no evidence that the trapdoor had been discovered—it was well concealed, and Kane himself had originally come upon the tunnel from its other end. This would leave him an exit from the warehouse once they knew he was inside. There was no way they could trap him inside—assuming the tunnel had not collapsed since he passed through many weeks before. That was a risk he could not escape at this point, though.

With soft steps Kane ascended the cellar stairs and crossed the darkened warehouse. At the side and rear doors he paused to make certain their heavy bars were in place. A smaller front door was similarly bolted. There remained only the massive main door through which to enter the warehouse. All doors were of thick, iron-bound timber, windows there were none, and the walls built from heavy sandstone blocks. Once the main door too was locked, long hard work with axes and prybars would be needed before entrance could be forced.

About him in the darkness lay boxes and piles of costly merchandise, waiting under a wrapping of dust and spider webbing for buyers who would never come. They formed fantastic shapes in the darkness, crouching patches of blackness against the night—all but invisible until they were brushed upon. Mounds of moldering rugs, rotting heaps of cloth and furs, shelves of tarnished metalwork, pieces of furniture standing in musty aloofness, broken boxes of spices imparting a sick pungency to the odor of decay. Wealth lay crumbling beneath the cold caress of time, and the same vermin now crawled alike over the bones of merchant and buyer and the corpse of their wares.

The warehouse ceiling stretched high, and the door which closed its main entrance was immense. A system of chain and pulleys lifted the main door vertically along grooves cut into the jamb, sliding the heavy barrier upward and down by means of a capstan. Entire wagons could be driven through the doorway when open; once closed it would require a powerful battering ram to smash through. For years the door had stood open, raised upward to the ceiling—the warehouse abandoned to the plague when death claimed its owners.

The capstan mechanism was mounted alongside the front wall. A thick iron chain strained from the winch, ran along heavy pulleys jutting from the stones, and fastened to the massive door. Kane had inspected the fittings on earlier occasions and was familiar with their operation. Now he drew his long sword from across his shoulder and crept into the shadow of some bales piled against the wall close to the capstan. A rat darted away from his boot and scurried off cursing into the darkness. Kane's lips pressed in a thin smile as he saw first flickers of torchlight streak the entranceway, heard shuffle of approaching steps, low mutter of voices. Tightness of anticipation slipped from him. Cunning or foolhardy, he was committed now.

Closer came the light, the sound—spilling echoes across the deserted darkness within. Light brighter. Figures appeared at the doorway. Entered.

They stood just inside the door, torches raised, eyes narrowly scrutinizing the shadows beyond. Kane mashed himself against the wall, unseen in the cover of the bales. Two had entered. The rest would hold back a moment.

"See anything, Mollyl?" came the call from outside.

"No. There's nothing here—as usual!" came the grumbling reply from the one who bore a hook for a right hand. Jan belligerently pushed his way into the warehouse, Mollyl beside him. They turned to inspect the wall behind them, just as the others moved to follow them inside.

Kane leapt from the shadows and reached the capstan in a bound! Framed against the darkness by yellow torchlight, his blade flashed a menacing gleam, reflected in his eyes!

"Kane! Here he is! Watch out!" Mollyl shouted in warning. From outside Gaethaa swore in triumph.

Only seconds were left to close the trap—or to be crushed in its jaws himself! Kane's right hand lashed out as he gained the capstan—seizing the brake lever and hauling it free! The lever snapped back in his grasp and ripped loose from its fitting! The winch now stood free from its pinion—no brake locked its mechanism to hold the main door suspended!

The door should have fallen. It remained in its place.

Dismayed by the failure of his strategy, Kane wasted a few seconds in sick conjecture. Had he miscalculated the capstan's operation then? Was the mechanism frozen after years of stressed immobility?

Snarling in rage, Kane threw himself against the horizontal crossbars, straining his massive bulk against the capstan handles! Another few seconds and he would be hemmed in by his enemies! Even now Jan and Mollyl were recovering from initial surprise to attack! Excited shouts, cold death knell of iron, boots pounding for the doorway!

Kane's shoulder struck the crossbar, and seasoned wood cracked. Muscle and timber rebounded. Jolted by the terrific impact, the capstan shuddered and recoiled in submission. With a dry, grinding snarl the mechanism began to rotate! Rusted chain groaned and cracked in protest! The immense overhead door shook itself in angry arousal and broke free of its bed of dust! Debris fell in a trickle—

then exploded through the night. An inch . . . three . . . ten . . .

Thunder roared in fury as the tons heavy door tore loose and hurled itself down across the entranceway—momentum building to blinding acceleration! The capstan shrieked on its pivot, spun like a gigantic top by the streaking chain. Crossbars whirled a vortex, the wooden arms driving Mollyl and Jan back in alarm. As he darted back from the berserk mechanism, a handle struck Kane across the side and sent him reeling against the wall.

The entire warehouse rocked as the door crashed against its sill with the finality of the gate of hell. Caught by the inertia of its fall, the chain snapped short on the spindle and ripped the spinning capstan free of its smoking mounting. Wooden drum and iron chain lashed across the warehouse like a beheaded python, sending all three men flat behind cover. The mammoth scourge cracked against a pile of crates and exploded into a storm of splintered wood and glassware.

Chips of stone pelted Gaethaa and the other two as they frantically drew back from the downrushing barrier. Clouds of dust blasted their faces, whipped the torches as the door thundered shut. Baffled rage again cut through the chill of death's brush, as Gaethaa howled orders. "Alidore, Missa! Left and right fast! Find an entrance! If they're all locked, we'll break through the weakest! Damn his cunning! Kane's split us up again, and we've got to get in there fast! Move!"

Within the warehouse silence droned as the dust and echoes fell away. Picking themselves up warily, three killers moved to renew the attack. Mollyl and Jan still held torches, giving light across the interior.

The crossbar had struck only a glancing blow, but Kane's side throbbed agonizingly as he straightened. He shifted weight experimentally, judging from the ache that no ribs had broken. With his right hand he drew his dirk.

"Kane!" Jan hissed. "Remember me? It's been over ten years though—ten years ago when I still had a right hand—and a home and family! But you and your Black Fleet saw to that—didn't you, Kane! Should have cut off my head then, Kane—instead of just a hand! I've hunted you since then, Kane! Missed you at Montes—they said you died there! But I knew you were still alive—still playing your devil's games in other lands! I knew we'd finally cross swords again! Fate ordained this—just as Fate ordained your heart should dangle from Jan's hook!"

"So you know me, Hook?" sneered Kane. "Sorry, but I've forgotten your name as well as your face. I ought to remember anyone fool enough to cross blades twice with me!"

From the side door came the shock of muffled pounding. But Kane knew the timber was sound.

With a snarl Jan hurled his torch at Kane's face! Several yards yet separated them, and Kane easily dodged the missile. Its flames fanned his red beard and smoke stung his eyes, as the torch shot past him to thud against some bales of cloth. Oil soaked fragments spattered across the bales, and the torch spread its flame over musty rolls of fabric.

"Don't lose our light!" cursed Mollyl, lodging his torch between two crates. "I know you for a black hearted pirate as well, Kane! Surprised to find two of the Island Empire dogging your twisted path even across the sands of Lomarn?"

"Spread out, Jan! We'll find out for ourselves how Kane can fight without his men behind him—see if the serpent can strike when he's chased out of hiding!"

Jan's sword was in his good hand now, and the torchlight caught the razor edge of his hook's inside curve. Dagger replaced torch in Mollyl's grasp, and the Pellinite rushed for Kane with sword thrusting. Jan slid off to the side to press Kane's flank. Behind Kane, flames streaked across the bales of cloth like sparks through tinder.

Crackling heat against his back, Kane's sword sprang across Mollyl's, driving the other man back in a powerful followthrough. His dirk rose to block Jan's blade at the same instant, sparks shooting as the hilt turned the heavier weapon. Desperately Kane backed to the burning mound, preventing his assailants from circling behind. Again and again their blades clashed together, Kane's blinding defense turning aside the attack of two skilled swordsmen. At the side entrance heavy blows shuddered the door against its bolt and hinges, but the thick barrier held. It would take some time for Gaethaa and his men to break through. Neither Kane nor his assailants fought with armor or mail—their duel would be a short one.

The fire at his back spread rapidly, licking across to ignite closely piled heaps of rugs, crates, furniture. Heat became scorching, forcing Kane away from the flames. Smoke stung their eyes and nostrils. Swinging his blade in a whirlwind of death, Kane drove back his opponents' attack and leapt between them. Jan's sword dashed past his shoulder by a finger's width.

Into the open now they fought, Kane pressing more on the offensive as he heard axes bite into the side door. The warehouse was brightly lit now, as the fire spread across one end. Sheets of smoke poured over the interior, shading the firelight to dark yellow. The countless piles of merchandise threw long, grotesque shadows across the floor and far wall—twisted shapes that drew away in fear from the destroying flames.

With a powerful effort, Kane forced his opponents apart. Before Jan could recover, Kane lunged at Mollyl. The Pellinite lacked the strength to match Kane blow for blow. Frantically he retreated, only barely parrying Kane's thrusts. The flames seared his back now, and his pale face twisted in fear and pain. His defense wavered an instant. Kane's blade slashed downward faster than Mollyl could turn, its tip slicing across the flesh of his sword arm. Dropping his sword with a howl of terror, Mollyl jumped back to avoid Kane's lunge. His impetus carried him over a low crate at the fire's advancing edge! Arms flailing wildly, Mollyl tumbled backwards into a blazing mound of furniture! Flames wrapped about him as he fell, smashing through a red hot jumble of carven wood and padded leather.

Screaming in agony, Mollyl lurched to his feet and stumbled from the blaze, tongues of fire dancing over his hair and clothing! Blinded by the flames, flesh seared and blackened, he flopped across the warehouse floor, smashing into objects in hopeless effort to escape the unendurable pain. Kane ignored him as he crumpled into a writhing, mewing smouldering mass.

Kane's concentration on Mollyl gave Jan sufficient time to renew his onslaught. In the seconds it took for Kane to drive Mollyl into the fire, Jan rushed his hated enemy from behind—his sword darting for Kane's back even as Mollyl tumbled onto his pyre. But Kane had not forgotten the other man, and sensing the danger as he heard the scuffle of boots, he twisted sideways to avoid the striking sword tip. Jan's blade shot past him narrowly, but a flash of pain stabbed across his right shoulder as he turned. Jan's hook slashed through leather vest and tore the flesh of his shoulder, but failed to lodge.

Reeling back, Kane thrust his dirk for the other's side. The agony in his shoulder slowed his movements though, and with a wild laugh Jan jerked his reddened hook against the dagger, skittering down the blade and meshing it into the hilt. The hook's tip gashed Kane's hand, and jerking back Jan tore the dagger from his weakened grasp. Jan yelled in triumph and slashed out with his sword. In red fury Kane beat back his attack and hammered his blade against his assailant's guard. The fire was spreading, and the side door was beginning to splinter. A brutal stroke stunned Jan's sword arm for an instant, and Kane struck before he could parry effectively. His blade tore through the other's side, shearing through ribs and lung! Jan toppled to the floor, eyes brimming hatred through death agony. His sword had fallen, but he crawled on his belly toward Kane, hook outstretched, its razor tip scoring the planks as he dragged his broken body onward. He died as his hook stabbed inches from Kane's boot.

Heat from the fire beat at Kane's face. He stepped back. Already the flames had engulfed the section where Mollyl's body had lain. The side door still held against Gaethaa's assault, but the warehouse was ablaze. Flames now had leapt over half the floor, and in places the planks had given way to collapse into the cellar. It was hard to breathe, even to see with the rapidly building smoke and heat. Hurriedly Kane retrieved his dirk and started for the cellar stairs. His enemies were outside waiting—the tunnel was his only escape now. But if the blazing floor collapsed over the cellar trapdoor before he reached it . . .

The trapdoor was still clear of flaming wreckage. Seizing a rough torch from the edge of the fire, Kane heaved open the trapdoor and descended the steps into the tunnel. Here the musty dampness of the earth was undisturbed by the holocaust above. Though stale, the dank air was relief from the burning smoke that choked the warehouse.

Rapidly as he dared, Kane passed through the tunnel. His torch offered poor light, but sufficient to pick out his way. Rotting timbers sagged overhead, bowed out from the walls. Dirt had trickled through to make soft ridges along the floor, and in a few places mounds of debris almost occluded the passage. Gingerly Kane crawled over these crumbling heaps of dirt and shoring, torch out-thrust to give light. Clods and sand fell over his back and legs, making a dark paste with the blood that flowed from his cuts.

At any second Kane knew the tunnel might give way altogether, sealing him in this tomb beneath the city of the dead. At one point a dull shock echoed through the tunnel, along with a muffled crash from behind him. The warehouse roof must have fallen, Kane guessed, nervously eyeing the tunnel walls. But by now he had come a good distance beneath the earth, and the tunnel seemed somewhat more solid as he approached its far end.

The floor rose, and a flight of steps appeared before his dying torch. Eagerly Kane ascended them and pushed open the concealed door in the inn's cellars. Moving confidently through the deserted inn, Kane found a door and stepped outside. Within the walls of Sebbei the blazing warehouse threw a glow against black skies soon to gray with dawn.

For the moment his enemies must believe him dead. Wincing at the pain, Kane paused by the inn's wall to wash his scorched, bleeding body and bind his wounds. Three yet lived of those who had hounded him, and neither injuries nor fatigue had abated Kane's fury.

X. Land of the Dead

When smoke began streaming from cracks and openings throughout the warehouse, and the splintering door began to emanate heat from the inferno within, Gaethaa called a halt to their frantic efforts to break in.

"This place is doomed!" he pronounced, laying aside his axe. "Anyone still alive in there has to get out in a hurry, or the smoke will kill them if the flames don't! Jan or Mollyl will open up if Kane hasn't finished them—and if he has, then we'll give Kane the choice of roasting inside or coming out to meet our swords! Either way he'll be burning in hell before dawn breaks! Spread out and watch the doors."

His men did as ordered. One man had always kept watch on the warehouse doors while the other two had attacked the side entrance. Clearly no one had escaped from within while they fruitlessly attempted to break down the door. Swords ready for instant use, they watched vigilantly for one of the doors to swing open, for a figure to stumble out in a shroud of smoke and flame, blinded and coughing. If it should be Kane who emerged, Gaethaa meant to give him scant time to draw clean air into his lungs.

But no door was flung open. No scorched figure stepped out. Crashes from within indicated the floor was giving way, and then came a ripping concussion as the warehouse roof collapsed ponderously upon the wreckage within. A cataclysmic blast of flame and cinders leapt into the night skies, transforming the yet standing walls of the warehouse into the cone of a volcano. Soon the doors crumpled from the heat, falling inward to reveal a blazing holocaust. Still stood the thick stone walls, red hot now from the furnace that raged within. But long before this, the watchers had ceased to guard the exits.

"Kane's funeral pyre!" observed Gaethaa triumphantly. "He took two more good men with him, but they died as

159

heroes." He turned to accept Alidore's congratulations. "Only three of us left. It's been a costly campaign—the most dangerous of my career clearly. But our goal was a great one, and we have at last met success. History's blackest monster has finally met the death that for centuries he had cheated. Mankind will be greatful for this work we have done. Once again I have cleansed a dark shadow of evil with the cold light of good."

A rustle from the alley behind them abruptly drew attention. "Why, it's the witch," Gaethaa announced, catching sight of her in the light from the blaze.

Rehhaile hung poised at the alley's entrance, almost concealed in the shadow of a building. Firelight shone across her face and limbs, as her blind eyes stared beyond them. She seemed to be summoning the courage to approach them, yet remained on the verge of flight.

Why had she come back? Alidore wondered. Surely her second sight told her she had been seen. Had Kane meant so much to her that she had thrown away all caution just to be present at his death? Alidore sensed a note of jealousy in his musing. "Milord," he began, "can't we forget about her . . . ?"

Gaethaa shrugged. He was in a jubilant mood, and if his lieutenant felt concern for this creature, he could easily grant him his whim. "Sure, Alidore, if this will assuage your misgivings. Kane is dead, and she was only his whore and dupe. She was punished for her tiny part in his crimes.

"Come on out of the shadows, witch," he called magnanimously. "We have decided to grant clemency. You need have no further fear of our justice. Come see the fate of the monster you served."

Sensing the leniency of the Avenger's disposition, Rehhaile stepped forward to join them. "Kane's dead," she informed them dully. "I knew when you at last cornered him, so I came to be in on the finish, however it turned out. But Kane was trapped within the burning warehouse. He died in the flames—I felt his death in my mind. You destroyed Kane as you had intended; your mission is complete now. Will you leave Sebbei at dawn?"

160

"So your witch's sight showed you Kane's death," Gaethaa smiled. "I envy you—that was a vision I would have given much to have shared. But see, Alidore—despite your concern for her, she only desires our departure. Well, my men and I will ride on as soon as we've rested and reprovisioned. I never care to wait around for the fulsome praise of those whom I have served—and Sebbei holds little attraction for me. But for now I'll soothe the strain of this mission by basking in the glow of my enemy's death pyre."

"I'll take some fresh air instead," Dron Missa yawned. "The smoke from this pyre is as redolent as a burning dump. Thoem! What kind of junk did they have stuffed away in there!" The Waldann strolled toward the city wall and climbed the steps to the parapet. His lean figure could be seen silhouetted against the graying skies as he leisurely paced alongside ghost guardsmen of dead Sebbei.

Gaethaa the Crusader settled himself against a wall and stretched his long legs out before him. Dreamily he smiled into the dying flames of the warehouse, reliving the excitement of the past days and wondering where the cold light would lead him next. First to Kamathae for new men and equipment. The death of Kane could occupy the court poets, but elsewhere there were others who needed the help of the Avenger.

Alidore and Rehhaile wandered on down the street. The witch was eager to draw away his lieutenant, Gaethaa mused. Still Alidore seemed fascinated with her, and he was entitled to the diversion.

The lake lay below him, its gray mist rising in the predawn darkness. Idly Dron Missa leaned against the parapet and felt the tight muscles of his back slowly loosen. A scrape of boot on stone met his ear, and he looked up, wondering who had joined him.

A figure approached him along the wall, striding through the mist as ominously as the angel of death. Menace radiated from the fog wrapped figure, shone in his killer's eyes, gleamed along his drawn sword. "Kane!" gasped Missa, recognizing the singed and bandaged swordsman. Only a second did he waste on amazed confoundment. Missa's own blade leapt from scabbard to answer Kane's challenge!

Kane rushed upon the Waldann, his sword hissing through the fog. Missa's blade moved in swift parry, then thrust past in a sudden lunge. Slipping away from the razor point, Kane swore and renewed the fight with more cautious tactics. His opponent was an excellent swordsman, and Kane's stiff right arm could wield his dirk only clumsily. Carefully he pressed his attack, Missa's darting blade baffling his own efforts to overwhelm his guard.

Left-handed opponents Missa had fought before, and he had no difficulty adjusting to the other's stance. Kane's speed amazed him though—astonishing agility for a man of his bulk. And as Kane continued to batter him relentlessly, Missa became conscious of the vast power that underlay his speed. Here was as skillful and deadly an opponent as he had ever confronted, and only Missa's own brilliant swordplay saved him from Kane's blade time and again. With growing concern, Missa coldly remembered the tales he had heard of Kane—recalled the spectre of violent death that had haunted them ever since Gaethaa began his mission to destroy Kane.

A twinge of pain shot along Missa's right thigh as Kane's partially deflected blade turned to slice shallowly across his leg. Ignoring the wound, Missa fell back a pace as if to stagger. As Kane stepped forward to follow his advantage, Missa raised his sword to parry and lashed out with the dagger in his left hand. Kane's recovery with his own dirk was too slow, and Missa's blade gashed across his ribs fleetingly as Kane twisted away.

Cursing in anger Kane recklessly hurled his dirk at the Waldann. Badly thrown, the blade cleanly missed the other. But as Dron Missa dodged to avoid the streaking knife, his guard fell for an instant. Kane's sword flashed down, slashing Missa's swordarm to the bone—only its downward course spared his arm from amputation. A return flick of Kane's weapon sent his opponent's blade spinning into the dawn mists. Badly wounded and armed with only his dagger, Missa saw Kane's killing stroke slash toward him with dreamlike slowness, nightmare inexorability.

In the split second of life that remained to him, Missa reacted with desperate speed. Darting back from the searching blade, he threw himself from the parapet and dived into the lake below. The darkness, the cold water, received him in a stunning embrace.

Surfacing quickly, Missa paddled away clumsily. His wounds were bleeding freely and stung even more fiercely as the water bathed them. Still they were not of themselves fatal, although disabling. Once he could bind them, stop the bleeding—with proper care they would heal, and not too many months would pass before he could wield a sword as expertly as before. But that would be for another lord and another cause. Gaethaa's insane missions had paid him well, yet the Crusader had not bought his life. Missa understood concepts of loyalty and duty of mercenary to his lord, but only within reason. Gaethaa's mission to destroy Kane had been cursed with dark fortune from the beginning, and Dron Missa decided it was time for discreet withdrawal. The gods plainly had given him this chance; it would be sacrilege to ignore their intercession.

He looked back at the hulking figure leaning against the parapet in the dawn light. "Go to hell, Kane!" he shouted back, then disappeared into the mists.

When Gaethaa had first heard Missa's shout and the clash of arms, he stared at the scene of combat in disbelief. Then through his astonished mind filtered the incredible truth—Kane still lived! The devil had not died in the flames—by some sorcery he had escaped! The witch had lied to complete the collapse of their vigilance! Now Kane had again returned to strike from the shadows! How many more times could the demon cheat death!

"Alidore! Alidore! Kill that damned witch and get over here quick!" He bellowed shrilly, watching the parapet duel. "Alidore! Run, damn you! Kane's still alive! He's attacked Missa on the wall!"

Forgetting Rehhaile for the moment, Alidore dashed to his lord's call. Against graying skies could be seen the deadly display of swordplay atop the wall. Swords in hand, they rushed to the steps that ascended the wall in this quarter. But the distance was considerable, and as they reached the stairs, they saw the fight's abrupt climax, watched Dron Missa plunge from the parapet into the lake.

"Missa too!" Gaethaa swore in rage. "Now he's killed Missa! I think we fight Lord Tloluvin himself! But we two have not fallen! We'll let Kane taste our iron before this sun has risen!"

Yet when they reached the top, Kane had stolen away into the mists of dawn, eluding them once again.

"He runs from us, milord!" Alidore exclaimed bewilderedly. "Strange Kane should slink off with only two to face. He won't face an opponent in the open it seems."

"No!" hissed Gaethaa, his eyes aflame. "See there on the stones! Blood! A blood trail! Kane's been wounded! Missa died not without giving account! No telling how badly wounded Kane might be! We've put him to flight now though—and here's the trail to lead us to him!"

But the trail of blood dwindled and vanished altogether after they had followed it for only a short distance through the streets of Sebbei, where now the rising sun was cutting through the concealing night. Grimly Gaethaa realized that Kane's wounds had not been as severe as he had hoped. However seriously he might be disabled, at least he had been able to staunch the bleeding. And now Kane had again hidden himself in the maze of dead Sebbei.

"The game continues," intoned Gaethaa heavily. "We have gained nothing. Again we must search for Kane through this damned labyrinthian ghost city, stalking him through his lair. Except today there are only you and I to hunt the tiger, Alidore. We can never destroy Kane like this."

Alidore looked at his lord in concern. There was a sharp cry of despair in Gaethaa's voice that his lieutenant had never heard before. But though the Crusader's lanky figure was slumped and his chin propped against fist, his eyes were lost in thought. His long face bore twisting lines of raw emotion as his keen mind sorted through and rejected dozens of strategems from past campaigns.

Abruptly his face broke into inspired smile, and a triumphant laugh barked from his lips. "We're not done yet, Alidore!" he cried wildly. "We'll burn this accursed city to the ground!"

"Burn Sebbei!" Alidore exploded incredulously.

"Right! Burn it all! Let it all burn to the ground! Kane's using these deserted buildings for cover—we'll smoke him out into the open. Thoem knows how he escaped that warehouse without our knowledge, but his cunning won't help him when all Sebbei is in flames! He'll burn with the town, or he'll head for open country. Even if we miss him at first, picking up his trail will be child's play in this ghost land. We'll run him to earth even if he tries to cross the Lomarn—wounded as he is, he won't get that far! No more playing into his traps!"

"Milord Gaethaa!" Alidore protested. "You can't be serious! Burn down the entire city to kill one man! What of the townspeople?"

"Their backbones have dryrot! Don't worry about them. We'll fire a few buildings across the city—enough for the wind to spread the flames over the rest! It will be done before they can lift a hand—not that I believe any man of them has the guts to stop us! Maybe we can tell some that Kane started the fires—might jolt them out of their cowering lassitude to the point they'll tell us where Kane is, though I doubt if they're worth even that!"

"No! I mean, we can't raze an entire city just to destroy Kane! These people will be killed—at best they'll lose everything they possess!"

Gaethaa shrugged impatiently. "The town has no more than a few hundred. Most should escape easily enough, and there's any number of empty towns and villages they can move into. And don't waste pity on them! Had they done their duty to mankind, they would have pitched in and helped us destroy Kane! By their cowardly negligence they're responsible for the deaths of all my men— as well as being traitors to the cause of good! Burning these whining rats from their rotten dens is a fitting punishment for their complicity! Come on Alidore, we're wasting time!"

Alidore's voice was strained, as he grasped Gaethaa's shoulder and turned him half around. "But to burn an entire city for one man! Kane isn't worth it!"

Face white with rage, Gaethaa threw off his lieutenant's hand. "Kane not worth it!" he roared. "Alidore, have you lost your mind! We've crossed half a continent to destroy this demon! All of your comrades have given their lives for this mission! And after all this effort, this sacrifice, the man I came to destroy still mocks me! I'll raze a hundred towns if need be to destroy Kane! Yes, and consider the price a cheap one balanced against the evil this man has committed—evil he will continue to bring upon mankind until he is hunted down and slain! What's the worth of this city of ghosts opposed to the greater good of mankind!"

The logic was inescapable, but Alidore still balked. "But the strategy may be entirely in vain!" he argued weakly. "Kane won't be trapped in the flames! He'll escape the city easily—we can't begin to guard the gates, let alone the entire wall! He'll flee Sebbei, and we'll never pick up his trail in the confusion!"

"A general who believes his plan of attack infallible is a fool!" Gaethaa snapped. "Tell me a better one, and I'll accept your counsel. The plain truth is that Kane has beaten us at this damnable game of cat and mouse! He knows Sebbei better than we do, so he has only to lie in wait for us to enter his traps! We failed yesterday with six men—it's hopeless to try again with two! We have to force him into the open—make him run instead of spin webs to ensnare us! Damn it, Alidore—what's wrong with you! Have you lost your ideals and your nerve together!"

The Lartroxian wavered, thoughts spinning in soul wrenching tumult.

A voice cried out from behind them. "Alidore! What are you doing? Have you completely sold your soul to Gaethaa? That madman and his band of killers have done more evil than Kane has ever been responsible for! Will you help him now to destroy Sebbei and its wretched people on the chance you might kill Kane with this atrocity! Alidore, if you have anything but iron left to your soul, leave Gaethaa! Stop him before he sacrifices more lives to his merciless gods!"

"Ah! I hear a witch!" Gaethaa whispered in knifelike tones. "The same lying voice that told me of Kane's death. Now we see the harvest of false mercy! But it's all apparent. The witch has perverted my lieutenant's soul—twisted his spirit with her sorcery—seduced him to serve the black powers of evil!"

He drew his sword and stepped toward her slowly, blade held low. "Come embrace me, witch!" he hissed. "I think this time you have overestimated my blind stupidity and your own dark glamour as well!"

Alidore leapt in front of him. "Stop, milord!" he pleaded. "She means nothing by her words—she has no sorcery!"

There was pity in Gaethaa's voice as he moved to push Alidore aside. "You're bewitched, Alidore—your reason no longer serves you. Stand back now while my blade severs her spell over you, and sends this witch back to the darkness she serves."

Resolution hardened Alidore's face as he planted himself firmly and drew his own sword. "It's not madness, milord—nor is it Rehhaile's sorcery! I recognize the truth in her words, understand the misgivings that have plagued my spirit these last months! I can't let you kill an innocent girl . . ."

"Innocent girl! She's a witch! She's lied to you! She's helped Kane strike at us from the first moment we entered Sebbei!"

". . . Nor can I permit you to burn this city just to destroy Kane!" Alidore rushed on. "Come on, Gaethaa," he begged. "Let's get out of this land of the dead! We'll return to Kamathae, raise a new army, and return with sufficient strength to destroy Kane!"

"Out of the question! Now Kane knows I intend to kill him! He'll hide where no man could find him—use his evil powers to build up defenses I could never hope to overcome! Stand aside, Alidore, and I'll forget your insane insubordination!"

"I'm sorry, milord Gaethaa," he returned slowly. "You'll kill Rehhaile and raze this city by yourself—but first you'll have to kill me!"

Sudden rage claimed Gaethaa. "Betrayal is it—and from you, Alidore! Damn you—if you stand among the forces of evil, stand against the cold light of good, then by the cold light you shall be destroyed! Get out of my way!"

"Don't force me to cross blades with you, milord!" Alidore's plea was a warning as well.

Gaethaa's face broke into a pale mask of vengeful fury. "You're a fool, Alidore!" he screamed. His sword streaked outward, all but tearing Alidore's weapon from his grip.

Alidore jumped back, blade weaving a defensive pattern. His soul was close to shattering with the conflicting emotions that raged through him. His entire universe had suddenly collapsed about him, so that now he found himself locked in deadly combat with the man for whom an hour ago he would have willingly given his life. Suddenly he was pitted against the beliefs and ideals he had sworn allegiance to all his life. Spurred out of his emotional maelstrom only by the instincts of self-preservation, he desperately parried Gaethaa's maddened attack.

It was not the state of mind to offer a chance against an opponent of Gaethaa's prowess. Rapidly, easily the Crusader wore down his guard. A sudden thrust lay open Alidore's side, and as he recoiled in pain, a glancing stroke tore off his helmet. Alidore was driven to the ground, blackness flashing through his skull, while his eyes were blinded by blood pouring from his gashed brow. A thousand miles away echoed a girl's scream.

Gaethaa surveyed his fallen lieutenant, madness still in his eyes. "I'm sorry, Alidore," he intoned with heavy regret. "You were a brother to me—a friend through many battles. Though I must kill you now to purge this evil spell that has stolen you from me, I'll always remember you as the loyal and courageous lieutenant you once were to me." He raised his sword for the *coup de grâce*. "The tales spoke of the evil curse that follows Kane—evil that destroys those who cross his twisted path. Now I understand the truth behind those legends. Good-by, Alidore—Kane has destroyed you, but die assured that you will be avenged!"

"Hell, kill him if you're going to—but don't give me credit for it. It bothers me to accept favors from a man I'm going to kill in another minute." The mocking voice grated from the street behind Gaethaa. "Or if you're embarrassed to kill a friend, let him lie there and I'll finish him after I've carved out your heart."

Gaethaa whirled to face Kane. His enemy stepped from out of the fog and smoke and casually strode toward him, sword poised. Rough bandages were bound across his ribs; others made crimson bands across his right shoulder. A murderous light shone from his blue eyes, brutal face drawn in a savage snarl.

"So the tiger has come out of hiding!" Gaethaa purred. "I had thought I'd be forced to smoke you from your lair! But now comes the final cast of dice in this game we've played, and it's only fitting that the principal players should meet at last. You've cost me every man in my command, Kane—it's for their lives you now must answer —and for the centuries of crimes that lie behind you like an accusing shadow!"

"You've achieved a fair number of atrocities in your own short career—soon to be lamented!" sneered Kane, raising his sword.

Gaethaa's silent lunge brought them together. Their swords clashed and locked, then Kane hurled the lighter man back. The knife in Gaethaa's other hand sliced empty air. Blow upon blow hammered a vicious cacophony to death. Kane's right arm was all but useless to him, but the dazzling speed of his sword arm made the loss seem minor.

"Call upon the forces of evil to aid you, Kane!" jeered Gaethaa, observing the crimson stigma of fresh blood spread over Kane's bandages. The wounds were opening, and soon his strength would waver. "Or have your dark gods left you in fear, just as evil must always flee before the invincible sword of good!"

"I serve neither gods nor fool's causes!" Kane growled. "And don't delude yourself into terming invincible principles that are meaningless except to the relative viewpoint of the beholder!" His apparent feint twisted into a sudden lunge that sliced across Gaethaa's cheek. "First blood!" he laughed.

The men struggled on in silence then, voiceless save for panting breath and animal grunts. Gaethaa was a deadly opponent—a shrewd and skillful swordsman with wiry strength driving his long frame. In addition he was relatively fresh, while Kane was fatigued and bleeding from wounds suffered in recent combat. Still his endurance did not falter before the Avenger's fanatical attack, nor did the lethal beauty of his swordplay grow strained. Relentlessly the two men slashed and thrust, parried and feinted —each confident that his attack would exhaust the other and soon bring an end to the stalemate.

Again their swords locked hilts. They strained against one another, man to man, blade to blade—a split second would see them thrown apart again! Gaethaa's dagger slipped past Kane's guard and slithered for his side. Heaving against the other blade, Kane threw Gaethaa back a step, dropping his own knife at the same instant. As Gaethaa fell away, Kane seized his left wrist in passing. Forcing the thick muscles of his injured arm to respond, Kane crushed the wrist in his grip and bent it back as his enemy lunged away. Gaethaa's dagger stabbed around to gash his arm. Then with a grating snap, the forearm bones cracked under the twisting pressure.

Gaethaa gasped and swung his sword wildly at Kane's arm, frantic to relieve the crushing agony. Kane released his grip and jerked his arm clear. At the same moment his sword flashed out at Gaethaa's unprotected trunk, before the other could recover his guard. The powerful blow clove down through Gaethaa's right shoulder, all but severing arm from trunk! Kane's reddened blade gleamed and slashed out again, catching his opponent as he spun about and sundering head from body! The head bounced twice with a hollow tolling.

Kane stood before the grotesquely strewn corpse of

Gaethaa the Crusader, sucking great gasps of air into his hammering chest. In the crisp dawn chill tiny tendrils of smoke seemed to writhe from the scarlet splashed stones, from his dripping sword, from his torn flesh. It blended with his steaming breath and vanished into the morning mist.

Shaking himself wearily, Kane frowned at Alidore's fallen form, stretched out across the deserted street, his head staining Rehhaile's skirt. Kane strode toward him purposefully.

"Don't, Kane!" Rehhaile pleaded. "Please don't kill this one! Alidore saved my life several times from those killers! Spare him now for me! Please, Kane! Alidore can't harm you now!"

Kane swayed before them, sword raised, murder lust still twisting his face. Alidore stared up at him blankly, face an expressionless mask. No move did he offer in defense or in flight; his eyes met Kane's in uncaring gaze. With a shrug Kane lowered his blade, blood fury slipping from his face—only to remain smoldering in his eyes, where its fires never slaked.

"All right, Rehhaile," he said. "I give him to you. But I doubt that your pity will be of much use to him. It seems that Gaethaa's blow knocked loose his brain inside that thick skull."

"No, Kane! It's his soul that's torn loose within him! I can heal his spirit's torment in time."

"So that's it," Kane laughed mirthlessly. "No point in asking you to come with me then, I see. Just as well. I'm leaving now, Rehhaile. I've had my fill of living among ghosts. I'm sick of morbid brooding—there's still adventure to amuse me in the world outside. Your companionship here has been interesting—soothing. I'm grateful."

"Good-by, Kane," said Rehhaile softly, turning her mind from the winter of his thoughts and spirit.

Kane muttered something she did not quite hear, then turned and stalked away down the empty streets. The ghosts of dead Demornte watched him depart. Go from

Demornte, land of the dead, world of shadows, where death has lain and life cannot linger.

Alidore stirred. Sitting up dizzily he reached for his fallen sword. With shaking hands he placed its point against his chest. His universe had toppled, pinning him in the wreckage of his unshakable beliefs, unassailable truths. What use to survive the death of his gods?

"Alidore! Don't!" screamed Rehhaile, sensing what he was about to do. "For my sake—don't! I want you to live! Together we can leave this land of the dead—we can go out into the world of life!"

"I thought I followed the cold clear light of right, of god," Alidore spoke in agony. "Instead I served the cold light of death!"

The swordpoint wavered against his chest. The soothing oblivion of death? Or try to return to life with Rehhaile? His soul was too wounded to decide.

Mirage

eath came shimmering through the afternoon heat.

In silence broken only by cursing, the battleworn band of mercenaries had fled along the dusty mountain road. Overhead the sun burned dismally, scornfully; its heat lanced through the ragged forest cover and seared the disheveled fugitives. Stumbling over scorched stones, they had plodded along in the weary desperation of flight, dust choking their panting breath and smothering them in a grimy blanket compounded of sweat and caked blood.

Half a hundred soldiers of a fallen cause. Men who had gambled their lives for the ambitious bastard brother of Chrosanthe's dainty king. But Jasseartion had proven no fool despite his laces and curious affectations; his spies, his personal army had been as meticulously efficient as his subjects foolishly loyal. In the end, his brother Talyvion had hung moaning in a tiny cage suspended from the great beams of the same throne room toward which his ambitions had lured him. Now the scattered remnants of his smashed army fled across the land, pursued by Jasseartion's tireless soldiers and vengeful subjects, a bounty on each man's head.

For Kane the bounty was great. Kane was the last of Talyvion's lieutenants still unaccounted for by Jasseartion's so very efficient servants. And although Kane had only entered into the conspiracy shortly before its downfall, his remarkable talent both for cloaked intrigue and open battle had impressed a particular enmity upon Chrosanthe's ruler, and upon his subjects as well. Even to a rebel would come full pardon and more gold than he might earn in ten years' soldiery, so promised the royal proclamation. True, Jasseartion's word had never been so inviolable as to inspire confidence among the fugitives from his well-famed justice, but it was nonetheless a most tempting proposal.

With this in mind, Kane had wrapped his face in bloody bandages, padded his belly to outsize proportions, and covered his mail with a filthy, voluminous cloak. So disguised, he had mingled with a band of fleeing refugees, hoping that neither Jasseartion's followers nor his own companions would recognize this dirty, obese foot soldier with bandaged face as the aristocratic stranger who had joined with Talyvion not long before the latter's fortunes had changed.

Then the searing summer air was filled with the sharp hiss of glinting arrows. Ambush! A detachment of Jasseartion's army had lain in hiding among the trees and the smoldering rocks that enclosed the dusty mountain trail.

Furious at having been caught in ambush along with the sheep he had hoped to masquerade among, Kane broke for cover, his right hand fumbling in the damp folds of his cloak for his sword. A deep wound from the last battle caused his left arm to be still too weak to use effectively, and although Kane was almost as dexterous with his right arm, he knew he was at a disadvantage in the chaotic fighting that enveloped him.

The king's soldiers rushed upon the stricken mercenaries simultaneously as the last arrows tore into them. Many of their number already writhing upon the burning mountain pathway, the desperate fugitives staggered to make a hopeless stand against their assailants. The first man to reach Kane he hurled back again with a crushing swordblow. Another charged past his comrade's husk and swung an axe in a glittering arc that took all of Kane's strength to turn aside. The axeman snapped backward and raised his weapon once more. Kane cursed impotently. The man would be gutted by now had Kane free use of his left arm. As he sought to face the axe, another soldier fell upon him from his left, just as the axe again swung down. Kane leapt back and caught the axe once more with his blade, frantically dodging his other foe. Twisting his blade, he slashed outward through the axeman's wrist, and as the other dropped his weapon in agony, Kane's return thrust caught him in the ribs.

A second to free the sword. Too long. The other soldier's sword was slicing for him. Kane forced his left arm into action, clumsily grappling with the sword arm that thrust for his trunk. A double wave of pain shook him as his wounded arm only partially deflected the swordblow, and the edge gashed through the heavy cloak and padding to smash against the mail beneath. Kane toppled, his powerful grip yet locked on the other's arm, pulling him to the ground along with himself, and impaling the soldier on his sword as they fell. And as he struck ground with the dying assailant atop him, an impossible weight slammed against Kane's skull. In a black wave of agony he lost consciousness, never knowing whether he had been purposefully struck, or simply kicked by some other pair of combatants.

I. The Forest by Night

His eyes opened into the cool of night. Groggily he rolled from under the soldier's corpse and sat up. Vision blurred, ground rocked with the roaring pain in his skull.

Kane bit his lip and forced himself to his knees. About him lay only the dead.

Gingerly he unwound the heavy bandages that swathed his head and ran fingers over the ache in his skull. It had been a hard blow, but the bandages and his thick red hair had effectively cushioned it. He rose to his feet and disgustedly threw off the enveloping cloak and the slashed padding beneath. His mail had stopped the swordthrust, but the force of the stroke had mashed the links painfully into his side.

A bad deal all around, mused Kane, once more cursing the poor judgment that had led him to seek to hide among the rabble rather than strike out on his own. Still, under the circumstances he had been lucky enough to escape from the collapse of the conspiracy, not to mention to survive this ambush. He looked about him, the light of the newly risen full moon casting sufficient illumination for his exceptional night vision to see clearly.

Silent. Still. Death. Cold moonlight cast over a strange panorama of white shapes strewn carelessly, hopelessly across the dark ground. Not even a hint of wind to break this frozen tableau. Black trees casting shadows—can moonlight cast shadows?—dark shapes clutching, covering the fallen. Contorted young face—had death been so dear with that slash through his belly? Perhaps the one who was asking Kane some forgotten question when the attack came. Perhaps not. The moonlight gave an unreal illumination to the scene, and faces firm and real by sunlight now seemed hollow, fantastic. Kane was not certain even that the pain in his tormented body was real.

Where am I now? he wondered, forcing thoughts into the blur of his consciousness. Nearly out of the lands claimed to be holdings of Chrosanthe—a very isolated area of the kingdom. Chrosanthians avoided this forest region, and with that in mind the fugitives had sought to escape along this route. Another bad idea, Kane reflected. Jasseartion's vengeance had ignored his subjects' dislike for this particular corner of the realm, but then Talyvion's mercenaries had earned an especial hatred for themselves during the abortive *coup d'état*.

The trees shimmered crazily when Kane gained his feet. At least the cool night air soothed where the scourging sun had lent additional agony to each move. Can't stay here, Kane realized. The soldiers would return for their dead with morning—certainly to loot the corpses. Only nightfall and their dread of the region had kept them from this ritual.

The ghouls. That was it. Kane remembered that the Chrosanthians had fought an uncommonly vicious civil war some two centuries previous. This region had been exceptionally torn apart by the struggle, with the victorious faction relentlessly slaughtering the great lords together with their tenants. Jasseartion's ancestors' handiwork. The area had never been repopulated—several strange legends regarding the fate of those victors who had attempted to establish themselves upon the unburied bones of their luckless predecessors. And that ancient carnage had attracted packs of ghouls to the area—or perhaps made ghouls of the few starving survivors, Kane mused. Yes, every reason to get away from this place as quickly as possible. Damn! For a horse of any description!

Wearily Kane recovered his fallen sword and limped away among the white shapes patterned across the dark ground, his feet slipping occasionally upon still darker patches. Wincing, he tossed his head, but the blur would not leave his vision. A large rock beneath the trees was enticing, and Kane stumbled to its rest, half reclining as upon one of the many thrones that fortune had cast him over the years, and later stolen again from his embrace. Thoem! So many long years! Could any man bear their weight! For a moment a kaleidoscope of bitter memories tumbled through the pain of his mind, doomed centuries of wandering, an outcast from mankind.

Brooding at a time when flight should be his sole concern. Delirium. The nightscape wavered in cadence to the throbbing within his skull, a hoarse roaring that at times engulfed him altogether. And Kane knew he had been struck harder than he had earlier realized. A concussion maybe. Just beautiful! By daylight Jasseartion's soldiers would return to find him sitting here mindlessly raving of fallen, forgotten empires.

His throat was thick with thirst, and he wondered if he might find some wine somewhere among the slain. That was stupid; the mercenaries had had little enough water among them. Wine tastes very good though, especially the white wine they brew in Latroxia. Although many consider it too sour. And wine is good to bathe wounds in, due to the purifying natures of the engendered sting. Salt water reacts similarly, but is useless for drinking purposes. A pity the oceans didn't flow with wine. Many shipwrecked sailors would have applauded this innovation, although it would probably disturb the fish. Once I ate an octopus pickled in wine. Subtle taste, but on the whole an unfortunate meal.

An ocean of wine lifted Kane in its tentacled arms, bobbing him up and down rhythmically, while about him the corpses of these pickled sailors swirled atop the purple waves, and octopi crept from their seaweed lairs to reach out cautiously.

Sound. Sharp snap. Reflexes cutting through the delirium. Startled into a semblance of alertness, Kane's cold blue eyes searched the battleground suspiciously.

Again cracked the sound, and Kane recognized it this time. It was a harsh, splintering snap such as an animal makes in crunching the marrow bones of its prey.

Now he could distinguish the ghoul. Crouched over its meal on the dark forest road, its dead-white body had resembled one of the corpses upon which it fed. And from the silent trees were slipping other pale, misshapen creatures, their stooped and twisted bodies a sick parody of the human form. So the legends had not lied.

Ghouls normally would not attack an armed man, Kane knew, but their numbers and his disabled state might prove too tempting. Besides, their hunger was apparent—ghouls abhor freshly killed flesh much the same as many men have little appetite for raw meat.

Carefully Kane limped back into the trees. The ghouls had interest only for the rich feast spread before them, hunger overruling their normal caution. A stone grated under his boot, and Kane froze to look about him apprehensively. A few pairs of dead, pale, almost luminous eyes stared in his direction, but none of the creatures seemed moved to investigate. Satisfied that he had not been detected, Kane slipped deeper into the shadows of the forest, and once the cover of trees and jutting rock outcrops shielded him altogether, he hurried away from this moonlit scene of horror.

It was Kane's intention to skirt the battlefield through the forest and then to pick up the mountain road once more. With luck he could put quite a few miles behind him by dawn, and during the daylight rest hidden within the forest. But the road twisted and meandered in a manner unknown to Kane—and as he wandered through the trees attempting to recover his trail, over his mind again crept tendrils of delirium, only momentarily pushed back by shock of immediate danger. An hour passed and Kane was not only utterly lost, but beyond caring as well.

Beneath his boots the earth pitched and yawed, but his sea-legs were up to treading any deck, and Kane strode recklessly into the storm, occasionally staggering against a mast for support. Then the trees whirled maddeningly about him, ensnared like himself in some cosmic vortex. Caves underneath the limestone shelves yawned at him, gaping caverns that snapped thunderously, some emitting rank, dismal breath. Under the staring eye of the moon danced thousands of colossal phantoms, tormenting the fool who stumbled through their eldritch circles. Long claws reached for his face, gnarled talons lashed out to knock him sprawling again and again. Faces of those long dead smirked at him from the blackness—sneering visages of ancient enemies, soft faces of old mistresses that abruptly grew stark with age. A spinning phantasmagoria of mocking smiles, and for half of them Kane could not even remember their names.

Eventually he found himself staggering through a ruined village. At least it seemed so—these crumbling walls remained solid to his touch, while other figures of his tortured mind faded mistlike into the darkness. He smashed a fist against the stones and studied the pain. Yes, it must be real then. An abandoned village, with vine-covered stone walls still carrying the charred signature of forgotten fire and pillage. All in ruins now—roofless dwellings, fallen walls—gutted structures whose gloomily gaping windows and doorways made them appear as monolithic skulls to Kane's fevered mind.

Desolation was all pervasive. Only the white shadow of half-hidden bones served evidence of former human habitation—at least Kane thought he could see these scattered relics discarded among the other debris. Had it not been for curious, narrow paths weaving through the rank underbrush, Kane would have believed no living creature had passed through this dismal artifact of ancient strife in many years.

Full moon silhouetted the deserted castle looming darkly upon the steep hill that overlooked its empty village. In that final battle the castle had fallen alongside the village which had paid it tribute in return for an inadequate protection. A fantastic mass of black stones piled against the moonlight, the crumbling fortress impressed Kane with an even more consuming sense of desolation than did these ruins which lay before its not quite unassailable height.

"There stands your funeral monument!" laughed Kane, pointing to the castle, and the empty windows winked agreement. "By the gods, a truly epic tombstone! Right?" The overgrown walls nodded.

Sharp, knifing pain from his wounds; dull, numbing agony of fatigue. Too much. A bed of moss among toppled stones was too tempting. Gratefully Kane dropped onto its cushion. To hell with what's-his-name's soldiers. A short rest was paramount, and no one would find him here.

Lolling his head upon the stones, Kane breathed in fitful gasps, his mind trapped in a black delirium somewhere between waking and dreaming. After a while he saw the destroyed village return once more to its old state. Gutted ruins blossomed into busy shops and bright houses; the weed grown paths became wide streets. Throughout this reborn village hurried its townspeople, most of them occupied with their own business and paying no attention to the stranger who reclined in their midst on a swaying litter of velvet.

But there were some who noticed the interloper. These few gathered about him and gazed at Kane with pale, hungry eyes. And even though Kane half realized that these were ghouls who surrounded him now, it mattered nothing.

Cautiously, like vultures fluttering down upon a dying lion, the ghouls slunk ever closer to Kane. Foul spittle hung from rotten yellow fangs as they reached with anxious paws for their indifferent prey.

"Back!" Her voice lashed them into fearful obedience. "All right, damn you! Get back, I said!" They tumbled backward before her anger.

For a fleeting instant full consciousness returned to Kane. In that dreadful interval he saw before him half a dozen pallid, twisted shapes cowering away from him, driven back by the awful fury of a girl whose strange beauty rivalled that of any his mind could recall.

Only for a startled second did he regain his senses; then came total oblivion. And as he sank into its welcome release, there echoed her joyous words: "This one shall be mine!"

II. Beyond the Forest

"How many days exactly?"

The elderly servant meticulously added five drops of yellow fluid to the wine goblet before answering. "Oh, three days, four days, something like that." Gently he stirred the elixir, taking care not to spatter his extravagant livery. "What does it matter?"

Kane's temper seethed within him. "I really would like to know how long I've been unconscious," he said with great patience.

"Mmm?" The servant handed him the goblet. Kane's hand shook somewhat as he accepted it, and a few drops flicked upon the rich fur pelts that covered his bed. A slight frown lined his attendant's lean face. "How long indeed. That's original. Trust a fool to come up with a line like 'Where am I?' or 'How long have I been like this?' every damn time."

"Yeah, sure! That's another question I'd like answered," Kane growled, as he sipped the tonic. It burned his throat, without totally masking a nauseously sweet undertaste. Kane paused in alarm, then reflected that his hosts could easily have killed him while in coma, and he gulped the rest of the mixture. "The last thing I remember was . . ." He groped for memory. "I seem to remember lying in a ruined village in the moonlight. There were ghouls too. A pack of them closing in on me as I lay there. Someone scattered them just as I blacked out for keeps. A woman, I think."

The steward laughed dryly. "That must have been some knock on the head, stranger! You were down in the deserted village, true enough. But it was just a few mangy thieves that my mistress chased off when they found you. Lucky for you she and her men were late in returning from the hunt. Beat up as you were, you wouldn't have lasted the night in the open." He accepted the empty goblet and gingerly placed the delicate vessel on a silver tray.

Kane shrugged and sat up. The elixir was potent. Already his head felt clearer. "So where am I now?" he asked.

"Why in Altbur Keep!" laughed the steward. "Didn't you see the castle as you came up?"

"The only 'castle' I can recall passing near," mused Kane with a frown, "was an empty heap of mossy stones atop the hill above the village."

"Heap of mossy stones?! Does this place really look like that to you, now?" The steward's airy gesture included the rich tapestries of the walls, the lavish furnishings of the room. "Well, I'll grant you maybe Altbur isn't as magnificent as in my ancestors' days, but still 'a heap of mossy stones'? Really!" He chuckled. "Jasseartion's boys must have really given you a knock on that thick skull!"

Kane's eyes flashed dangerously, but the servant only laughed again. "Oh, thought we couldn't guess who you were then? Seriously, how stupid do you take us to be! Sure we know about that ambush. Oh, don't get edgy now. We're no friends of Jasseartion—I promise you that! No sir, my mistress is surely no friend of that line of opportunistic bandits! Not quite! His ancestors ravaged this area, you know. No friends here, you can be certain! My mistress even took you under her protection out of spite. Just thank your gods that she didn't mistake you for one of Jasseartion's soldiers!"

"Who is your mistress? And when can I offer my gratitude for her protection?" Kane questioned.

"Her name is Naichoryss, if that means anything to you. And she'll accept your courtesy when the time comes. Until then just think about regaining your strength—although you seem to be doing that uncommonly fast, as it is." He stiffly recovered his tray and stepped for the door.

Kane called after him: "And how about you, steward? Do you have a name?"

"Now I haven't asked yours," was the reply.

Kane bit his lip in annoyance and swung his feet to the floor.

III. Altbur Keep

If you looked just so, Kane decided, you could almost see where the summer heat faded out against the chill of Altbur Keep. Maybe just a trick of the fading sunlight, but there was almost a perceptible aura formed where shimmer was blotted into haze. He shivered on his perch atop the battlements and drew his cloak more closely about him. His own clothes had vanished along with his weapons, he had discovered on regaining consciousness, but his still unseen hostess had given him far better apparel in their place.

No, he had no complaints in regard to his treatment. Superb apartments, excellent food and drink, and a staff of servants who gave him utmost attention. But still, his weapons had not been left him. And although he was free to roam the fortress at will, the gates of Altbur Keep were politely, emphatically locked to him. Well, if you were a prisoner, this was the way to do it.

Kane leaned out recklessly from the battlement and considered the castle walls. A sheer drop and easily killing height. Still there were several promising spots which should offer enough concealment. A matter of securing sufficient rope then. And no one actually guarded him, although Kane was aware that there were few times when someone was not unobtrusively going about his own business from a spot where an eye could be kept on the guest's movements. At the moment, in the shadow of a nearby watchtower a kitchen maid was in close embrace with a disturbingly grubby stable hand.

All in all a not overly difficult place to slip out of, if need arose; Kane had considerable confidence in his ability here. And maybe he was too uneasy—"paranoid" in the language of an obscure treatise he had read through long ago. His life had been saved quite likely, his treatment here was first rate, and it was essential that he have a safe place to hide until he was ready to escape Chrosanthe. Some caution in taking in a strange mercenary was altogether natural. And there had been no difficult questions to answer.

Yet Kane continued to be uneasy, and he had lived far too long to discount the forebodings of his inner mind. Of course he had little way of knowing just how much of what he had seen in his delirium had been real. From the castle the village looked forlorn, deserted—but not the sinister tangle of ruins seen that night. Altbur Keep seemed a bit empty and forgotten by the world—again it certainly was not the ruined fortress Kane had envisioned it to be. Should it be here at all though—in a region ill famed and by common knowledge laid waste for two centuries? Kane knew it was not extraordinary to find the dying embers of a once proud and glorious family that continued to dwell amidst the ruins of their ancient power and grandeur.

Other things lived in ruins too.

Silence. Chill. Events within the castle somehow frozen

186

moments of time, disremembered fragments of a dream strangely caught up again. And somewhere just beyond the power of recognition a hint of mustiness—flawing the representation as a mirror image tarnished with antiquity. Vague hints that in some manner the world of Altbur Keep was but a mirage.

Kane sensed it as he walked through its hallways. To be sure it was nothing concrete. Perhaps only for a moment a shadow would seem out of place, or a detail of a tapestry subtly altered. In the servants Kane thought it was most apparent. Almost as if they were actors in a grotesque play. To perfection did each one perform his role; no detail, no minor touch had been neglected in the characterization. Kane scowled at the impassioned couple in the shadows and wondered how often the scene had been rehearsed. Perfect servants, yet it seemed a perfection born of repetition. Polished as the hundredth performance of a popular drama—equally as brittle and unreal. Still there was nothing Kane could pin down to precision.

He wondered if the performance continued as he passed from one particular area to another, or whether the players called a break without their audience.

And his hostess. The mistress of Altbur Keep. Naichoryss. Where was she then? His questions received only politely noncommittal answers from her servants. Naichoryss. Fabrication? A character held in reserve for later in the drama? Or was she the author of the masquerade, who remained behind the curtains to watch the audience response? Naichoryss. Mistress of Altbur Keep, or Mistress of the Mirage?

Kane slid from the parapet. It was time he found out.

IV. Mistress of Altbur Keep

"This way, sir, if you please."

Kane turned to discover his acquaintance, the steward, had slipped up behind him unnoticed. That was a nice touch: seen and not heard. Withered creep was lurking behind a tapestry doubtless. Bastard could probably slide under a fresco. "This way?"

"Certainly. My mistress," he prompted. "Naichoryss has had prepared a small dinner in her chambers. She asks that you join her now."

That simple then. "So she's at last decided to have a look at her discovery."

The steward shrugged and quoted:

A woman's mind, friend Eistenallis,
Is a mystery;
Whose unfathomable depths,
Rival the uncharted currents of a god's whimsey.

"Curious that your quotation is that of Halmonis as he led Eistenallis to a rendezvous from which the courtier failed to return," remarked Kane, as he followed his guide.

"Ah! You know the work of Ganbromi then? A literate mercenary!"

"I knew Ganbromi," Kane muttered, hoping he would not provoke a further outburst of erudition from the supercilious prig.

"Here we are then," the steward concluded and rapped against a brassbound door. Seeming to hear acknowledgment from within, he swung it open and stepped aside, his expression correctly impassive.

Stepping within, Kane was received by two smiling maids dressed in identical garments of soft leather and interlocking brass rings. Silently they opened a second door and invited him to enter.

She rose from her couch to greet him as he pushed through the curtained entrance; her red lips parted, secretly smiling upon tiny white teeth. "I am Naichoryss." Her voice came clear and cold—distant as in a dream. "I welcome you to Altbur Keep." A long white arm stirred from the black folds of her gown and curved towards a couch across the low table from her own. "Please be seated now, and tell me of yourself. It is so seldom that I receive visitors anymore." A slight gesture to her maids,

188

then she returned to her couch with the quiet grace of a shadow.

Kane easily stretched his massive frame upon the indicated couch, watching as the serving maid filled his chalice with wine as clear and red as the rubies of the vessel's rim.

"My name is Kane," he began. There seemed no point in subterfuge under the circumstances, and he was too proud to be taken as a common mercenary amidst such splendour.

Naichoryss smiled. Thin lips poised over the red wine, dark eyes reflected its crimson, wave on wave of long black tresses wreathed a pale, delicate face, features finely chiseled. A study of eerie beauty, cold and aloof as an exquisitely carven masterpiece of gemset ivory and jet.

"Kane." Her lips caressed the sound. "A cruel name, I think. Not a common one." The light in her eyes was a mocking glitter. And Kane knew that Naichoryss had been aware all along of his identity.

Kane was not a man easily mistaken for another. His red hair and fair complexion, his powerful bearlike frame set him apart from the native Chrosanthians in a region where racial features leaned to dark hair and lean wiriness. And his rather coarse features and huge sinewed hands did not make him too exceptional from the mercenaries displaced from the cold lands far to the south. It was his eyes that branded him as an outsider. No man looked into Kane's eyes and forgot them. Cold blue eyes in which lurked the wild gleam of insanity, hellish fires of crazed destruction and bloodshed. The look of death. Eyes of a born killer. The Mark of Kane.

Kane returned his hostess's amused scrutiny with assumed indifference. "Since it's obvious that even here in Altbur Keep the details are commonly known regarding Jasseartion's quarrel with his lamented half-brother Talyvion, I won't bore you with stale news. As you can understand, it was urgent that I should outdistance Jasseartion's malice as rapidly as feasible. However, I was a little slow. Perhaps an underestimation of the flit's thoroughness, but it is startling to discover steel inside a violet. At any rate, his soldiers didn't recognize me, left me for dead, and I blundered about the forest out of my head until you chanced to find me." He went on to express gratitude for her protection and hospitality.

Her laughter was a symphony of silver flutes and bells; its sound light and merry, but underneath lay a shivery note. "So Kane is the gifted courtier that ladies praise him to be! To turn your own comment, how unusual to find polished graces disguised behind such brutal strength! But then I discover paradoxes at every turn with you, Kane! And what vitality! In a matter of days you appear altogether recovered from wounds that should have left you dead or disabled for weeks! I'm delighted now that I had you spared that night in my village!"

"My mind is a blank for that time, I'm afraid," Kane broke in. "Your excellent steward mentioned that there were bandits . . ."

Naichoryss's slender hand waved dismissal. "Bandits? Hardly! A few miserable sneakthieves and poachers who would have slit your throat for your boots. They fled like rats when my hunters and I rode by.

"Please, though! All these formal expressions of introtion and gratitude are so boring! And existence here in Altbur Keep is dull enough without that. You must tell me now of all the fascinating things going on in the outside world, or I'll spend the whole night yawning. Tell me of those exotic lands your wanderings must have led you through. Dispel my boredom, and you'll remain here until Jasseartion grows old and forgetful!"

The arrangement seemed satisfactory to Kane. The role of dinner partner was one in which he had enjoyed great experience, and an evening of anecdotes would keep his hostess from learning more about her guest than Kane felt she should know. So while Naichoryss's maids bore tray after tray of delicacies across the room, silent but for the jingle of their brass ringlets, Kane entertained the strange mistress of Altbur Keep with curious tales of old battles and intrigue in lands that were almost fabled.

The wine was of ancient vintage; Kane savored its rare and delicate taste with enthusiasm, and watched with high approval as the attentive maid kept his chalice brimming.

His mind seemed inflamed with its potency as he talked—so much so that he wondered if the wine contained some subtle drug. Yet his hostess was served from the same vessels, although she both ate and drank only sparingly.

And when the serving girls had taken away the last course and only the wine remained, Naichoryss rose to her feet and beckoned him toward the open balcony. Kane followed her onto the moonlit stones, his movements somewhat heavy from the wine and the magic of her beauty. For a moment they leaned in silence against the parapet, looking out over the valley where cold moonlight etched the ruined village in silver and black. Only a faint wind stirred, lightly rippling her raven hair with its chill breath, so cold, so empty for a summer's night.

Moonlight shone through her smoky gown, making almost luminescent the white skin it half veiled. Kane's throat grew tight with emotion, and his senses grew even more tumultuous. Here was beauty which drew him with a fascination more compelling than any he had yet experienced.

"Aren't you cold?" he began lamely, not trusting himself to an opening less conventional.

Naichoryss turned to him, only just beyond his arm's reach. "Cold? Yes. Yes, I am cold. Not from the night though. It's a far, far deeper cold that I know—one that can be warmed only . . ."

The moonlight glowed on her sharp white teeth, while the hunger of her eyes matched the invitation of her smile. "I think perhaps you can warm the cold that torments me."

Kane reached then to take her in his arms, but his movements were clumsy and she slipped through his grasp with secret laughter. Dumbly he stared at her, entranced hopelessly as an adolescent bumpkin in the hands of a talented courtesan. Where his fingers had brushed across her flesh they stung as if scorched by ice.

"Not so impetuous, my rough warrior!" she laughed. "This is a moment to be savored! With an eternity of nights before us, would you fall on me like a rutting bear?"

With extreme annoyance Kane fought to control himself. What was this woman's witchery, that it left him all

191

the grace of a horny plowhand? But the desire to possess this strange creature overwhelmed every attempt to restore sophistication to his usually polished manner.

Naichoryss gathered into her arms a lyre-like instrument, cradling it to her breast as she swayed mockingly a few paces from him. "A moment to be savored," she intoned huskily. "Fully. To the last glistening droplet. Shall I sing for you, Kane? Can you contain all that vitality for yet a few moments more?"

His hand shook as he raised the chalice to his lips, and though he did not trust himself to speak, Kane's eyes blazed with the desire that racked his soul.

Almost pensively her fingers slipped across the lyre strings, although Kane sensed that her casualness was altogether assumed. He thought of the seeming disinterest exhibited by a cat when it plays with its prey.

A tune caught her whimsy and she hummed to herself there in the moonlight. And from the moon and the cold and the loneliness and the night itself she wove the fabric of her song.

Come to me, my lover, join me here in the night,
In the moon's cold, clear light, stand before me,
And upon my altar of cold stone, offer to me your soul.
Touch my hand, my lover, feel my flesh like ice—
Rest your head upon my breast; it is a pillow of soft snow.
Caress my lips, my lover, taste my frozen breath—
Look deep into my eyes; they hold the chill of night.
Then let me take you in my cold embrace,
Come with me to my world beyond all pain;
And with my kiss, then shall you know,
That love's purest expression
Is in death, is in death.

With languid movement Naichoryss laid aside her lyre and stretched herself. Kane stared at her in utter entrancement. "There! So silent, Kane? I hope my song didn't lull you to sleep." She glided away from him, out of the moonlight and into the broken shadow of her bedchamber.

Kane followed her into the room; his every muscle stiff with tension, his mind in a delirium of wild emotion. "Naichoryss," he whispered hoarsely.

But she put a finger to her lips, and he was silent again. She faced him there beside her bed, and her dark eyes shone with her hunger for him. Then her slim fingers brushed the fastenings of her robe and it fell away from her like mist. A great band of moonlight framed her in the darkness, bathing every curve of her perfect beauty with new sorcery.

"Do you desire me, Kane?" she asked, laughter now vanished from her voice.

"You know I do!" he answered needlessly.

"And do you give yourself to me now, body and soul, for all the nights of eternity?" Was there still a hint of mockery in her eyes?

And even though Kane had now begun to understand the fate to which he was committing himself, he could not hold back his reply: "I give myself to you."

A flash of wild triumph crossed her face then, and she opened her arms to him. "Come to me now!" she cried joyously.

Kane crushed her in his powerful arms, melting her lithe body against his strength. Deeply they kissed, and the unholy chill of her lips seared the fire of his own. Almost unnoticed he felt the sudden thrust of her sharp fangs locking into position.

With surprising strength her hands tore through the fabric of his shirt, ripping it away from his throat and chest.

He watched dizzily as Naichoryss ended her branding kiss and settled back upon the furs of her bed. Feverishly Kane tossed aside the rest of his clothing, noticing even in his haste the long scratches her nails had slashed across his chest. Her fangs glinted evilly in the moonlight, quite obvious now, but Kane was beyond concern at this point.

Her cold arms pulled him down to her, and they entwined in an embrace of black ecstasy. Kane shuddered as wave upon wave of unendurable pleasure broke over him, and his sensations swirled in an impossible blend of flame and ice, revulsion and delight. He made no protest even when Naichoryss twisted over atop him and broke their kiss to trail her icy lips lower across his body.

When her fangs finally bit into his throat, it was as if the fires within him were suddenly unleashed. An unspeakable vortex of pain and ecstasy engulfed Kane, drowning him as he spun helplessly into its blackness.

V. Into the Mirage

Time became meaningless to him. It was as if all existence had become one endless night. Kane no longer knew the sun, although whether this was because he lay unconscious during the daylight hours, or whether time itself had ceased to move for them, he could not tell.

Reality consisted only of their nights together, and even then Kane could never remember how many times they had lain in dark embrace.

He would awaken. Outside there would still be darkness. Sometimes Kane would feel strong enough to walk about Naichoryss's chambers; other times he felt too weak to do more than drag himself far enough to reach the small dinner of wine and flesh that was set out for him. No sign did he ever see of the castle's servants, although he never ventured beyond her chambers to search. He even lacked the strength or curiosity to determine whether the door was locked; the possibility of escape simply did not occur to him.

When he looked at his reflected face in a mirror, Kane saw how haggard and gaunt he had grown, yet he felt no alarm. Without interest he contemplated the two close set wounds which made sullen red swellings upon the white flesh of his throat.

His only emotion was that of expectation—of anticipation for the disclosure of strange mysteries and secret pleasures for centuries denied to him. It was as if after an endless period of frustrated yearning, he were to have his every longing now fulfilled—at last to be free to embark

194

upon an eternally desired journey. In a delirium Kane waited there, too weak in spirit and body to feel concern, waiting for death.

She came to him always. Sometimes through the door, sometimes she just seemed to be in the chamber.

In mock concern Naichoryss would comment upon his weakness, insist that he take nourishment, drive him out of his lassitude. Always Kane made the effort to please the mistress of Altbur Keep, drawing failing strength from some hidden reservoirs within him. They would talk together, or Naichoryss might sing. But each time it would end in the same manner. Together they would make love. And when Kane lay spent and exhausted to the point of fainting, he would once more feel the searing kiss of her lips on his throat and know the pain of her hunger— that would drive him once again into darkness.

Sometimes Naichoryss would talk to him about herself, about her plans for him. For the vampire was certain of her prey now, and she knew that knowledge of his fate could not change Kane's powerlessness to escape her spell.

She told him of the fall of Altbur Keep two centuries before in the civil wars of that period, told Kane of how the victors had slaughtered all those within village and castle. On this same bed she had suffered the lust of the victorious troops, until someone had seen fit to strangle her. But violence and hatred were forces too powerful to vanish without legacy. Thus it happened that the mistress of the fallen stranglehold had drawn strength from the curses and the frustrated vengeance of a thousand slain—had become the focus of energies stronger than death itself. At night she had roamed the shadows of her plundered domain, and the light of dawn had exposed many a bloodless corpse to mark her unholy revenge. And eventually it was terror that drove all men from the region, leaving Naichoryss mistress only of ghoul-haunted ruins.

Many years had passed. The grandchildren of those on whom she sought revenge grew old and died; the war itself became a hazy fragment of history, its factions and issues now confused even by scholars. The stones of Altbur Keep grew weathered and mossy; most of the ghouls moved on to more propitious lands. Still Naichoryss remained to haunt the forgotten ruins of her realm, preying only upon the animals of the forests or a rare stranger who unwittingly passed through.

It was lonely. Only the undead can know all the loneliness of death without the final rest of the grave.

When she drove off the ghouls that had discovered Kane, Naichoryss had known at once what she would do. Bringing him back to her castle, she had raised Altbur Keep from the dust of centuries to all its former glory. Carefully she had nurtured her treasure while Kane regained his strength. Painstakingly had she ensnared him in her spell. And when she considered him fully recovered, Naichoryss had taken him into her embrace to feed upon his immense vitality.

But death was not to be Kane's fate, this Naichoryss promised. Kane's destiny was to become her eternal consort—to join Nairchoryss in the shadow realm of the undead! Slowly therefore was she draining life from him, carefully preparing Kane so that he might in death become as she—a creature of the night. And then together they would be rulers of this ghoul-haunted wilderness—together they would share the dark and unthinkable pleasures of the undead!

One night it happened that upon awakening Kane was too weak to leave the bed. He lay there, breathing in shallow gasps, his flesh pale and sunken, waiting for her to come to him once more.

Her dark eyes lit with exultation when she found him that last night. "At last!" Naichoryss's cry was as joyous as a bride's on her wedding night. "I had almost begun to believe your vitality an unquenchable spark!"

A note of tenderness crept into her voice then. "This is to be our final night like this, Kane beloved. Only for this last time must you know the pain of mortality—for when you next awaken it will not be from mortal sleep, but the sweet dreamlessness of death. And when you arise from death—then we shall at last be truly together! You and I, Kane—together for eternity!"

Kane smiled almost wistfully as she bent over him. Weakly he tried to speak, but her lips sealed his in silence.

Deeper and deeper burned her kiss. Needles of ice tore at every nerve of Kane's body, chilling his soul with unearthly cold. Cosmic emptiness was reaching through the darkness, engulfing him. Ecstasy and agony together assaulted and overwhelmed his failing senses, the two extremes simultaneously tearing him apart then fusing together to create an intolerable sensation.

Her raven black hair was tangled about his face and smothering him. The weight of her cold body was forcing the wind from his chest. Her insatiable lips were sucking the very life breath from his lungs. He could no longer breathe. He was falling . . .

VI. Return

Blackness. Kane drifted endlessly through infinite darkness. Not merely absence of light, but nonexistence of everything—matter, energy, time. Floating in the cosmic gulf between life and death.

Somehow through the darkness there extended a thread, a delicate web of substance that would not permit him to drift outward across the infinite void. A miniscule pull, it exerted upon him across the eons, its force weak and almost extinguished, yet too elemental to flicker away altogether. Life made one final attempt to reach Kane, relentlessly demanding expression of its most primeval instinct.

Centuries past, Kane had left the darkness of the womb, a squirming red creature whose first act of life was to draw squawling breath. And now through cosmic darkness this same instinct summoned him forth.

Kane gasped and opened his eyes. Hard stone walls held him tightly and his eyes saw only more darkness. The air in his lungs was stale and foul with century-old dust. Hoarsely he cried out, throwing his arms and legs in blind panic against the wall that pressed upon him. For an instant it seemed he had not the strength to break free, but then every primitive instinct within him howled in fear and loathing, driving his failing limbs onward with strength that surged forth from stores dormant since birth.

The wall gave under his straining heave and toppled away from him. Gibbering insanity only a breath away, Kane shot bolt upright in his sarcophagus and gulped down the cool, musty air of the sepulchre.

Kane sat there in the darkness, slowly breathing in the tomb air. As life streamed through his shivering body, his mind once more began to function clearly, rationally—freed from the enchantment that had so long imprisoned it.

He could see somewhat now, for the darkness of the sepulchre was daylight after the blackness that had so nearly claimed him. Kane decided that he must be in the family crypt that lay beneath Altbur Keep, for in the gloom he could discern the cobweb-hung shapes of other stone coffins, some reposing in niches of the wall, others set like his upon pedestals above the floor. With an effort Kane hoisted himself out from the confines of his sarcophagus and fell to the floor. Somehow he found the curiosity to wonder what had happened to the previous tenant, as he lurched across the dustladen stones. His feet encountered a stairway, which he stumbled his way up, following wan threads of sunlight that stole past the door to the crypt. Throwing his shoulder to this door, Kane forced it grudgingly open and staggered through the opening.

The hallway in which he stood was strewn with debris, and late afternoon sunlight shone brightly through collapsed ceiling at its far end. Painfully Kane dragged himself along the corridor to stand in wonder among the ruins to which it led him.

Altbur Keep was a deserted ruin. As Kane wandered through its silent hallways he met only desolation. No servants greeted him; only bats dwelled here now, along with certain wise-faced rats that scurried into hiding at his approach. The fortress walls still loomed solid upon the hilltop, although in places parts of the roof had given way. Signs of the castle's fall could still be seen in sundered gates and a few blackened walls where fires had sprung up. Many of its rich furnishings had been carried away by looters, although Kane encountered numerous mounds of rotting cloth and wood that indicated the tapestries and furniture of Altbur Keep's ancient magnificence. His own clothing was still the battle worn gear he had had with him, now showing signs of further abuse.

A bit of metal caught the sunlight, and Kane was pleased to discover his weapons stashed in a corner of one of the empty storerooms. Grimly he buckled on the battered sword and dirk, then made his way to the chambers of Naichoryss.

He paused often to regain his strength. His limbs shook and every cell of his body ached with numbing weakness. Nevertheless Kane felt a good deal stronger now than he had for a long while—shaken free of Naichoryss's spell, he ignored the dizziness and fatigue and willed his tortured frame to walk.

The sun was setting when Kane reeled into Naichoryss's chambers. Here too, all lay in dust and decay; yet there was a difference. The floors were not littered with trash and broken debris; here it seemed that the disorder left by the looters had been cleaned away and the room restored to a semblance of its old state. The walls still displayed tattered hangings, moldering rugs covered the stones, furniture reposed in proper order, vases and items that a woman treasures lay within dusty cobweb cocoons about the room. It was as though a loving hand carefully composed these chambers before their centuries of rest.

Kane warily examined the shadow haunted rooms, but no sign of life met his scrutiny. Much of her chambers was as he remembered, aside from the erosion of time—although he noted that many of the costly items which he had seen while he lay here were not present in this tableau. Her bed was still there, but Naichoryss did not lie upon its moldering furnishings as Kane had expected. For that matter, the dust that blanketed it appeared to be undisturbed. He frowned in consternation. Kane had supposed that the vampire would have chosen the bed upon which she had been slain as her resting place during the hours of daylight. This error was serious; he had wanted to confront Naichoryss once more—this time at his own advantage.

From the balcony Kane saw that twilight was growing deeper. He swore in frustrated anger then, realizing that Naichoryss had doubtless laid his all but lifeless body near her own in the castle crypt. And now he knew that his chances were slim of discovering her resting place before darkness called Naichoryss forth. Wearily he stumbled back into the darkening hallway, intent on reaching the crypt while Altbur's mistress yet slumbered.

He lacked the strength to win a race with nightfall. In a patch of light from the newly risen moon, Naichoryss stood awaiting him. Her beauty had not faded under that rough caress of time which had separated Altbur Keep of her spell from the ruin in which they now met. At least that unearthly beauty was not a trick of the mirage, Kane mused.

Her hungry lips smiled as she held out her white arms in welcome. "So I find you already up and about, Kane. Were you so eager to taste your new existence that you had to rush off without me? Perhaps . . ."

Her smile melted with distress then as Kane reached her. "Something's wrong!" she cried in horror. "You're still alive! You're not . . ."

"Yes, something is very wrong!' Kane smiled mirthlessly. "Despite your best efforts to the contrary, there's some little life left within me! Enough to recognize the world of the living once again! Enough so that your sweet invitation to join you in the crypts of Altbur Keep no longer tempts me!"

Her cameo face was a mask of dismay. "I don't understand! It's not possible that a mortal could stand living before me after he has known my kiss! Drop by drop I had taken from you your vitality. You were too weak then to resist last night as I sucked from your lips the very essence of your life force. It seemed that your body was already growing cold in my arms when I carried you to the crypt before dawn."

Naichoryss broke off pensively. "I laid you in the coffin beside my own. Those two had been set aside so long ago for myself and for the husband whom I was never to meet."

Kane sank onto a window ledge and gazed upon the vampire with brooding eyes, his thoughts hidden beyond their blue depths.

Naichoryss stood in silent contemplation, studying him. Somewhere in the shadows sounded the beat of velvet wings, while in the corner a rat rustled cautiously through dry leaves.

"I think I know now," she mused. "You recovered from your wounds so fast—even the scars are fading. Then it seemed that I would never sap your life force, though I drank of it each night. It was unnatural for a human body to replenish its lifeblood so rapidly. And only an extraordinary vitality could break the spell of my death kiss and fight its way back from the abyss of eternal night.

"The night spirits speak at times of one who bears the name of Kane. One of the first men, they say he is—a man cursed by the gods because he rose in rebellion against his creator, because he was first to bring violence and death to the paradise in which primeval man was nurtured. This Kane was given the curse of immortality— doomed to wander the earth for eternity, never to know peace, but to bring evil and destruction wherever he walked—until he might himself be destroyed by the violence that he had been first to give expression. That men might know him for what he is, Kane was marked with eyes of a killer."

Awe was in her voice. "An immortal body would be quick to heal any wounds that were not immediately fatal. Nor would it show age. Probably it would maintain itself in the exact condition it had known when the curse was pronounced.

"There was something unnatural in you, Kane—I had sensed it all along, but I had chosen to ignore it in my dreams for us. Now I see I was a fool to discount the whispers of the night winds."

Kane shrugged, still silently brooding.

Desperation edged her voice. "Stay with me, Kane beloved!" Naichoryss appealed. "You have only to cease this pointless resistence and surrender to my kiss! Please don't fight to break my enchantment again! Surrender to me just this last time, and then you will awaken to be my lover, my master, for eternity! I swear to you, we shall be lord and lady of Altbur Keep! We shall shall reign together here until the stars fall spinning into the sea of night! Our love—together in a world without age, without pain!

"Do these ruins oppress you now? Then gaze upon their sublime tranquility through the eyes of the undead! Did you prefer Altbur Keep in its former splendor? Our spells will restore it to all the magnificence in which you have lived these past days! If it is your whim, we can bring our entire realm back to its old glory and reign together in state, while in the outside world kingdoms rise and crumble!"

Laughter. Laughter of bitterness. "A mirage," Kane murmured.

Naichoryss hurried in alarm. "Mirage? The resurrection of Altbur Keep of my youth? Not so, Kane! To you and me it shall be altogether as real as these ruins are to us now! You spent days within the shelter of its ancient walls, attended by servants' long bleached bones, nourished by its food and drink, clothed in the luxuries of past centuries! Wasn't all of that real to you then? Can you truthfully say in your mind which vision of Altbur Keep is real and which one dream?"

"Reality and dream are often impossible to distinguish," mused Kane. "Philosophers have argued that reality is nothing more than man's personal interpretation of the microcosm in which he moves. Perhaps life then is only a dream from which death will awaken us.

"But you have misunderstood me, Naichoryss. Misunderstood me from the beginning, I think.

"Death. The mystery of death. Is it oblivion or a new adventure? Does it bring peace as so many have claimed? Is it some higher plane of existence? Is it a rebirth? So much has been theorized of death, but so little is known. I've spent years at a time brooding over death. Sometimes

I exult in my defiance of death, other times I ache with a yearning to fathom this forbidden mystery. In circles. Pointless circles.

"When I first regained consciousness here, I sensed that something was unreal with Altbur Keep. My curiosity was stimulated and I stayed on, even when I met you and later recognized you for what you are. You see, I could have broken your spell, I think—at least at first. Only I was so curious. Curious to sample death at last for myself.

"And I suppose I came as close as any man can come to knowing death, and yet return to life with that knowledge.

"But I found that death was a mirage. A promise on the horizon. Distant, unattainable. A vision of strange pleasures and mysteries. And once attained, there is only a waste of bare sand.

"Boredom is the nemesis which has stalked me without rest over the centuries. Life, unfortunately, tends to repeat its favorite and dullest patterns with monotonous regularity. Death seemed to me a new adventure—an escape from a world of which I grew weary ages ago.

"But death—or at least the variety of death in which you so nearly ensnared me—is only another endless waste of tedium. An eternity spent either hidden in a crypt, or else in haunting these forest choked ruins—or in reliving a stagnant dream of the past. The proposal strikes me as a greater boredom than any I have yet encountered!

"And so I found that in death I sought a mirage—only a mirage! It was this realization that sparked my rebellion to death and gave me strength to return to the world of life! This knowledge that now demands that I leave you and the world of Altbur Keep!"

Naichoryss appeared to tremble in the moonlight, her beauty flickering with warring emotions. "I see then that I cannot break your will. Even now you are too strong to succumb to the enchantments that held you earlier."

For a moment rage replaced tragedy in her voice. "If I can not make you my consort, you can yet become my victim! This time I can tear open your soft throat and drink every crimson droplet of blood from your veins! Yes—and leave you a dry hulk for the ghouls to fight over and devour! This has been the fate of all others who have intruded within my realm! You're too weak now to deny me should I desire your life!"

Kane's eyes glowed dangerously; his hand strayed toward swordhilt. "Don't force my hand, Naichoryss!" he snarled. "My stay with you has proven interesting and I bear you no grudge. Interfere with my departure and Altbur Keep will lose its mistress!"

Kane thought for an instant the vampire would hurl herself upon him, but instead Naichoryss chose to sigh. "Perhaps I should. I don't know. One way or another, it would be an ending."

She drew herself up proudly; an aristocrat does not forget her breeding. "Still I don't believe you'll be quick to forget my kisses, Kane." Her smile was resigned. "Go on and leave me now if your mind is made up! Take your chances getting past the ghouls and Jasseartion's soldiers! Only leave now before . . . while my hospitality lasts!

"But remember always that I am here in Altbur Keep. And when your existence grows more arduous than you can bear—when memories of my embrace, my kisses torment you in your dreams—remember then that two coffins await in the crypts of Altbur Keep! Remember the peace to be found in one, the love that lies dreaming of you in the other! And then, Kane beloved, come back to me here!"

Kane eased himself from the window ledge. "I'll remember. But don't delude yourself by expecting my return. Altbur Keep taught me something, and I won't travel this one road again."

"Are you certain of that, Kane?" Mockery had returned to her voice now.

"Good-by, Naichoryss," was his answer.

Cautiously Kane picked his way down the slope from the lonely ruins of Altbur Keep. If he avoided the deserted village, there should be little chance of encountering any ghouls in the few hours left before dawn. Then sleep in a tree perhaps during the day. A rabbit or two would do wonders toward improving his condition. Once past the Chrosanthian border . . . Several possibilities suggested themselves to him.

He paused at the base of the hill to glance back, thinking of the beautiful child of death who walked those forgotten hallways alone. Kane knew full well the agony loneliness could be—understood the pain Naichoryss had felt when he had left her there alone in the moonlight.

Pain? Can the dead feel pain? Tears from dead eyes would coldly sparkle in the moonlight.

KARL EDWARD WAGNER

NIGHT WINDS

KANE

—The Mystic Swordsman
ranges Earth and Time to confront
the demons of darkness

Where once the mighty Kane has passed, no one who lives forgets. Now, down the trail of past battles, Kane travels again. To the ruins of a devastated city peopled only with half-men and the waif they call their queen. To the half-burnt tavern where a woman Kane wronged long ago holds his child in keeping for the Devil. To the cave kingdom of the giants where glory and its aftermath await discovery. To the house of death itself where Kane retrieves a woman to love.

The past, the future, the present—all are one for Kane as he travels through the centuries.

CORONET BOOKS

KARL EDWARD WAGNER

DARKNESS WEAVES

KANE

indestructible swordsman—invincible
sorcerer—immortal wanderer through
strange worlds

Efrel, Empress of Pellin seeks vengeance on the
King of Thovnos for the treachery which changed
her from a siren of unearthly beauty into a
shrivelled nightmare with no face. Her twin
weapons are her mighty land and sea armies, and
the Black Arts, her lifelong passion.

To lead her attacking forces Efrel requires a
Commander—and in all the lands only one man
could lead her to victory . . . Kane. But can even
the Mystic Swordsman survive the insane urges of
Efrel, as well as the hideous secrets thrown up
from the depths of the Bottomless Sea?

CORONET BOOKS

ROBERT SILVERBERG

BORN WITH THE DEAD

BORN WITH THE DEAD contains three superb new novellas from Robert Silverberg, major science fiction writer and winner of the Hugo and Nebula Awards. The title story, BORN WITH THE DEAD, describes a world in which the dead are re-kindled into mysterious zombies who no longer relate to their still living friends and lovers. In THOMAS THE PROCLAIMER a reformed criminal turned evangelist makes the sun stand still in the sky—with disastrous results for mankind. Finally in GOING a world-famous musician decides to 'go' and contemplates the mysteries of state-aided suicide.

'At the top of his field'   *Publishers' Weekly*

CORONET BOOKS

EDMUND COOPER

THE DEATHWORMS OF KRATOS

They were THE EXPENDABLES—some genuine volunteers, others not. They were the chosen ones—the people who had been 'selected' to travel far into space and find new planets for human colonisation.

KRATOS was the first planet of call, inhabited by gigantic creatures that swayed and roared, that were blessed with seven eyes and mouths cavernous enough to suck in a handful of humans at a time.

THE DEATHWORMS OF KRATOS will wrench you into the most terrifying of unknown worlds . . .

Read these other exciting adventures of THE EXPENDABLES from Coronet

THE RINGS OF TANTALUS
THE WAR GAMES OF ZELOS
THE VENOM OF ARGUS

THE DEATHWORMS OF KRATOS was first published as Book 1 of Richard Avery's THE EXPENDABLES

CORONET BOOKS

EDMUND COOPER

THE TENTH PLANET

'Each Cooper novel is a unique experience . . . he is one of the most entertaining and philosophically constant writers producing science fiction today.'
Science Fiction Monthly

The *Dag Hammarskjold* takes off from Woomera, Australia for the new human settlement on Mars.
   Planet Earth is being eaten away by uncontrollable pollution, starvation and disease. Its life expectancy is nil.
   This is the last spaceship, its passengers the last people on earth with any hope. But it is never to reach its objective. Five thousand years later its captain wakes up to a new world undiscovered in his time and to a bitter experience he must fight alone.

CORONET BOOKS

JACK VANCE

THE ANOME
Durdane Book 1

Durdane the Imprisoned

A world of strange ways and stranger people. A land where men and women are marked for life. Where they are bound to irrevocable destinies by the proclamations of the Faceless Man—an unseen power which terrorises and controls the world.

Durdane is a place where defiance is punished with death. But this kingdom of myriad mystery and incalculable peril is now threatened by a menace from without—the dreaded Rogushkoi. And only one youth, Gastel Etzwane, dares to challenge the unchallengeable, the power of the Faceless Man, in an extraordinary struggle for mastery and for the survival of Durdane . . .

CORONET BOOKS

JACK VANCE

THE BRAVE FREE MEN
Durdane Book 2

Durdane in Peril

The Faceless Man is a prisoner in his own palace. His power over the people of Durdane is in the hands of Gastel Etzwane, a youth whose thirst for vengeance against the dreaded Rogushkoi would be slaked only by oceans of their blood. For these invincible foes who threatened Durdane had taken and killed his mother and sister.

   To destroy the Rogushkoi Gastel would have to unite a world that survived only through its separateness. It was more than dangerous, but he had no choice. If they were to fight the people must regain control of their own lives. Only then could Gastel recruit an elite corps of the liberated—the Brave Free Men—to fling against the Rogushkoi and fight to the death . . .

ALSO AVAILABLE

THE ASUTRA
Durdane Book 3

CORONET BOOKS

POUL ANDERSON

THE ENEMY STARS

Journey to the ends of space

They built a ship called the Southern Cross and launched her to Alpha Crucis. Centuries passed, civilisations rose and fell, the very races of mankind changed, and still the ship fell on her headlong journey toward the distant star.

After ten generations the Southern Cross was the farthest thing from Earth of any human work—but she was still not half-way to her goal.

Here is an absorbingly exciting tale of the far future from one of the giants in the field of Science Fiction writing.

CORONET BOOKS

POUL ANDERSON

THE REBEL WORLDS

The Barbarians in their long ships waiting at the edge of the Galaxy . . .

. . . waiting for the ancient Terran Empire to fall, while two struggled to save it: ex-Admiral Mc-Cormac, forced to rebel against a corrupt Emperor, and Starship Commander Flandry, the brilliant young officer who served the Imperium even as he scorned it. Trapped between them was the woman they both loved, but couldn't share: the beautiful Kathryn—whose single word could decide the fate of a billion suns.

CORONET BOOKS

ALSO AVAILABLE IN CORONET

KARL EDWARD WAGNER
☐ 21812 6	Bloodstone	85p
☐ 22002 3	Darkness Weaves	95p
☐ 23472 5	Night Winds	85p

ROBERT SILVERBERG
☐ 21297 7	Born With The Dead	80p
☐ 21978 5	Unfamiliar Territory	90p

EDMUND COOPER
☐ 20512 1	The Tenth Planet	85p
☐ 04364 4	A Far Sunset	75p
☐ 19472 3	The Deathworms of Kratos	85p

JACK VANCE
☐ 19827 3	The Anome	75p
☐ 19828 1	The Brave Free Men	75p
☐ 19830 3	The Asutra	75p

POUL ANDERSON
☐ 16338 0	Rebel Worlds	70p
☐ 16480 8	The Enemy Stars	75p

All these books are available at your local bookshop or newsagent, or can be ordered direct from the publisher. Just tick the titles you want and fill in the form below.

Prices and availability subject to change without notice.

CORONET BOOKS, P.O. Box 11, Falmouth, Cornwall

Please send cheque or postal order, and allow the following for postage and packing:

U.K.—One book 30p, 15p, for the second book plus 12p each for additional book ordered, up to a maximum of £1.29.

B.F.P.O. and EIRE—30p for the first book, 15p for the second book plus 12p per copy for the next 7 books; thereafter 6p per book.

OTHER OVERSEAS CUSTOMERS—50p for the first book plus 15p per copy for each additional book.

Name ....

Address ....

....